FROST BURN

A Midnight Rising Novel
The Depths of Winter Trilogy
Book 3

THIA MACKIN

AUTHOR'S COPYRIGHT

Frost Burn
Copyright © 2020 *Mackin Works, LLC* and *Thia Mackin*
Excerpt from *Tequila Moon* copyright © 2020 *Mackin Works, LLC* and *Thia Mackin*
Print Edition

ALL RIGHTS RESERVED

Editing by: Meredith Bowery
Cover by: Covers by Julie
Interior Design and Formatting: BB eBooks

No part of this publication may be reproduced, distributed, or transmitted in any form or by any means, electronic or mechanical, or stored in a database or retrieval system, (other than for review or promotional purposes) without the prior written permission of the author, except for the use of brief quotations in a review.

This book is a work of fiction. Names, characters, businesses, places, events, and incidents are either the products of the author's imagination or used in a fictitious manner. Any resemblance to actual persons, living or dead, or actual events is purely coincidental. The author acknowledges the trademarked status and trademark owners of various products possibly referenced in this work of fiction, which have been used without permission. The use and publication of these trademarks is not authorized, associated with, or sponsored by the trademark owners.

BOOKS BY THIA MACKIN

Midnight Rising Novels

<u>The Depths of Winter Trilogy</u>
Hard Frost (Book 1)
Cold Comfort (Book 2)
Frost Burn (Book 3)

<u>Eiffel Creek Pack</u>
Tequila Moon (Coming Summer 2021)

Visit my website at www.thiamackin.com

ACKNOWLEDGEMENTS

So many people carried Kinan to the final book in the Depths of Winter trilogy. I'm so blessed to have them along for this ride.

As always, to my Alpha reader and co-creator, **Kat Corley**. Even though *Cold Comfort* is my favorite book, she swears this one is hers. Without her, Midnight Rising would not exist, and we are both so happy to see the family Rankar and Kinan built.

To my fantastic beta team—
Barb Jack, I hope my first fictional assassination was everything you wanted; **Lisa Simo-Kinzer**, thank you for your feedback and emotional investment in the characters; and **Jessica Slavik**, your comments were pure gold. These amazing people shaped this book into something bigger and better than it would have otherwise been.

To my amazing editor and friend, **Meredith Bowery,** who stayed on board despite the big personal happenings in her life. She tried to keep my scenes moving and on task. Any meandering is on me and my misinterpretation of her notes. And many thanks to **Christine Sullivan Mulcair** for her eagle-eyed proofread. As an editor in my other life, I am the absolute epitome of "don't edit your own work."

Thank the gods for her! (Any remaining typos are my fault.)

To **Kallypso Masters**, whose sprints motivated me to complete this book and start the next. Also to **Marisa Scolamiero**, whose constant presence kept me sane during this pandemic.

While all of our circles shrank during 2020 with the insanity in the world, it will always take a village. I'm so proud and grateful to mine.

And if I forgot to name you, I'm sorry. I still love you!

~Thia

AUTHORS' NOTE

Dear Readers,

This adventure began over fifteen years ago when two nerdy best friends took a writing prompt and began a universe. We—Kat and Thia—were both avid readers of fantasy and urban fantasy. So when someone invited Thia to do text-based roleplay in an urban fantasy world, she wanted to jump in with both feet! Except... the premise wasn't believable. The creatures were a mishmash from different worlds, and she couldn't suspend her disbelief to enjoy it.

We had always shared our books and ideas, which was what happened as we sat in Kat's bedroom after Kat's graduation party. She agreed. Whoever put it together created it for the "fun" factor, to make it flashy. But... what if paranormals *were* real? What if something pushed them over the edge until they could no longer stand peaceably in the shadows? How could we make people *believe* that vampires, shapeshifters, and other paranormals had remained hidden for so long—and were more powerful than we humans could ever imagine?

So we tore it down to this base idea that paranormals were going to take over. We established the *What*, *When*, *Where*, and *Why*. Then we built the *Who* and *How*. All we had left was... well... everything else. But we pored over legends of established creatures, like vampires, and separated "fact" from fiction. It needed to make sense.

There needed to be a scientific or logical basis. We want you to *believe* while you read our stories, enough that you can wander happily lost in the pages.

For about six months between 2005 and 2006, we invited others to play in our world through text-based roleplay. Unfortunately, though the members were phenomenal and we loved them greatly, it didn't feel right to have others creating characters in a world we crafted. So we shut down the ProBoards account after a heartbreaking goodbye and went back to our pre-RP basis before we continued layering, growing, and writing. Today, here we are with Thia's final novel in the *Depths of Winter* trilogy—the next book of what will hopefully be many to come from each of us.

On May 25, 2005, Midnight Rising was born. However, it grows daily. Now we invite you to visit—and we hope you stay.

Yours truly,
Kat Corley and Thia Mackin

CONTENTS

Acknowledgements	v
Authors' Note	vii
Dedication	xi
Character Name Pronunciation Guide	xiii
Chapter 1	1
Chapter 2	13
Chapter 3	19
Chapter 4	29
Chapter 5	48
Chapter 6	61
Chapter 7	68
Chapter 8	79
Chapter 9	83
Chapter 10	94
Chapter 11	105
Chapter 12	118
Chapter 13	129
Chapter 14	140
Chapter 15	149
Chapter 16	162
Chapter 17	176
Chapter 18	183
Chapter 19	192
Chapter 20	199

Chapter 21	219
Chapter 22	229
Chapter 23	244
Chapter 24	257
Chapter 25	275
Epilogue	286
Glossary	297
Let's get social!	307
Sneak Peek *Tequila Moon*	309

DEDICATION

For the survivors.

You outlived your trauma.

You overcame your trauma.

You built a life for yourself.

Here's to your happy ending.

Character Name Pronunciation Guide in IPA format

Aaron Michael Locke /ɛrən ˈmaɪkəl lɑk/ Male Tuatha de Danaan

Alala Veracruz /əleɪlʌ vɛrakrus/ Female Tuveri

Alera Sinton /ʌliərʌ sɪntʌn/ Female Tuatha de Danaan

Alika Sirach /əlikə siɹak/ Female Tuatha de Danaan

Alyson Asez /alisɤn əsæ/ Female Human

Ardal Sinton /ɑrdɔl sɪntʌn/ Male Tuatha de Danaan

Arisha Kinatnya Sheldon /arɪʃu kɪnatnja ʃɛldən/ Female Tuatha de Danaan

Asher Sirach /æʃər siɹak/ Male Tuatha de Danaan

Athanasia Serei /æθəneɪʒə sərei/ Female Tuatha de Danaan

Belisario Veracruz /vɛlɪsɑrɪo vɛrakrus/ Male Tuveri

Bretinoc Eshrai /brɛtɪnɑk ɛʃreɪ/ Male Tuatha de Danaan

Caitlyn Kinan /keɪtlɪn kɪnɑn/ Female Tuatha de Danaan

Chaz Haversham /ʧæz hævɜrʃæm/ Male Tuatha de Danaan

Cire Lyksva /saɪər lɪksvə/ Female Ferente

Cruce Alishion /kruʧeɪ æliʃɪɑn/ Male Unknown Demon Breed

Damienn Katataros /deɪmɪən kætʌtɑroʊs/ Male Tuatha de Danaan

Davis "Davie" Greene /deɪvəs "deɪvi" grin/ Male Tulevi/Tuveri

Derek Dukon /dɛrɪk dukɑn/ Male Tulevi

Devon Laoch /dɛvən leɪɑk/ Male Tuatha de Danaan

Eliecha Bhinj /iliɛkʌ bɪndʒ/ Female Tuatha de Danaan

Erykah Sirach /erikə siɹak/ Female Tuatha de Danaan

Faela Sirach /feɪlɑ siɹak/ Female Tuatha de Danaan

Fhin Kinan /fɪn kɪnɑn/ Male Tuatha de Danaan

Flechwe Katataros /flɛʃweɪ kætʌtɑroʊs/ Male Tuatha de Danaan

Fwen Panthrus /fwɛn pænθrʌs/ Male Shapeshifter

Garfell Reykjavik /gɑrfɛl rɛkjəvɪk/ Male Tuatha de Danaan

Garth Haversham /gɑrθ hæv3rʃæm/ Male Tuatha de Danaan

Gavyn Laso /geɪvɪn lazo/ Male Unknown Demon Breed

Gerald Brock /dʒɛrəld brɑk/ Male Bouda

Ghevan Chiwa /gɛvæn ʧiwɑ/ Male Barcki

Ilyetik Hoxez /ɪljɛtɪk hɑkseɪ/ Female Unknown Demon Breed

Irhic Bhinj /irɪk bɪndʒ/ Male Tuatha de Danaan

Ivan Karl /aɪvən kɑrl/ Male Unknown Demon Breed

Jarrett Atkoy /dʒɛrət ætkɔɪ/ Male Human

Jeannitra Patric /dʒɛnitrʌ ˈpætrɪk/ Female Barcki / Human

Jeremy Sinton /dʒɛrəmi sɪntʌn/ Male Tuatha de Danaan

Jorvan Abshoc /dʒɔrvæn æbʃak/ Male Unknown Demon Breed

Karma Delaney /kɑrmə dəleɪni/ Female Mixed Breed

Karyn Sirach /kærən siɹak/ Female Tuatha de Danaan

Keawyn Asez /kiæwɪn əsæ/ Female Tuatha de Danaan-Human

Killian Winstead /kɪljɛn wɪnstɛd/ Male Unknown Demon Breed

Kismet Sirach /kɪmɛt siɹak/ Male Tuatha de Danaan

Kitry Abinaleh /kɪtri æbɪnɑleɪ/ Female Unknown Demon Breed

Kiss Yleva /kɪs ɪlɛvʌ/ Female Ferente

Leara Sinton /liɑrə sɪntʌn/ Female Tuatha de Danaan

Lucienn Katataros /luʃən kætʌtɑroʊs/ Male Tuatha de Danaan

Lyonos Katataros /laɪənoʊs kætʌtɑroʊs/ Male Tuatha de Danaan

Marcul Zuhavi /mɑrkʌl zuhɑvi/ Male Tuatha de Danaan

Mebrid Choalite /mɛbrɪd koʊliti/ Male Tuatha de Danaan

Michelle Craig /mɪʃɛl kreɪg/ Female Human

Miguel Vicar /migɛl vikɑr/ Male Lykos

Mycal Sirach /maɪk(ə)l siɹak/ Male Tuatha de Danaan

Penelope Sirtis /pəˈnɛləpi sɜːrtɪs/ Female Vampire

Rankar Donovan Sirach /ɹankɑɹ donovan siɹak/ Male Tuatha de Danaan

Rendle Cavallo /rɛndʌl kævɑloʊ/ Male Tulevi

Renfri Grem /rɛnfri grɪm/ Female Ferente

Ries Jacobs /ris dʒeɪkəbz/ Male Unknown Demon Breed

Riknare Katataros /rɪknɑreɪ kætʌtɑroʊs/ Female Tuatha de Danaan

Sage Jaxon /seɪdʒ dʒæksən/ Male Unknown Demon Breed

Sareya Montgomery /sɜreɪʌ mɑntˈgʌmri/ Female Barcki

Sarki Elayne Kinan Sirach /sɑrki ɪˈleɪn kɪnɑn siɹak/ Female Tuatha de Danaan

Tier Sheldon /tir ʃɛldən/ Male Tuatha de Danaan

Tiernia Sirach /tirnjə siɹak/ Female Tuatha de Danaan

Treyv Osman /tɹeɪv ɑzman/ Male Shapeshifter

Triswon Kowi Bhinj /triwɑn kowi bɪndʒ/ Male Tuatha de Danaan

Ulvin Xavic /ʌlvɪn zɑvɪk/ Male Tuatha de Danaan

Will Allan /wɪl ælən/ Male Unknown Demon Breed

Xander Sirach /zændər siɹak/ Male Tuatha de Danaan

Zanta McCarthy /zɑntɑ məˈkɑrθi/ Female Tuatha de Danaan

Zeer Rezqwa /zir rɛzkwɑ/ Male Unknown Demon Breed

— Charles /ʧɑrlz/ Male

— Gerin /gɪrɪn/ Female

— Graver /greɪvər/ Female

— Ising /aɪzɪŋ/ Female

— Keem /kim/ Male

— Mab /mæb/ Female

— Sandhill /sændɪl/ Male

"You will stand firm until you break.
Your broken shards kill your enemies but cut your allies.
Flames destroy you, but fire mends you.
Death protects you as it hunts you.
You will lose everything you treasure
to find that which exceeds value."

Eliccha Bhinj's Prophecy
<u>Hard Frost</u>, Book 1

CHAPTER 1

THE MOON WARRED with the sun for dominance in the sky, neither willing to give up that coveted position. The clouds wept pastel pinks and purples, coating the heavens with a delightful array of color. *It's too godsdamn early to deal with people,* I mentally groaned as someone in an official-looking uniform walked briskly in my direction. I resigned myself to not reaching the cafeteria before the seven-a.m. crowd. So much for getting back with fresh muffins and fruit before Rankar, my husband, finished showering.

For a moment, I flashed back to almost a year ago when someone in similar attire had delivered a postmortem letter from my soulsibling. Aaron Michael Locke died in the war, killed in action on the final day of fighting. My fingers gripped the ring hanging from a leather cord around my neck, and my feet stopped moving as he continued toward me. While I knew my loved ones were safe this time, I doubted the envelope in his hand contained good news.

"Sarki Kinan, Tuatha de Danaan?" the official asked, already offering the letter over. I grabbed one end and pulled. He didn't release it, though.

"Yes, I am Kinan." I tugged again, this time successfully.

"You have been served."

Slipping my finger under the flap, I opened the envelope and scanned the papers. A rage filled me so cold that my next breath fogged the air. "This bitch…" The words chimed like a promise, and I didn't regret the curse. A second, slower read only confirmed that the fear creeping into my anger was justified.

I turned on my heel and jogged toward the main compound. If Councilwoman Keawyn Asez did not rein in her out-of-control employee, perhaps I would volunteer to bring the woman down a peg or two myself. Unsurprising for six-thirty in the morning, the hallways to Keawyn's office were deserted until I came face-to-face with her personal guards.

"Good morning, Kinan," Fwen Panthrus greeted. The second lieutenant had probably heard my angry footsteps echoing down the corridor long before I came into sight.

I returned the pleasantry before getting to the point. "Is the councilwoman available?"

The corners of his mouth turned down. "No. She left with a small guard contingent just after midnight for a meeting with the other council members. When she gets back, she'll go to bed." He raised a shoulder. "She's keeping vampire hours right now, but she'll have meetings on Monday. Want me to pencil you in?"

I glanced at the summons gripped in my fist. "I think so, yes."

Fwen grimaced. "Anything I can help with?"

Almost. I almost made a half-joke about him assassinating someone. However, he'd once been my husband's boss, and he was still third-in-command of the guard.

Instead, I shook my head and went back the way I'd come in.

Once in the courtyard, I called to Hypnos. The cat-sized blue dragon appeared a short distance in front of me. As with all drakyn, his Gate was invisible to the eye. When any other creature traveled through the Void, someone paying close enough attention could see through to the other side.

"Where's Rankar now?"

He sent an image of his other bondmate nursing a cup of coffee at the kitchen table in our apartment. In the projection, Rankar checked his watch, though he hadn't bothered to put on his boots or weapons yet.

"Tell him to stay there?"

Hypnos disappeared, and I quickened my steps. A few of my coworkers were feeding the horses in the stable when I entered and headed up the ladder to the loft. I waved back to those who greeted me, comfortable in not sticking around to talk since it was my day off. Then I pressed the code into the keypad on the door and walked through the wards. Rankar and I had layered them together, training them to recognize us and close friends.

As soon as I shut the door, he stepped out of the bedroom with his boots in hand. His brown eyes looked me over, his brow crinkling slightly when he didn't see the breakfast my note on the pillow had promised. I shook my head, striding across the room and wrapping my arms around him. His body relaxed in my embrace, his hands gently resting on my hips and his cheek against the side of my face.

We'd learned through trial and error that this gentle

hug wouldn't set off one of my panic attacks, which I'd never appreciated more than I did now. The skin-to-skin contact somehow eased the racing of my heart, slowed my breathing. His proximity warmed me physically while cooling my rage.

After a couple minutes, I stepped back, handed him the envelope, and walked to the table. He had made me a cup of coffee, and I sipped it as he read the letter.

He looked at me, and I could see he was nearly as upset as I was. That reassured me.

"We're going to fight this."

I wrapped my hands around the mug, mostly for something to hold onto. "Of course we are. But how do we win against her family? Zanta McCarthy is one of Leara's closest living relatives—her grandmother—and her petition is for full custody and a restraining order against me. While I can't see Keawyn granting a restraining order without grounds, there is zero reason for her to deny custody of Leara to her grandmother." Tears filled my eyes, and I smeared them away with the backs of my hands.

"Kinan, I can think of a handful of reasons," Rankar began. However, the door slammed open, interrupting.

"Don't you dare let her take me away!" Leara shouted, drowning out the sound of the door closing behind her. Her eyes and nose were red, as though she'd cried the entire way from her cousin Alera's room. Obviously, she had overheard something while having her regular Friday night sleepover.

Pushing my chair out, I stood and opened my arms to her. "Warrior-girl, I would never give you away, and I'll fight for you against any comers."

She almost knocked me over as she ran to me and squeezed me tightly. With her tear-streaked face buried against my shirt, I barely understood her when she spoke. "You can't let them keep me from you. You can't."

Staring up at the ceiling, I sent a prayer to the Goddess asking for Her to do the best thing for Leara. Personally, I doubted at least once a day that she should be with me. When we'd been locked in the internment camp together, I hadn't been able to save her parents. After they'd removed me from her cell, I'd thought for months she had been killed. Then I hadn't even been in a position to search for her when I found out she lived. Rankar sent a team for me. And months after we'd been reunited, I still kept her awake at night with my nightmares. Then there was the fact that I had zero blood relation to her, though sometimes I imagined more than trauma bound us together.

"Stop that," she ordered. "Stop thinking that I'll be better off without you. It isn't true."

I sniffled, lifting a hand to smooth the flyaways that had escaped from her ponytail. "Leara, I know it's hard to see that your grandmother has your best interests…"

"No!"

Her hands pushed against my stomach. Startled, I let her go.

"No, she doesn't! Zanta doesn't have my best interests at heart. *You do.* She didn't stop to ask herself if maybe I'm better with you. *You did.* She's doing this out of spite. I belong to her, and she can't stand that I prefer you. She hates that I love you more than I do her."

My feet carried me toward her. "Leara, my warrior-girl…"

I reached for her, wanting to wipe away her tears, but she dodged me. Standing still, I waited and watched her panting in a mixture of anger and grief. Her shoulders rose and fell quickly enough I worried she might pass out.

When she swayed, I tried again. "Leara?"

A sob broke free, and she stared at me. "Why doesn't anyone want me for me? You're willing to let her take me. She only wants me to keep me from you. My brother hates everything about me. What did I do that was so terrible?"

An invisible knife stabbed my chest, the phantom pain strong enough that I put a hand over my sternum as I walked toward her. "That's not true, Leara. I don't want to lose you. You mean the world to me."

Rankar moved on her other side. "Leara, you've done nothing wrong. Your brother is the one in the wrong. He's a piece of shit, and it has nothing to do with you."

Her head snapped toward him, like a snake catching a scent. "I know."

The coldness in her tone caused my gaze to swing between the two of them. Had something happened I didn't know about?

"My brother treats me like you treat Alika. Neither of us did anything to deserve it. But no one will stand up for us, so we just have to live with it." Her fists shook, and her eyes gleamed behind the tears. "And I hate you both!"

Before I could catch her, she'd darted for the door. I reached the door just as she slammed it behind her, leaving me shaken. "Hypnos?" I called, voice breaking. "Follow her. Tell me if she leaves Asez Holding's walls."

His chirp as he Gated out sounded panicked, and I fully sympathized. A long moment passed before I forced my hand off the handle and turned back toward Rankar. He had sunk into a chair, his elbows on the table and both hands covering his face.

Crossing the room quickly, I sank to my knees beside his chair and placed my hand on his thigh. "Ran, hey. She doesn't really hate us."

He slipped his right hand beneath mine, linking our fingers together. Long minutes passed in silence. Then Hypnos reappeared, sending us the image of Leara sitting with her head down crying in the stables below. She hid in the corner of Pantheon's stall.

Rankar squeezed my hand then let it go. "Go to Leara. She needs you."

Torn between needing to reassure them both, I rubbed his thigh but glanced over my shoulder at the door. "Rankar, you okay?"

He laughed, but it sounded wet with emotion. "No, but Leara is young. She needs you most. Go make sure she is alright."

I swallowed, hesitating as I felt his heartbeat racing beneath my palm. He was right, though. Leara had to come first. Standing, I wrapped my arms around him and hugged tightly. "I love you, Rankar. She does too. We'll have Hypnos find you in a bit."

As I touched the handle, he whispered my name behind me. My hand paused, and I half-turned toward him.

"Is she right?"

Panic filled me. "Of course not! We want her. She is wanted."

He shook his head. "Not that. Have I treated Alika like that fucking bastard Ardal treats Leara?"

My lips gaped, not expecting the question. "Rankar, I…" Words stuck in my throat, but I couldn't lie to him. "I don't understand everything that's happened between you and Alika, but I think… yes."

He nodded, the barest movement. Then he rested his forehead in his hand again.

I twisted the door handle and the invisible knife in my chest in the same motion. As I stepped into the hallway, I whispered Hypnos's name. "Find Thanatos and you both go to Rankar. Don't leave him until I come back."

Immediately, the drakyn disappeared, and I climbed down the ladder and headed toward Pantheon's stall.

Leara needed me most. But for the time, I'd send him Sleep and Death for company.

PANTHEON SHOOK HIS dark mane and neighed as I approached the stall, but his feet never moved. The blue roan's coat shone in the dim light, so some brave soul had brushed him last night. Probably my partner, Davie Greene, because no incident reports had been filed. He and Rendle Cavallo were the only two people beyond Leara and me that the horse wouldn't take a chunk out of without a direct order.

Rukchio, a gangly two-month-old colt, snorted impatiently in the stall beside him. When I showed him empty hands, he huffed at me in disappointment. His black coat showed dimension, and Leara had decided to take weekly photos both to monitor his growth and document the changes. When he came of age, I planned to put mine and Leara's name in for him—whichever of us he chose to bond. If either.

"Hey there, boys," I greeted, running my hand down Rukchio's neck and patting twice before moving to the next stall.

I lightly rubbed Pantheon's muzzle, because the soft skin felt delightfully dry and warm. However, he disliked being touched there, so I shifted my attention to his cheek. That, he appreciated much more.

"I know you know I'm in here." Her voice held tears, snot, and a lot of emotion. "Hypnos snitched."

Resting my arms on the top of the stall door, I peeked into the corner. "I was hoping for an invitation." She didn't say anything. I waited another few seconds. "May I please come in?"

She exhaled, and the sound made me wish for a handkerchief to give her. "I guess."

Opening the lock and the latch, safety against Pantheon accidentally getting free and braining someone, I slipped inside and redid everything back behind me. I slid down the wall to sit in the clean straw beside her. She pulled her knees up to her chest and hugged them, so I crossed mine in a meditation pose and leaned back.

"I'm sorry," she whispered as the silence dragged on.

"Leara," I began, still trying to find the right words but realizing time had run out, "neither Rankar nor I want you to go anywhere. We're a family. But that doesn't mean my reasons for wanting you with me are less selfish than your grandmother's."

Her head jerked toward me, and I saw she intended to interrupt.

"No. Listen for a minute. If you are right and your

grandmother's only intention is to keep you away from me, is that less acceptable than me wanting to be around you because you ease the pain in my soul? When I look at you and see how smart and strong you are, I am proud that I can be part of your growth. Aren't those things selfish?"

Her derisive laugh caught me off guard, a sound I'd expect from someone much older, and I shot her a startled glance. "Kinan... I... Look, you don't know what selfish is. You do the dumbest shi-stuff. And you do it for other people, to try to rescue stupid families time after time. You have *zero* concept of selfish, and you can't seem to see it in other people. Even when they *literally* take you to court for it."

"First, I am as selfish as the next person. Second, this isn't about me. It's about you." I rested my hand on top of her linked ones. "What I'm saying, Leara, is that I—selfishly—want to keep you. Forever. I want you to be my ward on paper, because you already are in my heart. And, if you don't believe my being your guardian in the eyes of Orion and the Council and Zanta McCarthy would be disrespectful to the memory of your parents, I will go to court and plead for them to make it official."

Her arms went around me, and she awkwardly half-stood to crawl into my lap. Her growing teenage frame, though still much shorter than mine, wasn't meant to be there. That didn't stop me from wrapping her up in a hug as tight as I could.

"You forget, Kinan, Mom and Dad trusted you with me in the camp. And you proved their faith was founded. You are the right person."

"Then we'll see what the councilwoman decides, and

we'll go from there."

Her body shuddered, a further sign she'd been sobbing before I arrived. I rocked her gently side to side, my legs already half-asleep. She not-so-subtly wiped her face on my shoulder, sniffling.

"Will you tell Rankar I don't really hate him?" she whispered.

I kept rocking and rubbed her back reassuringly. "No. I don't think he'd believe me anyway. If anyone tells him how *you* feel, it needs to be you."

She sighed. "Li doesn't talk about Rankar when we chat after my Gift training sessions. She talks about all of her siblings, even Tier sometimes, but never Rankar unless I ask about him. But sometimes when I talk about him taking me riding or shooting, she looks so... wistful. Not like she wants to do those things, but like she wishes Rankar had done those things with her. And she once told me when I was really nosey that she was happy Rankar was that way with me, but he wasn't that person with her. When I got nosier, the other siblings became evasive."

I kissed the top of her head before resting my chin on it. "I know, Leara. I've seen the defensiveness. The odd comments and pointed jabs the siblings throw at Rankar. Something happened between Rankar and Alika long before either of us was born. And I think, maybe, the rift wasn't either of their faults at first. They both were dealing with pain the only way they knew how. But now no one knows how to fix it."

Her thoughts were so loud that I felt telepathic.

"Leara," I continued, sternly, "I know you want to help, but they have almost a century of issues to overcome.

You should leave this be."

She rested her cheek against my shoulder, relaxing gradually.

"I should apologize to Rankar," she whispered after a long pause.

I sighed, hugging her closer. "I think emotions definitely took that conversation over the line. I don't want you to feel like you can't talk to us about your feelings, but we need to do it in a way that isn't unnecessarily hurtful to our family. And I think you realize that now."

Pantheon pawed the ground, telling us that he'd tired of our company. "That's our cue," I murmured, hugging her tightly for long moments until she moved to stand.

She stood, patting the back of her pants and legs to try to remove the straw clinging. I rose and did the same before opening the stall and motioning her out. Once we stepped into the aisle, I latched and locked Pantheon in. Pulling a piece of straw from her hair with a flourish, I gave her a small smile as I dropped it back inside. "I'm going to go grab us whatever is left for breakfast. I'll be back in about twenty minutes."

She straightened her shoulders like she prepared for battle. "I'm going home to see if Rankar is still there."

I ruffled her hair and nudged her toward the ladder. Then I took off at a brisk pace toward the kitchen. Hopefully, my errand gave them enough time to say things they needed to say but not so much that they could make the situation worse.

CHAPTER 2

W HEN I ARRIVED at the apartment with breakfast, Leara and Rankar were playing a quiet game of chess at the kitchen table. The two black-and-tan puppies tugged a rope toy between them, occasionally growling at one another. Though the room throbbed with emotions, the two chatted as they played about moves that could have been. He used it to teach her strategy, but he also enjoyed having someone to play against. Right now, though, he looked like he'd been raked over hot coals and still smoldered a little from the heat. While I could tell Leara had cried more, she otherwise seemed okay.

After lunch, Keawyn called Rankar in for a meeting. Since Leara planned to take a nap, I grabbed my three favorite weapons—including my Heckler & Koch PSG1 rifle—and ammunition bag from the safe before heading to Asez Holding's gun range. Surprisingly, only two people used the first section. I headed through the opposite door and to the far end to set up, as far from them as possible.

When an earlier owner of Asez had commissioned building the gun range, they'd taken a lot of precautions. The thickness of the walls helped protect the families who lived in the compound. The range was split into three separate rooms with cement block and metal walls for the safety of the users. The main entrance opened into the center room with ten lanes. Metal doors with double-paned glass windows containing chicken wire separated the other two rooms, also allowing ten individual shooters at a time each.

The design reduced the sounds and also the amount of time the range needed to be clear as people replaced targets. And it allowed me to avoid people on days like today when I just wanted to block my emotions and feel only recoil. Ear and eye protection on, I began with the Glock from Locke's house.

Inhaling slowly, I pulled the trigger. The bullet ejected, and my center closed around me without my mental hand even touching the door. Emotions fell away, leaving me with the feel of invisible snowflakes on my skin and a peacefulness I'd yearned for earlier. Methodically, I emptied the magazine, aiming for the same bullet hole each time.

To my right, I sensed movement as I reloaded. I nodded toward the newcomer, looking up slightly to meet his gaze. He smiled and nodded back, tapping his ear. Setting my weapon down, slide open, I tugged off my hearing protection. "Hey, Treyv."

Treyv Osman's smile turned to a grin. From my first time meeting the shapeshifter almost two years ago, he'd been friendly and outgoing. Before the war, we had celebrated his birthday at a bar with him, his husband, and his sister-in-law—Belisario and Alala Veracruz. Most recently, he helped rescue Leara.

"Do you mind if I join you?"

Calmly centered, I waved my hand to the line of aisles.

He chose the one beside me, and I realized he stood about the same height as Rankar, around six-two.

I waited for him to put on his hearing protection, mine in my hand meaningfully. However, he did a leisurely weapons check before looking at me. "You know some of the guards have bets about who you are and what you're doing here? And I have to admit, I'm a little curious about the second part myself. After all, you were a mercenary before the war, and you still carry yourself like a fighter." He paused, leaning against the separating wall. "You're armed and *training* like a soldier, but you're *not* a guard. At least not for Asez."

I blinked, startled. We'd jumped into the deep end without warning, and for a minute, I forgot how to swim. What exactly was he implying?

Luckily, he kept talking, and I didn't have to guess. "And you should be an Asez Holding guard." The blue eyes that studied me were much darker than my own. "Belisario says you might not be ready for conflict again so soon after the war, and I get that. Mister Cavallo is a fair boss from what I hear. But even my blind grandfather could see you weren't cut out for stable work on a regular basis. And yet here you are working in the largest stables in Orion."

Treyv's voice was neutrally friendly, his thumb hooked casually in his pocket. He held perfectly still, apparently trying hard not to startle me before I gave him the answers he wanted. But I wasn't certain how to respond. And I didn't figure he wanted me to answer the only question he'd actually asked.

When the silence stretched on, the shifter continued. "Me, I don't much care. And by that, you should take it to mean I don't have any serious cash invested in the betting pool." A light entered his eyes as he continued. "But if you wanted to make up something crazy and let me know ahead of time so I could put money in the pool, I'd split it with ya. Sixty-forty."

The laugh escaped, and I rolled my eyes at him. "Gods, Treyv, you don't need my help winning money from the books."

He lifted his free shoulder in a carefree half-shrug. "That doesn't mean I wouldn't accept it."

Shaking my head, I twisted the muffs of my ear protection gently. "I'm in the stables because that is where I fit at Asez when I arrived. And I'm incredibly lucky it was an option."

He slid his glasses on and picked up his gear. "I get it. But both you and Asez would be a lot better off if you were in the guard."

I didn't disagree with him. However, the biannual guard tryouts—called the Trials—had been cancelled in Spring since we hadn't been certain whether Keawyn's challenge of Mebrid Choalite would end with her dead and all of us exiled. Luckily, she'd stepped out of the challenge arena traumatized but alive—as the new council member representing the Tuatha de Danaan of our country.

The next tryouts would be in Fall. Any guard applicants would compete in skill tests against each other to fill open job slots. They also fought against the four officers in their chosen arena—Rankar in mounted combat, First Lieutenant Alala Veracruz in blade work, Second Lieutenant Fwen Panthrus in ranged weapons, and Sergeant Major Belisario Veracruz in hand-to-hand combat. The winner of each assessment received an automatic perfect score in that round. Then the other competitors were given a score by the overseeing officer based on their competency in that arena. Typically, it lasted about ten days. Then the top performers would be accepted and begin actual training.

"Thanks, Treyv. And if I decide to make up a ridiculous lie, I'll make sure you are the first to know."

A grin creased his face, and he put on his hearing protection. Sliding back into my lane, I waited until he asked if I was ready for the range to go live. Then we practiced in near silence, with occasional breaks to reload or switch weapons. As I fired the H&K, I felt him move to stand a few feet behind me. He watched without urging me to stop, so I finished the twenty-capacity magazine.

His admiring whistle caught me as I removed my hearing protection. "Has L-T seen you shoot?"

Turning on the stool, I raised my eyebrow at him. He had to be talking about Fwen, as I'd never heard him call Alala by title. "Why would he have? I only ever practice here in the range."

He held his palms toward me, as though holding me back. "Whoa. I just asked a question. Panthrus used to watch the videos and hunt down the sharpshooters."

I set the rifle down, packed Locke's weapon back into the case to clean that evening, and placed it in the ammunition bag. Then I picked up the unopened longbow case. "I'm sure the new safety protocols have kept him quite wrapped up. Besides, I'm just a hostler. I don't imagine he'd concern himself with stable hands anyway."

Treyv's shrug was a little too casual, but he let the discussion drop. "If you ever need some company, come find my patrol on the early morning shift, from three in the morning to nine in the morning. I'm off tomorrow, but remember what I said. Three to nine, come find me. Mister Cavallo knows where I'll be." As he walked away, he whistled a tune I didn't catch.

I headed back to the apartment and checked on Leara, who still napped. After changing out my weapons at the safe and penning a note to Leara and Rankar to let them know where I was going, I went downstairs to saddle up Pantheon. He pranced past Rukchio's stall, and I patted the colt's nose in consolation. Poor guy was much too young to be anywhere outside Asez Holding, and the Elysii Plane tended to be full of surprises.

Within minutes, I checked the shields around Pantheon and me, making sure we were both completely protected. Then I opened a Gate as close to the Banded Traveler as the laws of the capital city allowed, and Pantheon confidently walked through.

CHAPTER 3

No one assaulted me in the streets, and Pantheon didn't try to take a chunk out of anyone in the Banded Traveler's courtyard. I counted both things as a win as I placed him in one of the temporary guest stalls. The man who ran the stables, my friend Zeer Rezqwa, had invested in magnetic signs to warn people to stay away from the areas with the more contrary mounts, and I placed one on Pantheon's door.

Crossing the main courtyard, a former coworker stopped and greeted me. As we finished catching up, she let me know Rezqwa visited family off-Elysii but that both Eliecha and Triswon Bhinj were inside.

The front door wards washed over me, like a hit of static electricity. From somewhere deep in the kitchens, Triswon's booming voice echoed. "Snowflake!"

Someone oomphed followed by the sound of something shattering. Then he appeared in the doorway, his beaming smile surrounded by an impressive mustache and even more impressive beard. Considering the fae took days to grow a five o'clock shadow, his amount of facial hair truly inspired. Eliecha had once confided that he'd already grown it when they met; one of the first times she had ever seen a beard was on him. In the century since, she came to like it. In the past years, it came to remind me of home.

"Did you kick that good-for-naught Sirach boy to the curb and come here to live out the rest of your life?" he asked, stopping six inches in front of me with his hands in his pockets to keep from hugging me and sending me into an anxiety attack.

"My husband—your nephew—is doing fine, and he would have sent his love if we'd talked before I left," I countered, carefully hugging over his arms. If I initiated and controlled the contact, typically, I could avoid becoming a nervous mess.

His wife stepped up behind him, peeking around his much larger frame to wink at me. Her arms wrapped around him, sliding beneath mine to keep from trapping me but not to be excluded. "He loves Mycal's children fine; he even believes they've grown into good people. He just doesn't think anyone is good enough for his favorite."

I smiled, squeezing them both a second before letting go. "I'm not sure how I earned that title, but I am grateful every day."

Eliecha linked her arms through her husband's. "I feel like the coming discussion deserves more comfortable chairs than the main dining room." She waved to the young man behind the bar, a Barcki demon I did not recognize. "Ghevan, please bring a pitcher of the new ale and three steins to the private dining room."

Nodding thanks to him, I followed along. As we moved along the narrow hallway, I wiped my sweaty palms on my pants and breathed slowly to try to quiet my heartbeat. In my many visits to the Banded Traveler, we had only used the back room once—when I killed the man who betrayed and caused the deaths of people he'd hired to do a job.

Triswon held the door for us, and Elie led us to the grouping of chairs around the lit fireplace. I extended my palms toward the fire, and the flames warmed me like Rankar's touch did. When I looked up, the soulmates were making hard eye contact, as though speaking telepathically. "Everything okay?"

Elie smiled softly at me. "No. Tell us about the summons."

So I began with my morning visitor and continued through Leara's reaction. Recounting it didn't diminish how torn I felt, only bringing the emotions I'd spent the second part of the day suppressing back to the surface. "Rankar and I don't want to lose her, and she wants to stay with us. We give her security that she doesn't seem to feel otherwise. But worse than her no longer living with us would be someone honoring Zanta's request for a restraining order. *Never* seeing Leara again? I cannot imagine."

Eliecha gripped my hand, squeezing. "Oh, Snowflake, you aren't going to lose her. Nothing Zanta McCarthy can do will take that sweet girl out of your heart. Besides, I've made it quite clear to my clan that I consider you to be my daughter and Leara to be my grandchild. No one will back Zanta in standing against my right to see my granddaughter. And if I see her, you will also."

Immediately, my chest squeezed, and I choked on my tears. "I love you both. You have been the best parents I never imagined I'd get the chance to have. If not for you, I wouldn't recognize how special my feelings for Leara are." Leaning back in the chair, I tried to choke down the overwhelming helplessness clawing at my throat. "If I knew my parents' clan, I might run to them with Leara to hide. I should have asked you all to tell me what you knew about them…"

A loud pop, as though I had just hiked up to a high elevation and then swallowed to clear my ears, sounded. The internal pressure caused me to wince and raise my hand to my head. Across from me, Triswon also held his ears, but his eyes were wide with amazement. Eliecha simply appeared relieved.

"What was that?" I asked as Triswon shouted, "Did that do it?"

Before Eliecha could reply to either of us, Triswon quickly scooted to the edge of his chair and leaned forward toward me. "Ghouski. Russia. Kinatnya. Cold."

Startled, I instinctively set back in the chair. "What?"

He opened his mouth, but Eliecha's hand on his arm stopped him. "Did you feel the binding break? Like a mental bubble that popped?"

My eyes darted between them. "I heard something." For the second time since I arrived, dread filled my chest.

Eliecha smiled, waving away my worry. "No, this is a good thing, Snowflake. It means I can finally tell you a story I have yearned to let out over these past years."

"What was stopping you?" My left hand gripped the arm rest of the chair, and I slipped my right one under my leg to warm it. Even the fire didn't seem to be helping now.

"That's part of the story," she murmured as Triswon scooted his chair closer to hers and gripped her hand in his. "And, while the story could begin almost a century ago when Fhin and Caitlyn met, it has waited quite long enough. Instead, we'll start around Yule 1980 when Caitlyn Kinan walked into her daughter's nursery to see her beautiful six-and-a-half month-old little girl cooing and creating tiny ice creatures above her bassinet."

I swallowed hard, scooting all the way back in the chair and sliding both hands under my legs. Already, I could tell I was not going to like this story.

Beside Eliecha, Triswon nodded his head. "That was you. You were the baby. Sweet as chocolate pie and as beautiful and unique as a snowflake."

"She called your father home immediately. They realized they had to make a choice, because an infant displaying Gifts would expose paranormals to the world. Either they could send you back to the Ghouski Sithen to be raised by their family—the Kinatnya clan—as your Gift continued to develop or they could desert the life they'd spent decades creating on the Terra Plane and return with you. While they realized they could never abandon you, your father was much too loyal to his men to disappear on them for what would likely be decades or more. Then someone told them to find a fae capable of binding a powerful Gift manifesting long before its normal time."

The picture painted itself, like a vision unveiling in my mind. "They traveled here to you, someone outside the Sithens but still strongly tied to them."

Millennia ago, when the Danaan Plane became unstable, those with Gifts of Prophecy gave the strongest fae time to save the race. They created Sithens—miniature Planes or pocket dimensions—where their clans could live. The clans without enough powerful energy-workers joined with larger ones, like the Kinatnya did with Ghouski. And they linked their new homes to places on the least developed but most stable Plane they could find then: Terra.

She inclined her head to me. "When you create a binding ritual of that magnitude, the details have to be firm. We spent two days arguing the fine points. For example, they wanted no one to be able to speak of the binding until they brought you back as a young girl to have it undone. However, though I did not See their deaths, I *have* seen too much to commit to such a choice. Especially since information like your clan and Sithen name were tightly tied in. Triswon countered that any request you made to us for information about your family or that specific Gift would break it, and they accepted."

Triswon grunted. "We've been waiting years for you to ask us literally *anything* to break the binding. Elie is so powerful that the ritual wouldn't even let me try to lead you to a question. Instead, I'd have the worst headache for at least a day when I tried. Ghouski Sithen is in Siberia, Russia. Your clan is Kinatnya. They are the smallest of the clans in that Sithen. Technically, Fhin is Kinatnya, but your mother's mother didn't claim one of the clans. One of the Gifts that line is known for is manipulating the cold—thus the nickname… Snowflake."

I stared at them both, speechless. It hurt that they hadn't told me, though the binding prevented them from doing so. An irrational reaction, but one I couldn't control. "Are my grandparents still alive?" I finally managed.

"Your grandfather is still the biggest dic—" Triswon trailed off when his wife elbowed him.

Eliecha chimed in diplomatically. "Your paternal grandfather is known to be unpleasant. It's the reason your father left when he realized that Caitlyn was his soulmate and his family would never approve. However, your maternal grandmother is delightful. If you ever visit, she'll be nothing but happy to see you."

Since I turned thirteen, my family contained only people who shared no blood relation to me. While the part of me who'd lost her parents as a teenager felt only joy at hearing I had people who shared my name, another part of me needed to process that Mom and Dad had chosen to cut me off from my Gift rather than change their lifestyle for what would have been such a short time in their lives. If they had chosen differently, they might still be alive.

"I'm sorry, Kinan," Eliecha murmured.

I shook my head, shutting down the negative thoughts. "Don't defend them, and I'll try not to blame them. Perhaps, perhaps things would have worked out that I still showed up in time to save you and Leara. Or maybe—if they'd chosen differently—I would have a child in the Sithen and never met Rankar. Moral of the story: My dad's dad wouldn't help me hide Leara, but I have family here who will make sure I see her again."

Triswon grumbled something about knowing how to hide a body, but Eliecha shushed him again before continuing, "Thank you for understanding, Snowflake. We didn't want to hide this from you. We had no choice."

I replayed the conversation. "What about the Gift? Can you unbind it now? Should we even try?"

I'd done pretty well for myself without it, and Gifts that manifested in adults often caused unpredictable issues.

It could do more harm than good.

Eliecha winced. "Do you remember when the anti-energy arrow hit you? The Goddess sent you to the Sirach's land. And shortly after, the room started cooling off when you felt strong emotions..."

Waiting for her to continue seemed like the best option. Obviously, she knew that I remembered those things, though I didn't recall ever telling *her* about the odd side effects.

"When that arrow hit you, it apparently damaged the ritual energy. Since rituals and spells are different than typical energy-working, which is what the arrow primarily aimed for, it did not completely destroy the binding like it did your shields. However, it—it's hard to explain. If the ritual is a vine, the arrow cut the stalk near the root. As time goes on, the core energy that kept the leaves alive cannot reach them. The leaves slowly shrivel and drop away. Eventually, it completely dies, but not overnight." She waved her hand, gesturing at me. "Those moments where the room cools or you feel cold are leaves falling off the dying plant."

"So tearing the damaged binding away now might cause more problems than letting it fail over time?" The analogy made sense. If someone ripped the vine off a tree, it often tore up the bark and might kill the tree instead of saving it.

She nodded. "And the Goddess has not deigned to show me that part of the future. Perhaps the binding continues to fail in tiny ways or maybe your Gift peaked when you were an infant. That often happens with early developers."

Triswon patted my leg once before pulling his hand back. "You're perfect the way you are, Snowflake. You are powerful in the best ways."

I smiled hopefully at him. "We'll find out if the councilwoman agrees with you at the hearing next month."

HOURS LATER, I told Rankar and Leara what I found out as I curled against Rankar in one bed and she drifted toward sleep in the other. Leara thought the whole thing was amazing. When I checked, my husband's expression turned thoughtful, though.

I tilted my head and caught his eye. "What's that look?"

His half-smile reassured me. "It explains a few things. The temperature suddenly dropping in the middle of a desert in summer, for example. But, mostly, I was thinking that Tier's mom is from there. She was a Kinatnya before she met and married Tier's dad. I wonder if she knew your parents."

I'd never met Tier's mom, but I liked Rankar's soulsibling a lot. "Tier and I are cousins by Tuatha de standards!"

He made a face. "Technically, we are too. By fae standards."

I grinned. "I was raised outside the Sithens. Family is love, not blood. But cousins should be blood, not a game of five degrees of separation."

Leara laughed behind us in the other bed. "It's true! Everyone in a Sithen and half the people outside are 'cousins' by the definition we use."

Long minutes later, Leara's breathing evened out into sleep. Hypnos curled on her second pillow, and Thanatos perched at the foot of our bed. The puppies slept in their kennel in the other room, close enough for us to hear if they needed an emergency overnight outing. Even the stable underneath us was silent. Yet Rankar's heart still beat hard under my hand, and I couldn't sync my breathing.

"It's gonna be okay," I murmured, hoping to convince us both.

"Everyone knows she belongs with us," he agreed, just as softly.

Except her grandmother and brother. Her closest living relatives.

Who hoped she never saw us again.

CHAPTER 4

A MONTH LATER, I tapped my fingers nervously against my pants leg, exhaling slowly as Rankar and I sat in a small room off the main hall. We'd only been in the room for five minutes, and my nerves must have worked on Rankar's. He slipped his fingers between mine, rubbing my wrist with his thumb. Gripping his hand, I stopped the tapping.

When we had entered the main building, two members of Keawyn's personal guard brought us here and advised they'd wait outside until it was time. Their words implied they intended to escort us to the hall, too, once the councilwoman was ready for us.

"Do you think this is a bad sign? Do you think she's already made a decision?" I whispered, aware that the guard outside the room had paranormal hearing.

Rankar kissed my forehead, lingering just a second. "No. I've found Keawyn to be fair and just in her dealings with her people since she came to Asez. Becoming a member of the council is not going to change that, I don't think. I expect she will be thorough and fair. Whatever she decides, we have to believe it is best for Leara."

Again, I sent that prayer up to the Goddess. *Please help Keawyn make the best choice for Leara's future and wellbeing.*

Even if it means she doesn't stay with me.

Someone knocked twice on the door before opening it. "Please follow me," the woman murmured. Her partner waited until Rankar walked out to shut the door.

"Thank you, Jeannitra."

She glanced over her shoulder. "You're welcome, Captain."

One of the double doors was propped open, and she moved aside once we arrived. "Right side. Front row," she murmured, her quiet voice barely heard.

I paused as I stepped through, trying not to hyperventilate.

At the front of the room, four guards stood on each side. Keawyn and Councilwoman Penelope Sirtis of the vampires sat at a long table with four chairs. The other councilwoman's presence made the late hour of the hearing understandable.

Between the women was Leara. Her hands were clasped, knuckles a little white. Otherwise, she looked much calmer than I imagined I did. One chair remained empty. About fifteen feet from the table, in the center, was a podium with a microphone. Then behind the podium and to either side were rows of chairs four wide.

To the left sat Leara's grandmother, brother, and cousin. Only Alera, her younger cousin, turned when the door opened.

On the right, in the front row where we were supposed to sit, were Eliecha, Triswon, and two empty chairs. Behind them were Mycal, Karyn, Kismet, and his wife, Tiernia. In the third row, Asher, Alika, Faela, and Xander sat. In the fourth row, having stolen four chairs from

Zanta's side, were Belisario, Treyv, Davie, and Rendle.

I glanced at Rankar, wondering if he knew his entire family intended to make an appearance. He shook his head, silently urging me forward with a light hand at the small of my back. Moments later, I squeezed Triswon's shoulder as I slipped into the seat beside him. I noticed that his eyes were as damp as mine.

After a moment, Keawyn stood, motioning everyone else to remain seated. "We are here today by the request of a Tuatha de Danaan citizen of Orion to determine the best suited guardian of fellow Tuatha de Danaan Leara Sinton. As news of this hearing spread, I received a few requests for attendance, which I decided to allow. However, anyone who interferes in the proceedings without being called upon will be escorted from the room. Does everyone understand?"

All present, including me, agreed in unison.

Councilwoman Sirtis stood and addressed Zanta. "Zanta McCarthy, please rise." As soon as she stood, the councilwoman for the vampire citizens began. "Do you agree that you are a Tuatha de Danaan resident of Orion under the jurisdiction of the council—specifically Councilwoman Asez? Do you agree to abide by all decisions made in this hearing by Councilwoman Asez?"

Zanta stared straight ahead. "I do."

"Please be seated," Keawyn said.

Then the procedure repeated with Ardal, Rankar, and me. As I stood, my knees felt weak, but I met the gaze of both Penelope Sirtis and Keawyn, lingering for a moment on Leara between them. My warrior-girl appeared so strong. I couldn't fail her now. "I do." I felt relieved when the councilwoman told me to sit.

"Zanta McCarthy, please approach the podium."

As she glanced at me, I forced my expression to remain neutral. Then she faced the councilwomen and Leara with her back to us. I kept my shoulders straight by force of will. The Goddess would do whatever was best for Leara, as it should be. *As it should be*, I reassured myself.

"Please tell Councilwoman Asez why you brought this complaint before her," Councilwoman Sirtis advised from her seat.

"I am here today to plead for my granddaughter, the youngest child of my son Jeremy Sinton, to be returned fully to my custody. My beloved son and his beautiful wife were both callously murdered by the humans during the war while incarcerated in an internment camp. Since the Goddess safely returned Leara to us here at Asez Holding, she spends her days running rabid with no structure or schedule."

A sniffle escaped the woman, and she wiped her face with a handkerchief. I wanted to make her cry in truth for the lie. Leara's life stayed ridiculously structured, and today was the first day she had even missed school, despite us giving her one free pass to use. Rankar's hand gripped my leg, as though he could feel my anger. I set mine on top to let him know I wouldn't actually kill her in front of this many witnesses.

"Children need structure to properly develop. In my care, Leara will attend classes regularly. Furthermore, she will join her cousin Alera in her daily instrument and herbalism lessons. She will have her own bedroom to sleep in at night inside the main building, not in a horse stall, and we will purchase her a wardrobe appropriate for a fourteen-year-old girl.

At the table, Keawyn jotted notes onto a legal pad without looking down. However, everyone watched Zanta as she continued.

"Leara deserves to be surrounded by her family, and she and her brother, Ardal, are all who are left of my son's line. I want her to remain safe, which is why I also filed the petition to eliminate her contact with Sarki Kinan. She has taught Leara how to use weapons no child should wield, has placed Leara in the presence of dangerous, guard-trained Deylura horses in the stable, and allowed her to wander around the extended grounds in the presence of people who are not intended to watch children. I have it from reliable sources that she has been seen following guards on their rounds, sometimes in the early hours of the morning. Each of these activities is dangerous of itself. Combined? They endanger her life to an extent that proves Sarki Kinan cannot be trusted with the care of my granddaughter."

A long minute passed. Beside me, Rankar's breaths were so regular that I knew he had to be timing them. Thankful, I also tried to release the negative energy and lower my heartrate by matching his rhythm. Then Councilwoman Sirtis looked at Keawyn who shook her head. "Is there anything further you would like to add at this time, Zanta McCarthy?"

"No, Councilwoman."

"Then please be seated. Ardal Sinton, please approach the podium and advise why you believe that your grandmother is the best person for Councilwoman Asez to assign as guardian of Leara."

The fae's nervousness was palpable, but he didn't glance at us as he passed. Instead, he gripped the sides of the podium and stood tall. "My grandmother raised me and is raising Alera, both since we were young children. Her dedication to her bloodline is admirable, and she wants to continue her stewardship over her family with Leara. That Leara receives everything necessary to grow into a woman worthy of the Sinton name is quite important to her. Plus, I know my mother and father would have wanted Leara to be in a position to continue her studies. Education was paramount to my mother. Even while they were in the middle of nowhere traveling in a wagon, she always made sure to give Leara lessons. That's—uh—that's all. Thank you."

He stepped back, but Councilwoman Sirtis held up a hand to stop him until Keawyn finished taking her notes. Then she waved him away and asked Rankar to move forward.

Rankar walked to the podium. I heard his slow, measured breaths and did not doubt everyone else in the room did too. "Councilwomen," he nodded a greeting to both Keawyn and Penelope Sirtis, his voice telling me more than his breathing how hard he fought for control of his temper.

"Rankar Sirach, why do you believe that you and Sarki Kinan Sirach are appropriate guardians for this child, who is not of your blood? Also, how do you address the issue of the alleged danger Leara has been exposed to in Kinan's care?" Councilwoman Sirtis questioned.

"I think Kinan and I would be the best guardians for Leara Sinton for several reasons. First, to answer Zanta's points in order: Leara attends daily classes with the instructor here at Asez and has never missed a single class session until today—something I'm surprised Zanta would be unaware of, considering that I have personally invited her to each and every parent-teacher conference that has been scheduled in Leara's time at Asez. Leara has had the opportunity to participate in both herbalism and musical instruction, from some of the most qualified musicians and herbalists on this Plane. She has declined, because she is profoundly uninterested in both of those things. Instead, she is taking extra instruction in linguistics, languages, and strategy in the form of chess lessons.

"She is also able to learn a great deal about animal husbandry by spending time with the Deyluras and other animals at Asez Holding—which I'm sure you can appreciate, Councilwoman Asez, seeing as you yourself are a veterinarian and you inherited one of the largest and most well-respected horse ranches in the western hemisphere, a ranch which Zanta McCarthy has been employed by for nearly thirty-five years. Any time Leara spends in the stables with the Deyluras and Deylura crosses, she is under the eye of at least one trained hostler who is ready to intervene if needed. And she takes self-defense classes, because after surviving multiple attacks on caravans with her parents, the internment camp, the war with the United States, and the anarchy after the war was over, it's important to her and to the people who love her that she be able to take care of herself in the event that the worst happens to her again."

He paused, and I drew in the breath with him. Together, we exhaled.

"Leara does not sleep in a horse stall, and it's absurd for Zanta to say she does. The current living situation isn't ideal, because the apartment only has one bedroom, but there is room to remodel to make it into a two-bedroom apartment. The plans for that remodel are currently on your desk, awaiting your review and approval, Councilwoman. In the interests of maintaining some stability in Leara's life, I haven't pushed as hard as I maybe should have to drastically change Kinan and Leara's living space once I moved in. However, as soon as we receive your go-ahead, we're ready to move forward with the renovation to the apartment.

"I don't know what could be inappropriate about Leara's wardrobe; her clothing is new, in good condition, fits her, and suits her needs and style. Where possible, Leara picks out her own clothes because she is fourteen years old, not a four-year-old child. Kinan and I purchase these clothes without financial input from Zanta."

I scooted forward on my seat, urging him to stop grinding his teeth between sentences.

"We feed Leara with no financial input from Zanta six days a week, excepting when she stays with her cousin. We shelter her and provide for her schooling, with—once again—no financial input from Zanta. I will acknowledge that family may very well be important to Zanta. That's why we ensure that Leara spends the night with her and with her cousin Alera every Friday night. Ardal has had the opportunity to spend more time with his sister; when Leara was rescued, I offered him paid time off so he could make sure his sister was okay and adjusting to Asez. He declined at that time and continues to decline at every opportunity. Zanta had the opportunity to organize a search party for her missing granddaughter; she did not. Ardal had the opportunity to be part of the search parties that I organized, at Kinan's request rather than Zanta's; he declined.

"At every opening to do the right thing for Leara, to do something that would make her happy or keep her safe in a productive way, Zanta and Ardal have declined to do so. The reason I think Kinan and I would be better guardians for Leara is because we've each entertained the possibility that maybe we aren't the right choice. We've thought about whether or not it's selfish for us to keep her with us rather than passing custody to Zanta, because family *is* important. But to Leara, Kinan is her family. Kinan protects her, teaches her, and helps her heal. Kinan knew she didn't have the time or knowledge to adequately train Leara's Gifts, and her biological family wasn't making any effort to take over that aspect of her training, either. In response, Kinan went out and found the best possible teacher on this Plane to train Leara's Gifts. She knew Leara needed the help of a professional to begin to process everything that had happened to her, so Kinan found a professional to help Leara."

He placed his hands on top of the podium for a moment. "I would do anything to make sure Leara was happy and safe, including give her up if that was what was truly the best thing for her. But I don't think taking her away from our family is the right thing for Leara."

"Anything else to add?" Keawyn asked, nodding to him.

"No, Councilwoman."

She excused him and called for me. I passed Rankar as I approached the podium and fought against reaching out to him for reassurance. Instead, I subtly rubbed my sweaty palms against my pants once hidden from the councilwomen's sights. I offered Leara a reassuring smile, because her eyes had filled with tears. If I could loan her just a little strength to get through this, I'd risk the ire of the others. Her lips turned up a tiny bit, but it was enough for me to know she was okay.

"Sarki Kinan Sirach, please tell us all why you believe that you and Rankar Sirach would be more appropriate guardians of Leara Sinton than her grandmother. Also, address the issue of the alleged danger you have exposed the minor to while in your care."

My brain blanked, and I said the only thing that came to mind. "Because we love her." Somehow, the words broke the barrier, and I continued. "Rankar and I love Leara, not for who we want her to be but for who she already is. This warrior-girl is so incredibly strong that I know grown men who don't measure up. She watched her loved ones murdered, and she remained positive and optimistic in the most dismal place I never could imagine. At thirteen, she took a few basic self-defense moves taught to her inside a concentration camp cell and *survived* on her own for months. Without formal training, she would have made it to Asez Holding on her own if the grounds hadn't been locked down after the war. She soaks up every language I throw at her with almost no effort, always ready and willing to learn more."

I inhaled, wanting them to understand her. Needing them to see Leara for herself. "Leara had an unconventional upbringing for a Tuatha de Danaan. Her parents traveled with a caravan across various Planes. Her mother taught Leara about demon cultures, Planar history, math, languages, and many of the regular subjects. She didn't learn instruments or herbalism, because those things didn't interest her parents or her. But she throws herself wholeheartedly into things that *do* attract her interest, like self-defense and horseback riding. And... her personality is such that she naturally draws everyone to like her, which is the reason every person in this room is here. It's also the reason that my guard-trained, contrary Deylura would never harm her."

I shook my head. "Leara is a very intelligent teenager who has been in situations much more dangerous than Asez Holding's stables where a dozen different people would give their life for her without second thought—including me. She reads every language used in our signage system more than well enough to know the dangers warned about. Furthermore, in her time spent at Asez Holding throughout her life, her parents and Rendle taught both her and Alera how to maneuver safely around horses."

A small smile teased my lips at a persistent memory. "My parents did not allow me to wield anything more than a bow or dulled-edge sword at Leara's age. To her frustration, I have no intention of moving from those weapons until she has mastered them. However, when we inevitably train her in more powerful weapons, she will first and foremost be taught the safety protocols required to protect both her and all inhabitants of Asez Holding."

Exhaling, I glanced over my shoulder at all of these

people, proud of the family that Leara had drawn around her. "Councilwomen, before my arrival at Asez Holding and on rare occasions since, Leara *has* followed members of the guard on their shifts. However, these men and women are highly competent and are aware of her presence. Second, they are absolutely intended to watch children. These are the people trained and trusted to protect all of the noncombatants—men, women, and children—of Asez Holding. There is no safer place for anyone to be than under their watchful eyes."

I hesitated a moment, but they needed to know everything to make the best choice. "I don't know if I'm the best person to raise Leara, honestly. I ask myself that question at least once a day. But I am always going to do what seems best for her, even when it is difficult. If you decide that Leara is better off without me, I will forever have been privileged to be part of her life." I nodded to Leara, who stared at me. "And you'll always be my warrior-girl."

Councilwoman Sirtis met my eyes. "Do you have anything further to add?"

I swallowed. "No, ma'am."

"Please have a seat."

I slid into the seat beside Rankar, and he gripped my fingers hard. I squeezed back, needing the support.

When Keawyn Asez stood, my heart slammed against my chest. How could she have made such an important decision this quickly? Didn't she realize it would affect Leara—and us—for the rest of our very long lives?

However, she glanced over our heads. "Alika Sirach, please come forward. You requested to speak during these proceedings. What would you like to say to your councilwoman on the matter of guardianship of Leara Sinton?"

Rankar's fingers froze around mine as she walked past us, but I placed my other hand on top. In this especially, I trusted his sister to do the best thing for Leara. In many ways, she knew Leara better than we did. Leara could reveal things to her that would be difficult to tell to a parent or guardian. Also, she would never tell a lie that would endanger one of her charges. Like all the Sirachs, she had compassion and integrity.

"Thank you, Councilwoman Asez. Councilwomen, as you may know, I am employed by the Albuquerque City Medical Center as a Gift instructor. My duties are to teach the general basics of things like centering, shielding, and Gating to young paranormals, as well as offering specialized instruction to any child or adolescent whose Gifts fall within my purview of water, healing, and some minor divination. For Tuatha de Danaan students, I offer history lessons as well, both of our people generally and of their Sithen and clan specifically if the information is available. Because of my training pre-Enlightenment, I am also qualified to act as a counselor for children and adolescents who have survived trauma. I'm here today to offer my professional opinion of the best guardianship arrangement as Leara's social worker.

"Since October 31, 2006, I have been seeing Leara Sinton as a student and as a therapy client. These lessons were arranged by Sarki Kinan, because she felt Leara needed instruction that Kinan was not qualified to give. The therapy sessions were arranged by Kinan, because Leara was imprisoned in the Kansas Internment Camp and, as a result, had seen and experienced things in her first decade-and-a-half of life that you or I could scarcely imagine enduring as adults. Kinan chose me to be Leara's teacher not because of my familial relationship with her husband, but rather despite it, because I myself have undergone extensive training in both my Gifts and my profession as a clinical social worker.

"During the time that Leara has been working with me, Kinan has brought her to Albuquerque twice a week, every week, for more than six months. During our sessions, Kinan stays in the waiting room with the other parents and guardians. She sometimes studies Leara's schoolwork to ensure that—if Leara has questions—she is prepared to answer them or help Leara work out the answers for herself. Leara has never missed one of our sessions, regardless of what is happening in Kinan's life, which is rare for a fourteen-year-old.

"During that same period of time, neither Zanta McCarthy nor Ardal Sinton have come to my office even once to check on Leara's progress. They have not introduced themselves to me as her family members. If I may be perfectly frank, I sincerely doubt either of them knew that Leara was in either training or in therapy.

"It's a bit... unusual, in my practice, for a Tuatha de with acknowledged living relatives to be in need of the ACMC's Gift training services. Children are so special to our people that we tend to be insular and devoted to training them ourselves in our family's Gifts and histories. Under normal circumstances, given that Leara's parents are unable to do so, I would have expected that—as her grandmother—Zanta McCarthy would have made the necessary arrangements for her granddaughter's training.

The fact that she did not, the fact that Leara came to the ACMC knowing only what she could piece together on her own and what a twenty-five-year old mercenary could teach her in the midst of one of the worst internment camps in the United States, was shocking to me. The fact that Leara came to the ACMC when Zanta could very easily have taken her to their family's home Sithen, which has a stable and permanent entrance in Orion, demonstrates a distinct lack of care and concern for Leara's well-being.

"Untrained Gifts are as dangerous to the Gifted as to those around them. Untreated trauma has lasting and devastating effects, especially on children and adolescents. Zanta and Ardal's gross negligence in this regard is ameliorated only by Kinan's devotion to Leara's health and well-being."

Zanta made an angry noise, like a cat whose tail had been stepped on. When I looked over, though, she sat calmly on her seat with her grandson's arm comfortingly around her shoulder. Rankar eased his grip on my hand slightly, and I patted his.

"Based on these facts alone, I would suggest that regardless of how guardianship is settled, no restraining order should be entered against Kinan."

A long breath escaped, and I felt Rankar relax more also.

"However, there is also the matter of what Leara has spoken with me about in our sessions, which for the sake of preserving patient confidentiality I will not discuss aloud in this venue. But because I believe this to be extremely relevant and pertinent to the facts at hand, I have brought a redacted copy of my treatment notes from my sessions with Leara. In these notes, I have flagged where Leara has discussed her familial relationships with both her blood relatives and with Sarki Kinan, Rankar Sirach, and the members of the guard and the stables who are present here today to support Leara and Kinan."

Keawyn motioned one of the guards forward. He accepted the papers from Alika and handed them to Keawyn. She scanned the first few pages before noticing Leara covertly trying to see what they said. Slipping the stack of papers under the legal pad, she nodded for Alika to continue.

"Given that information, I believe that allowing Zanta McCarthy to have full or partial physical custody of Leara Sinton, and granting Zanta's request for a protective order to be entered against Sarki Kinan, would be contrary to the best interests of Leara and would, in point of fact, be extremely harmful to her. In the slightly more than six months that I've known Leara personally and professionally, neither her grandmother nor her older brother have shown any evidence of caring for Leara as a person rather than as an object to be fought over and controlled or, in Ardal's case, as anything other than an obstacle to be overcome. Granting custody to Zanta McCarthy would be a mistake, and the significant risk of harm to Leara must outweigh whatever minor rewards could be found in preserving and enshrining this biological family unit."

Councilwoman Sirtis noted Keawyn's nod and excused Alika. My sister-in-law nodded to me as she passed, and I returned it. Taking Leara to see Rankar's estranged sister had been a very difficult decision for me, especially as I wasn't sure Rankar would forgive me for doing it without talking to him first, but Alika proved time and again that Leara could trust her in every way. Leara needed a big sister figure to help her through the issues that I'd never be able to touch.

Keawyn flipped through the paperwork Alika had given her, leaving the hall in complete silence and not appearing to care. At her side, Councilwoman Sirtis whispered something to Leara, who nodded once and then stared down at her hands resting on the table. Finally, Keawyn looked up. "We have one more person who would like to speak. Before that, does anyone else here have anything they want to say or anything they would like to add?"

Movement behind me caused me to turn around. Treyv stood at parade rest in front of his chair. "Councilwoman, can I say something?"

At her nod, he approached the podium. "Rankar asked me to join the search party who rescued Leara when we ended the lockdown at Asez. Kinan had called the captain from one of the last surviving payphones in the country because she'd had a premonition that Leara might still be alive. Leara had been trying to get to Asez on her own, because Kinan told her this place would be safe. She tried over and over but couldn't get through the wards that were in place. Unfortunately, Leara was on her own for months after surviving Kansas."

He paused for a moment. "I was part of a group who liberated the Kansas Camp during Orion's Vengeance, Councilwomen; I've got some idea of what happened to both of them there." My hand tightened around Rankar's even as Treyv clenched his fists and took a deep, slow breath. I hadn't known that Treyv had gone in during Vengeance. Of course, as dark and hectic as that night had been, I would not have recognized him even if he'd been in the unit with Locke and me.

"After the rescue party found Leara, she shadowed me on my patrol shifts when she could not sleep. Without Kinan here, Leara didn't feel safe. Even having her *grandmother* as steward and her older brother here as a guard, Leara would rather follow a stranger who had shown her care and kindness than those two."

The word 'grandmother' was said with such venom that it was honestly surprising he didn't spit on the floor after it crossed his lips. He had never indicated in any of our conversations—or to Leara, as far as I knew—that he felt so strongly.

"Zanta never approached any of the guard—or, I presume, the leader of Asez—about organizing a search party, either for her so-beloved son and daughter-in-law or for her granddaughter."

My brain stuttered as his words sank in. Not only had Zanta not searched for Leara, she never tried to find her son either. Glancing at Leara, I caught her smiling at Treyv from her chair, and I realized I'd missed some of his speech. Tuning back in, I appreciated how he reinforced many of the issues Rankar had brought to light—especially that he praised how well we cared for Leara.

"I've never seen Leara look even twenty percent as happy in Zanta's presence as she is in Rankar's and Kinan's. Given what I've seen and heard today, excuse my saying so, I don't know how you could conclude that Zanta is the best choice when you have Rankar and Kinan here willing to continue raising her."

Keawyn glanced at Leara but quickly looked back down at her notepad. She excused Treyv, still rereading something on her legal pad. Finally, she asked for anyone else. This time, no one stood up.

"Jeannitra?" The guard stepped forward, behind Leara's chair. "Miss Leara, Jeannitra is going to escort you into the back office. Come here, Alera. Why don't you keep her company?"

Alera jumped up and rushed forward. However, alarm crossed Leara's face, and I felt it to my soul. The last time a guard had pulled her from a room with me, I'd been worse than killed and we'd been separated for months. "No, I won't leave," she argued, voice shaky.

Keawyn's face remained stern as she stood. "Leara, I won't prevent you from saying your goodbyes when the time comes, but please leave now with Jeannitra without forcing her to remove you."

Leara's eyes met mine, pleading with me. I tried to tell her it would be okay with a look. Linking my fingers with Rankar's, I lifted our hands high enough for her to see. I wasn't alone. Nothing bad would happen to me this time. And I would be forsworn before I let anything bad happen to her.

Her eyes shiny with tears as she stared at me, she nodded and pushed her chair back. Keawyn looked at me, but I refused to take my gaze off Leara. I had to make sure she made it safely out of the room this time. Not that Jeannitra would ever harm a child.

She wasn't a monster.

CHAPTER 5

THE DOOR CLOSED with a click behind Jeannitra, who went through last of the three, and Keawyn sat back down. "Please approach, Mistress Bhinj."

When Eliecha stood, Triswon did also. Together, they walked to the podium. Her turquoise jewelry and the bright feathers in her hair contrasted with his dark clothing. They waited, side by side, until both councilwomen nodded at them. Then Eliecha began.

"I am Eliecha Bhinj, thrice blessed by the Goddess. Through Her, I have Gifts of Prophecy, Healing, and Empathy. Though I am not nor will I ever be ruler of my Sithen, my word is law there by grace of the Goddess as yours is law here. Though not of our line, we consider Sarki Elayne Kinan Sirach to be our daughter." She nodded respectfully to Keawyn and Councilwoman Sirtis. "This is my husband, Triswon Bhinj. We have consent from Irhic Bhinj, our ruler and first in our Sithen, to speak for him as your guests here today."

"Eliecha and Triswon Bhinj, we are blessed to have one touched by the Goddess as a guest, and I apologize for the inconvenience in asking you to come to this Plane on short notice. However, after our previous conversation, I made a few inquiries and thought it best that you present your accusations here." She gestured to the crowd, and Faela stood and walked to the table to take the seat beside Keawyn. "While I am a descendent of the Serei Sithen, I have asked Queen Athanasia Serei's heir Faela—Fayeliah— to join Councilwoman Sirtis and me to speak in her esteemed mother's stead. Do you object to this?"

The news that Keawyn Asez belonged to the Serei Sithen surprised me. Her power lined up, but that she had publicly dropped the surname on this Plane definitely didn't. Faela's mother required all members of the Sithen to keep the Serei name.

While I couldn't see Eliecha's face, I heard controlled amusement in her voice. "I have no objections. I am privileged to face two so-valued by the queen of the Serei Sithen, including her beloved daughter."

If this were Sithen politics, I never wanted to go to one. For a moment, I looked around as the ridiculous interplay continued. Only then did I notice an olive-skinned man with dark hair standing against the back wall. He stared straight ahead, looking oddly comfortable in his double-breasted suit. The lines were obviously tailored to him, the fit perfect and expensive.

I nudged Rankar, wanting him to identify the newcomer. However, Faela and Keawyn each stood in unison. Keawyn bowed her head to him while Faela only smiled. "Well-met, Lyonos Katataros, favored son of Riknare and Flechwe Katataros."

He grinned and shook his head as he passed us, obviously familiar with her. "Well-met, Fayeliah Sirach Serei, favored daughter of Athanasia Serei."

"Only daughter," she corrected, laughing.

"Only son," he reminded, showing teeth.

She motioned him to take her chair, moving to Leara's. "I saw you arrived for introductions. All present, we are graced by Lyonos Katataros, second heir to the Katataros Sithen. He is here at Councilwoman Asez's request so all parties in this hearing have a representative from their Sithen present."

Keawyn gestured to Eliecha. "Please continue."

"On March 26, 2007, Asez Holding faced a dire threat. You had a plan in place to protect all of your people in the event that you lost the challenge to Mebrid Choalite. You trusted your people, and you deserve to know if you cannot trust someone to do the duties required of them as Asez continues forward during what our allies have advised is a trying time where evacuations are practiced weekly."

Across the aisle, Zanta stood. "I object. Councilwomen, what does the challenge have to do with Leara?"

Councilwoman Sirtis addressed her as Eliecha paused respectfully. "Zanta McCarthy, you have no power to make objections. I asked you if you had anything further to say earlier. You did not. You will keep your current thoughts to yourself until we request otherwise. If not, you will be removed under guard. We trust that the representative from your Sithen can remain in your stead."

Anger radiated off the fae, but she returned to her seat. Then the four leaders, nearly in sync, nodded to Eliecha to continue.

"On the day of the challenge, Kinan Sirach brought Leara Sinton to the Elysii Plane to remain with my husband and me until the challenge completed so she could man her post to the very end. Kinan had attempted to locate either Zanta or Ardal initially to send Leara with Alera to the evacuation point, believing that the children would benefit from the other's company. However, none of them could be located within the grounds, though hours remained prior to the ordered evacuation time. They had abandoned Leara to her fate, obviously trusting Kinan and her husband, Rankar Sirach, to keep their beloved kin safe. Which they did in the chaos."

Eliecha lifted her hands, palm up. "I presented to you the vision the Goddess sent me, and you asked that I recount it here."

I knew from her posture that she stood with her chin slightly up, eyes open but looking to the ceiling. Undoubtedly, they glowed with the power she channeled via her Gift. Penelope Sirtis looked quite interested, but the other three had apparently seen her commune with the Goddess before.

"Zanta McCarthy walks quickly through the hallways, half-pulling Alera Sinton behind her. Their surroundings are minimally lighted and deserted. Overhead, footsteps rush in the opposite direction. She ducks slightly, looking around. Then she stops at a door. Using a large ring of keys, she opens it, and they go inside. It is dark, no lamps shine in this room. However, she walks to a trunk against the far wall, uses a different key, and opens it. Light from the hallways glints off… gold? Copper? She closes it. Alera asks what is inside. She tells her granddaughter it is 'payment.' When she creates a Gate to the stationary Gate outside the Katataros Sithen, she gestures Alera through before lifting the trunk and exiting also. The incredible weight would have been too much for any two humans, but she manages with barely a limp."

Again, Zanta came to her feet. Her hands fisted at her sides. "Eliecha Bhinj speculates! She was not present during the challenge!"

Eliecha's hand gripped Triswon's wrist, holding him in place. However, she did not speak as the vampire leader gestured for a guard from each contingent to go to Zanta.

"This is your final warning," the councilwoman growled. "Proceedings are nearly at close, and it would be a pity for anyone to miss the conclusion."

Swallowing hard, Keawyn stood herself. "All rise," she ordered, and those of us still sitting followed her command. "We came here today to determine what is in the best interests of teenager Leara Sinton. Though orphaned, she has living blood family from her Sithen, and her clan is the second smallest in Katataros. Lyonos Katataros informs us the blood line is greatly valued, and we see the importance of that. As Alika Sirach mentioned, the culture of a clan is pertinent to continuing the traditions and creating a lineage the Sithen can be proud to call its own."

I squeezed Rankar's hand, and he held mine just as tightly. My chest cramped, and I felt a soft hand against my back to steady me as I swayed.

Keawyn paused. "Zanta, why did you not ask anyone to speak for you? Every member of Rankar Sirach's immediate family seems to be here, plus coworkers and the people who consider Kinan daughter."

Zanta raised her chin, lips curled slightly. "I needed no one to stand with me. I am Leara's *grandmother*. She belongs with me."

Keawyn looked between Rankar and me. "So why did

you two request these people come?"

"We didn't." Rankar and I spoke in concert.

"You didn't?" Her brow wrinkled.

Triswon raised his hand, and Keawyn's mouth tightened, as though holding in a smile. "Yes, Triswon Bhinj?"

"They did not ask any of us to come, and many of us didn't come for them—as much as we love them. We're here for Leara. We want our granddaughter to be happy," he offered gruffly, turning his hand in Elie's grip until their fingers linked.

Keawyn exhaled slowly. "Thank you for clarifying. As I mentioned, Sinton and McCarthy clans fall beneath the purview of the Katataros Sithen, though you have all agreed to abide by my decision. I believe, though, it is only fair that the Serei, Katataros, and Bhinj representatives understand my choice that they may direct me if I overstep."

She looked down at the legal pad before meeting my concerned gaze. "I spoke to Leara last night as she stayed with me. She told me about her life before she and her parents were taken to the camps, life traveling the Planes. She told me of the first time you—Kinan—rescued her, and Karyn Sirach filled me in this morning on what that nearly cost you. Leara also told me what happened in the Kansas camp, that you tried to stop her parents' death but could only keep her safe in the end. She told me... a lot. About her rescue, the relief she felt and how close she'd come to being killed while on her own. There is no doubt you saved her life more than once. However, I hear you have saved many lives. That is not a solid basis for guardianship.

"I have researched a few of the accusations this past

week. According to Leara's teachers, she is never late to class and she never skips class. She has the highest possible grades, and she speaks more unique languages at least passably than all of the teachers combined. According to the stable hands I spoke with, including Master Rendle Cavallo, Leara has never been in danger while in the stables. She obeys all of the rules—posted and otherwise—while in that purview. She has her own bed, her own wardrobe, and even a computer to complete her homework. Furthermore, her only injury since she has returned to Asez Holding post-war was a gash that required stitches when she was playing with her cousin Alera. With all this information and the testimony of Alika Sirach, I deny the request for a protection order against Sarki Kinan Sirach. She is not and never has been a danger to Leara."

The loud buzzing in my ears kept me from hearing her next few words, but I swallowed hard to try to clear them. "… believe that family is paramount to the upbringing of a child. As such, I do award full and permanent custody to Leara's family."

Karyn appeared to my right, her arm and Rankar's around me to keep my legs from buckling. My chest hurt, but for once, the anxiety had nothing to do with being held. It had everything to do with losing my warrior-girl.

She can still come see you. You haven't lost her.

"First, though, we need to address the accusations Eliecha Bhinj made today." She paused, but my vision still blurred from the tears in my eyes. I couldn't see her face, only her silhouette. "I reviewed the video recordings from March 26th. While I fought a battle to the death, hoping to save my people from a monster, the steward trusted by my beloved grandmother, Alyson Asez, to preserve Asez Holding stole from storage. According to the manifest provided by the accountant, the value of the items in the trunk exceed half a million dollars—including a solid gold rose with a six-carat ruby bud gifted directly to Alyson Asez from Queen Athanasia Serei for her service to the Sithen in housing my father—a Serei diplomat—while he visited the Terra Plane."

Beside Keawyn, Lyonos spoke. "Fayeliah Serei brought these accusations to our doorstep, asking if we harbored those who committed theft against the Serei Sithen. Though the rulers of the Katataros Sithen advised that we would never disrespect Athanasia Serei, we performed a search of Zanta McCarthy's quarters to appease the heir." He gestured with his left hand, and a reinforced trunk appeared beside him. When he gestured a second time, a golden rose with a bright red gemstone sat on the table before him. Placing it against his chest a moment, he then handed it to Keawyn. "Unfortunately, we must admit that one of our own did steal from the indomitable Athanasia Serei."

The guards beside her gripped and held Zanta. Another two grabbed Ardal and pulled him toward the back to keep him from interfering. I leaned as close to Rankar as possible, holding him as tightly as he did me.

What is happening?

Keawyn turned the rose slowly in her hand before passing it to Faela, who put it back on the table in the middle. "Zanta McCarthy of the Katataros Sithen, you have been found guilty today of stealing from the Serei clan, of violating your oath of loyalty to Asez Holding when you forsook your post in our time of need, and of betraying your own blood and the Katataros clan when you abandoned your granddaughter Leara Sinton to possible death in your greed. Asez Holding, against whom you sinned, sentences you to banishment from the entire country of Orion. As I promised, you will be able to say goodbye to Leara if you so choose."

Faela shook her head. "Athanasia Serei would want your head, literally. You are lucky I stand here for her. Instead, for your crimes against the Serei clan, you are no longer welcome within our Sithen or any allied Sithen. My mother will be sending messengers to all we consider friend that anyone who harbors you after this hour has declared the Serei clan their enemy."

Lyonos Katataros stared at Zanta. "Your mistake nearly cost us more than an alliance. You nearly caused the Serei clan to war against us. We are smaller, and our numbers would not have held against theirs. You almost destroyed us all. The Katataros declare you *gan treibh*. To all Tuatha de Danaan, you no longer exist. Any fae assisting you after this Terran day ends will share your punishment. You do not value your clan, so you are nothing to us."

Behind me, I heard someone inhale sharply, and I remembered that Tiernia's father had suffered the same fate. Everything seemed to be falling apart. Without Zanta, Ardal would be Leara's closest blood relative. If he received guardianship of her... *We'll run. I'll be forsworn. We'll run.*

More guards entered the room to encircle Zanta and Ardal, who fought their hold. Zanta shouted, but her words were indecipherable—no language I'd ever heard. However, Lyonos Katataros snapped his fingers, and she became completely silent. Her mouth still moved, but nothing came out.

"I believe Keawyn Serei would like to say something further," he murmured.

Keawyn thanked him. "As I said earlier, family is paramount to the upbringing of a child, and I award Leara's family custody. Effective immediately."

Barehanded, she knocked three times upon the wood of the table. "Rankar and Kinan Sirach, as her family, you have co-guardianship."

Only my unbreakable grip on Rankar kept me from collapsing in relief. A few of our family behind us expressed their own happiness. Though I couldn't form coherent words, I appreciated all they'd done.

"You will complete the apartment remodel, ensuring Leara has appropriate privacy within the next sixty days. Please submit a statement of completion with photos before the end of that timeframe. I also want a monthly report from her social worker through the end of this year. She will continue both her therapy and Gift training through at least that long, I assume."

Keawyn looked over the people who'd gathered in the room. "Anyone who has ever lived in Asez should know that family has little to do with blood or clan. A shifter, a Tulevi demon, a Tuveri demon, and a half-dozen fae from at least five clans are united for one child. And her newly appointed guardians mentioned two things most important to her wellbeing: happiness and love. You wanted what was best for *her*. Not for yourself, not for your clan, and not for the memory of the deceased. I am certain this is the right decision, and if you prove me wrong, there will be considerable consequences."

Lyonos Katataros nodded. "Well-stated. Along those lines, the Katataros clan would never allow a minor to be erased with a non-parental guardian. Alera can return to clan with me, or Asez Holding can take over her guardianship. As you mentioned, there is a sense of family here."

Keawyn's mouth gaped a second. "We'll let Alera choose. She has clan at your Sithen, but she's lived her entire life here." Squaring her shoulders, she looked at the crowd. "Leara's family, please step outside. We need to explain to Leara and Alera what has happened and give them and Ardal the opportunity to say their goodbyes to Zanta. Captain, please make sure Ardal's next shift is covered so he has time to grieve after the guards escort Zanta to her rooms and on to the border of Orion to begin her exile. We'll send Leara out to you."

Rankar supported my weight, my legs still too weak to hold me up, as we walked out the doors. A couple of the guards patted his shoulder as we passed. Then we stood outside the main hall with the doors shut, and everyone celebrated. I saw suddenly what Keawyn had. Even if something happened to Rankar and me, Leara would never be left to fend for herself again. Her family was too large, too stubborn, and too powerful to ever let her go.

Leara walked between Rankar and me back to the apartment. Xander, Triswon, and Mycal wanted to take a look at the remodel plans before we went to dinner, plus double-check a few things that were apparently important during construction. Though her face still held some of the blotchy redness from when she'd walked out of the main hall, she beamed as we headed back to the apartment as a group.

Belisario and Treyv excused themselves halfway across the courtyard, and Rendle congratulated us at the base of the stairs. In the fastest Gate I'd ever witnessed, Triswon and Eliecha moved from the ground to the catwalk. Tiernia laughed as she climbed the stairs with Kismet right behind her. Leara and I followed them up with Rankar's arm so close I felt the heat. Everyone else cheated and met us at the top.

Leara cut to the front, unlocked the door, and stepped inside with a twirl. "Welcome to my home!"

I picked her up, carrying her over my shoulder and to the kitchen table. "It's been your home for as long as it's been mine, warrior-girl."

Everyone split into groups. The older three brothers, Mycal, and Triswon checked how difficult it would be to wall off the sitting room and rearrange the main room. Karyn, Eliecha, Alika, and Asher sat with Leara at the table, trying to decide where we'd eat—we'd all been much too nervous to attempt it before the hearing. And I moved to the safe to add a few weapons to my outfit since we'd been ordered to arrive before the councilwomen unarmed.

Armed and ready, I rested my hands on Leara's shoulders as she talked to Faela about Alera's decision to remain at Asez Holding for now. Keawyn had promised that a family in the compound wanted her to live with them. Once the apartment transformed into a two-bedroom, the girls asked to begin having the Friday night sleepover here. "I think it'll be nice for Alera to at least alternate Fridays here," I agreed. "She's your family, after all."

Faela and Alika both smiled approvingly at me. I couldn't resist returning it. Eliecha, though, studied Leara with no expression on her face. That level of scrutiny made me feel suspicious, especially since not much escaped the thrice-blessed fae, which was only compounded when Leara stood up—slipping from my hold. A worried expression crossed Elie's face before she closed it down.

Leara waved at the men, who carried the last of our living room furniture out into the open. "Oh! That reminds me! Rankar, could you come here a second?"

Eliecha stepped into Triswon as the guys all approached. She whispered something into his ear, and he shot a startled look toward Leara before moving to stand beside where Xander joined Faela. Kismet leaned down between Tiernia and his sister to ask a question as Rankar walked up.

I moved forward, planning to intercept her. Whatever she was about to do, we needed to talk about it *outside* first.

Too late.

"Today was all about family, and I'm incredibly blessed and proud to be a part of this one. The only thing that would make it better would be if... Rankar, please apologize to Alika. You two need to work things out. You love each other. I know you do."

I froze a second before borrowing Locke's favorite word.

Fuck.

CHAPTER 6

THE ENERGY IN the room froze then pulsed, creating a low but noticeable buzz. Triswon's hands gripped Xander's shoulders, while the middle brother focused his attention on Rankar. Kismet crouched down beside Tiernia, wrapping his arm around the empath's back. If her expression was any indication, the emotions in this room had dialed up to catastrophic levels. Faela, on the other hand, seemed torn between staying with her husband, going to support her soulsibling, or heading straight for Rankar.

Alika cringed, her body poised as though she wanted to Gate out of the room. She looked cornered, like a coyote with her foot in a steel trap ready to chew her way out. Though I couldn't see Rankar's face, his body was rigid.

Too many people spoke at once.

"Leara, that's really not—"

"I don't think this is the right—"

"Let's just focus—"

"I think you're absolutely right, Leara." Xander's voice was flat, dry as dust, and void of any emotion as he cut through the cacophony in the room.

Triswon's hands were on his shoulders, but that wasn't stopping Xander from speaking. People often said Xander's sense of "proportionate response" fluctuated wildly between "the mountain does not bend to the wind no matter how hard it blows" and "leave no stone touching another, salt the earth that nothing will grow there." The fact that he was speaking up now did not bode well for his state of mind.

"Rankar, don't you agree that you owe my baby sister an apology?" Xander continued, absolutely still except for the roiling emotion in his eyes.

Rankar's hands twitched as he gritted out, "I don't—I wouldn't—what do you want me to say?" he demanded. "What do you want me to be sorry for?" He'd switched to Welsh, his and his siblings' native language.

I suddenly wished I hadn't spent the last years learning it for him. Perhaps, if I hadn't lived in his parents' house for so long, I could ignore this argument. Glancing at Leara, I saw that Eliecha had wrapped her arms around the teenager. While she hadn't practiced enough to follow the family speaking in their native tongue, the tone of the conversation had to be slapping her in the face.

Somehow, sympathy escaped me. I'd rather be anywhere than this fallout. We'd discussed how terrible an idea it would be for her to do this. Yet... here we were.

"I don't know, Rankar. How about being sorry for blaming me for not being there when your fiancée died, even though you never seemed to blame Asher for the same thing?" The Welsh poured out of Alika, sounding heartbroken but resigned to the pain. "How about being sorry for never even telling me you'd been engaged in the first place? I found out by accident that my own brother had been widowed before he was a husband because I did an independent research project in undergrad. Or, and here's a thought, maybe you could be sorry for blaming me for the fact that, while you were captured during the war, you were waterboarded by Viet Cong fighters? You could apologize for the fact that you never seemed to care or believe I was just as scared as everyone else in our family when you and Tier were both captured within a month of each other and we weren't sure if we would ever see either of you alive again. Could you be sorry for that?"

Asher reached out, his hand touching her back. However, Alika never paused for anyone else to interject, not that anyone seemed to know how to stop this disaster now that it had started. The youngest Sirach's bitterness welled up and spilled out through her words, decades of pain boiling over. "No, I'm sorry, Rankar, that's probably too much for you—the fact that I can drown someone with my Gift makes me guilty by association, right?"

"Alyssa Rhiannon Si—" Karyn started to speak to cut off her daughter, voice stern and disappointed.

"No, Mother, he asked what he should be sorry for. If he doesn't know, then I should tell him. He'll apologize because Leara told him to, but if he can't think of anything he should be sorry for, I am allowed to remind him."

"Mom, you don't need to drop the full first and middle names on her when she's telling the truth. Li's right."

Rankar's voice was hoarse, like he fought back tears. Quietly, I stepped up behind him and slipped my hand under his shirt to touch the small of his back. Hiding behind him, I let his body buffer the emotion and silently urged him to mend this rift, if he could, for not only his and Alika's sake… also Leara's.

Eliecha stepped forward, her palms down as though trying to lower the energy in the room. "Rankar and Alika do have something to discuss. While everyone in this family has been brought into the conflict over time, *now* is the time for *them*. It has been a long day, and it is late. Everyone is exhausted, and too much outside emotion will only muddy things, as shown by the strain on young Tiernia's face. Perhaps, Kismet, she'd like to check on little Erykah? I believe Asher is willing to stay with his sister while we go to the Banded Traveler to dine." She met my eyes. "Gate into the back room when they're ready."

For a moment, energy filled the room as all but the four of us left. Rankar spoke again once the rest of their family had Gated away. "You're right. I've treated you like an enemy because I was jealous and afraid and more than a little fucked up when I came home. I blamed you for things that weren't your fault, I treated you like shit, and I haven't been a good brother. I don't know how to make that up to you; I don't know if I can make that up to you. I'd like to try, if you'd let me. I would have told you this in person without an audience, but—for good reason, I guess—you aren't ever in a room alone with me where I could have."

He paused, started again in Welsh. "Alika, I'm sorry. I'm sorry it took this long for me to apologize to you. I'm sorry I was too self-centered to see what an asshole I was being until I saw someone else being the same kind of asshole. I'm sorry I never told you about Bridget, and I'm sorry I continued to blame you for not meeting her before she died. I'm sorry for the way I cut you open on my broken pieces when I came home; I'm sorry I dismissed you when you tried to help. I'm sorry I never gave you the benefit of the doubt. I know I made things worse for you whenever one of us was going through a shitty time."

I gripped his belt loop, wanting him to know I supported him. As upsetting and emotional as this made me, I couldn't imagine how he felt facing Alika after decades of tension and unrest. Even with weeks to think about it, he'd undoubtedly had a hard time reconciling this.

The tears dripping onto Alika's face evaporated as quickly as they appeared. She didn't bother wiping them away or acknowledging them; her Gift hid her vulnerabilities. "Great, you're sorry. Fantastic. That and four dollars will get me a latte in the café at work. I've had to watch my back against my own brother for my entire life. I've sat in six months' worth of twice-weekly sessions with a teenager who's lost *everything* and been *jealous* because even though her brother treats her like what happened to their parents is her fault, my brother treats her like she's family. Do you know how shitty that is for me?"

Rankar flinched under my hand, and Alika stopped. After a long moment, she sighed. "What do you want from me, Rankar?" Her gaze focused on the table top, and she didn't look up. "I'm so tired. Please just tell me what would fix this so it stops hurting Leara." Alika's voice sounded defeated, like exhaustion was dragging her under.

"If I found us a therapist—one that you don't work with and that I'm not in charge of their safety," Rankar clarified, "would you go with me?" His voice was hesitant, but a tinge of hope hid there.

Alika's hand snaked over, grabbing Asher's free one. Both their knuckles lightened with the force of her grip. "You mean like family counseling?"

"Yes. Leara's proof that it works, right? Surely there's someone in this country that we're not related to and don't work with who can deal with our family bullshit. There has to be. And if there's not, I'll find one. I don't know how to fix this, but someone has to, right?"

Alika stared at him, silent, before nodding slowly. "I can ask around, see if anybody at work knows of someone. Why not ask someone I work with, though?"

Ranker tensed under my hand, obviously struggling to put his thoughts into words. "Because you don't deserve to have to sit in the cafeteria with someone who knows all the worst shit about our family and wonder if they look at you differently because of it. When I said I was sorry and that I wanted to fix this, I didn't just mean because I don't like who I've been; I meant because you deserve to have a brother who looks out for your well-being. I haven't been that, but I want to try. I want to fix this, if I can."

Alika nodded, and Rankar exhaled beneath my hands. "Okay," he said in English.

His hand reached back and found mine. Carefully extricating it from beneath his shirt, he pulled me up to his side and rested his lips against my forehead for a moment. Closing my eyes, I waited for him to gain his bearings.

Asher met my eyes when I opened them, and I had to clear my throat to speak. "I'll Gate us to Elie's."

Pulling the energy, I pictured the private room at the Banded Traveler. As it snapped into place, I could see the fireplace and people sitting around the table. I motioned Rankar through first and Asher urged Alika next. I fell into step behind him, reaching up to pat his shoulder and earning myself a smile.

The silence of the room closed around us as I stepped

out and shut the Gate. Tensions in this room matched those from the apartment, like stepping out of one hell into another. After a moment, Eliecha picked up the pitcher and poured two glasses. Triswon accepted them and carried them around to us.

"Elie made the jam yesterday. Have a piece of bread and settle your nerves," he murmured as he handed Alika then me the drinks.

Alika murmured a thank-you, but her gaze locked on Leara. "Leara?" she asked, motioning to the far corner.

I watched them walk over and felt energy flare as a soundproofing ward went up. Rankar bumped my hand with his. Our fingers linked together, and he pulled me to the table to sit across from Eliecha and Triswon.

Triswon smiled at us. "Mycal and I ordered everything we think you'll need for the additional bedroom. They should be delivering it within the hour. With you, Xander, Kismet, and Treyv, we can probably have it all but sanded and painted tonight."

"Thank you," Rankar and I said at the same time. I noticed his voice sounded almost normal, and I squeezed his hand in support.

The ward around Alika and Leara collapsed, and Leara wiped her face on her shirt before coming back over. Alika, though, said her goodbyes and excused herself with Facla following behind her.

Mycal sighed, and Triswon looked at him a moment. My father-in-law nodded. "We should fix the things we know how to and figure the rest out when emotions have time to calm."

Triswon stood. "Let's build Leara a bedroom!"

CHAPTER 7

THE PAINFUL LIMP that caused me so much grief pushed to the back of my mind as I ran the distance between the Sirach home and stables without hesitation. Already smoke billowed from beneath the stable's double doors, despite the downpour. How could the flames flourish despite all the water soaking the world around them?

Not waiting to remind Asher to send someone to get his brothers, all of whom could be useful in dousing the flames if they moved their asses, I calmly threw the heavy doors open and called for the family dogs by their nicknames. "Trouble! Clif! Come!"

Pulling the rain-doused tunic up slightly to cover my mouth and nose, I barreled inside while calling to the two beloved pets. If they found me, they would surely follow me into the fresh night air. I moved forward, heading toward the occupied stalls and using my hand to feel my way down the line of stalls. Cloth touched my hand, and I realized it was a saddle blanket I'd left hanging upon an empty stall's door. I pulled it toward me, gripping the slightly singed material in my fist. The open door allowed oxygen to replace the carbon monoxide. The fresh air fed the flames and doubled the amount of smoke, burning my eyes as I tried to see through the dense wall the heavier air formed.

Heat beat at my uncovered limbs, tugged at my red-tinged eyes. Still, I touched my hand against the wooden stall doors and counted silently. Two. Three. Four. "Romtal? Pantheon? Rukchio?" I coughed as I heard the panicked whinnies. The horses were all shuffling anxiously beneath the roar of fire and confusion of the smoke.

Slowly, I opened the stall door. I barely heard the gelding's worried neigh before he made a fearful plunge to get past me. Grabbing the halter firmly, I pulled him down and held him trembling as I soaked the blanket in his water bucket and tossed it over his eyes. I spoke to him quietly as I led him—blinded—in the direction of the second door at the back of the stable that led to the recently built corral.

Someone seemed to be calling out behind me, and I thought I heard the sounds of fearful screams, but I couldn't distinguish the words over the occasional crash of something falling through the loft floor. *Where is Asher? Where is everyone?* Opening the smaller door, I yanked the blanket from the terrified horse's eyes as I slapped its flank to motivate it away from the danger zone. For a second, I was tempted to run after it into the cool, quenching wetness of the rain. However, I resisted.

Moving back into the flames, I heard a horrendous crash. A terrified equine scream filled the air. *The loft is coming down!* Rushing toward the stalls, I started throwing the doors open. Blindly, I bumped into one that had already been thrown open, likely Asher's way of letting me know he'd already rescued the horses from that stall. Was that stall Pantheon's? In the smoke, I couldn't tell. Already, I'd nearly lost my bearings and thinking too deeply would likely distract me until I didn't know up from down.

"Yah! Get on!" I screamed, waving the blanket wildly in an attempt to spook the Deylura to the back exit. Without knowing if the loft had caved in near the double doors, I took the only sure escape. Still yelling, I had to make a wild grab for the second horse's halter as it reared threateningly over me. The horse's hooves missed cleaving my head by inches, but I still pulled the stubborn beast the last few yards to freedom.

A loud, threatening creak caused me to back up warily, aiming for the unpolluted air of the corral.

"Kinan!"

Distracted, I turned toward the sound of my name. Someone had spoken from the center of the building.

Rankar!

I opened my mouth to tell him to get out, but no words emerged. The crack of timber breaking caused me to look up. When I tried to speak again, the only sound that emerged was a scream as the burning loft collapsed on my husband.

My knees gave out.

"Kinan, *eirlys*, we're here. You're okay," Rankar's voice assured me from far away.

"Kinan, wake up. You're dreaming," Leara asserted firmly, closer.

The remnants of a scream echoed through the room. I inhaled deeply of the unpolluted air. No smoke, no heat, and no dying horses. Leara patted my hand as I pushed myself to sit up. Then she slipped away.

Rankar held his arm out, offering to let me cuddle into his shoulder. Seeing him alive and unburned left me without hesitation. I leaned into him, head resting in the crook between his neck and collarbone.

"Wanna talk about it?" he murmured.

I half-laughed, half-choked. "No. But it was the fire in your parents' barn. Except different. Raining. I was alone. And then you showed up as the loft came down... still inside."

He rubbed my back as Leara came back in and handed me a warm mug. She sat on the edge of the bed, watching me. My hands trembled. I lifted the rim to my lips to hide it.

"Karyn's blend," she assured me.

I could already smell the barest hint of lavender, verbena, and only the heavens knew what other herbs. However, the taste was neither too bitter nor too sweet, and I could typically fall back asleep after a cup of it. Whether or not I stayed that way depended on an entirely different situation, but her concoction at least gave me the opportunity.

"Better?" Rankar asked, covering one of my trembling hands with his own.

I finished the drink and set it aside. "Back to bed, Leara. I'll work on the soundproofing wards tomorrow so you can't hear through the wall. I'm sorry I didn't think of it sooner."

She snorted, resigned. "Don't apologize. It's my fault you had the dream. That fire led to the camp, right? You reacted to protect people you loved, and it was stupid, and you regretted it. Just like what happened last night. I wanted to help the people I love, and I was in over my head."

Her eyes shone in the bedside lamp for a second before she hurried out of the room. Her bedroom door slammed, rocking the shared wall. *Definitely needs more soundproofing.*

Rankar lay tense beneath my arm, but emotions were too high from the recent trial and sibling makeup for anything I said to make a difference. Instead, I reached across him and turned out the light before urging him to slide back down until his head rested on the pillow. I curled against his back, arm around him and mind racing.

An hour later, he slid back into sleep, and I stared at the cougar eyes tattooed on his shoulder. For a short period of time, things had seemed to flow forward without our direction. Now we stood at a crossroads.

Leara was ours forever. We had to balance what was best for her with what kept us sane. A good first step would be leaving my comfort zone. The time had come for me to contact Tier and get my United States bank accounts unfrozen—whatever it entailed would definitely need a lawyer of his skill. And perhaps I would never work as a mercenary on the Planes again, but Treyv had been correct when he said that I wasn't meant to spend eternity in the stables.

I would try out for the guard.

Rumors whispered of a merger between Asez Holding guards—the soldiers who protected Asez—and Orion's Arrows—the policing force for the country of Orion—in a coordinated effort to make sure both were fully trained. That probably meant we'd hire on fewer guards in August, despite losing a number to the war. I needed to train more, work harder.

The thought made it less likely for me to sleep, so I quietly crawled out of bed and dressed in workout clothes. I grabbed my bag hanging in the bedroom corner as both drakyn watched me from the foot of the bed. Quietly shutting the door, I headed to the bathroom. In the kitchen afterward, I jotted a short note at the table.

Going to the exercise room. Let the pups out. Send Hypnos if you need me. Love you. –Kinan

I left all my weapons in the safe, knowing there'd be nowhere to safely store them in the gym with me. About three a.m., the walk across the courtyard was dark and mostly quiet. Shifters called to one another outside the compound; some guards preferred patrolling as their animal selves. As a Tuatha de Gifted with excellent hearing, I didn't need to change shapes to gain better reflexes or enhanced senses. I understood the appeal, though.

Someone had designed the exercise areas beneath the main barracks with an external and internal entrance. Both doors required a fingerprint scan, and they were monitored by video twenty-four seven. It took less than thirty seconds for the person to match my fingerprint ID to my face. The light turned green, and I pulled the handle.

The first set of rooms contained rows of lockers. Every guard had one assigned. Others could rent one for a small monthly fee. Luckily, our apartment had a safe. The fee went toward upkeep of the equipment—all top of the line and designed specifically for paranormals. However, if someone carelessly broke a piece of equipment, the repair cost would be taken out of their paycheck in installments until they paid it off. Signs hung on every wall warning patrons to use the equipment as intended only.

To each side of the locker room were unisex showers, changing rooms, and bathrooms. Straight ahead, through the first set of doors, were lines of ellipticals, treadmills, rowing machines, and various other devices that looked like torture implements. Only about ten people used the ramped-up machines. Two people appeared to be racing on the treadmills, their feet moving so fast that the motion was a blur.

I crossed through to the next room, which contained an impressive assortment of free weights. Jeannitra Patric nodded at me as I passed through, and I waved back. Her spotter glanced over his shoulder and returned my wave. A couple other people used the room, but they concentrated on their workouts.

The third room was empty. Punching bags ringed the outside edge and rows of wrestling mats ran up and down the middle. The signs on the walls advised that anyone who damaged the bags would be required to replace them and that removing hard-soled shoes was required for use of the mats. A set of stairs on the far side led up to Alpha Barracks. Fingerprint scanning was required to get in or out of that door, and only guards could pass through except in case of emergency.

Digging in my duffel, I pulled out my sparring shoes and hand wraps. After a few minutes of prep, I started stretching and warming up. The first punch felt glorious, though hand-to-hand was my least favorite method of fighting. Stress seemed to flow out of my hand and into the bag as I used snapping punches to avoid causing rotation and push. Breathing steadily, I controlled the movement, making sure my fist never lingered after connecting. The combination of punches consumed my attention, moves I hadn't used in years.

Suddenly, a semi-familiar voice broke into my field of concentration. "Keep your hands up. The bag might not hit back, but you'll develop lazy habits. You're throwing good punches. Remember, you're tall, but most of the men you encounter will be taller. Punch higher when you are taking headshots. It'll keep your shoulders from tiring when you find yourself fighting someone five to six inches taller than you," Sergeant Major Belisario Veracruz commented casually.

Without glancing in his direction, I followed his advice. After all, he was the person who trained all of Asez Holding's guards in hand-to-hand combat. He knew what he was talking about.

Once I finished three series of punches his way, I paused to wipe the sweat from my brow. Belisario's lean frame rested against the wall. He studied me carefully, closer to me than he'd probably been since admitting me to Asez Holding over ten months before. And I could see Belisario's ability to lead reflected in the way he carried himself.

Now if I can just figure out what he's about, I'll be set, I admitted as I thanked him for the advice.

When I'd traveled with the caravans, I spent a lot of time listening to any gossip about the Terra Plane. Two demons from the Lredv sept—the clan leader Vyckintlredvn's children—were rumored to be working as guards on the Terra Plane. It had caught my attention because I had thought, *Goddess have mercy on me. Never let me be caught in a fight against them.* Around Asez, it was quietly whispered that he and Alala were members of the Lredv sept. Putting the two pieces of information together led to a very scary conclusion. Alala and Belisario's father was Vyckintlredvn, the leader of the Vyckintlredvn clan.

Son of a bitch.

The demon in question smirked at me, hazel eyes glimmering with good-natured mirth. I swallowed quietly, thanking my benevolent deity that mind reading was not a Teharan Gift. "I'll be honest. Treyv is quite fond of Leara, and he's transferred some of that to you. I promised him I would speak to you about trying out for the guard, which is why I came down when I saw you on the monitors." After a short pause, he continued, "Your instincts are admirable, and I see why Treyv asked me to convince you." A wry grin graced his features briefly. "Maybe we don't tell him that he's right."

I smiled back, bouncing lightly to keep moving and avoid cooling down. "I doubt Treyv often doubts that. But I agree with him too. I am going to go for a guard position."

Belisario studied me, and I returned the favor. The more I watched, the more certain I became that if I never battled a full-blooded Tuveri demon descended from Vyckintlredvn it would be too soon.

He stood upright and walked toward me, a rolling motion as fluid as a river flowing. It took everything in me to ground my feet and not back away. "If this were a drill and you were one of my recruits, I'd explain that you'll hardly ever find an opponent who knows how to box properly and will follow the rules, much less ascribe to the flow of practiced drills. I'd also explain that unless you are actually *in a ring* with a referee watching you, I don't ever want to hear that you followed those rules."

I didn't know anything about the rules of boxing. However, I forced myself to listen to his breakdown. If he could help me strengthen my skills, it would be a win. Rendle told me no one had beaten the twins during the Trials since they arrived at Asez Holding. Perhaps I could hold my own longer than the other recruits, but that was my best-case scenario. Hand-to-hand was easily my weakest arena of combat.

Circling me, he began his critique of my performance. I felt his hazel eyes boring into me, as though he watched me closely just to catch my reaction to his criticisms. "When you get tired, Kinan, you'll throw punches at your opponents' head or chest. In a knife fight, that's fine. In hand-to-hand, it's a waste of time. Aim for the throat or the kidneys or the abdomen. Hit them where it'll do the most damage in the shortest amount of time, where you won't have to worry about them instinctively defending themselves. If you're going to feint toward their head, hit them hard enough elsewhere that they won't get up again."

When Belisario finished speaking, he dropped to the ground on a mat and crossed his legs tailor-style. Hypnos apparently considered the seated demon to be less of a threat to him and dropped from wherever he'd been watching to perch upon the nearby garbage can beside the demon's green drakyn.

::Lorna!:: He provided her name to me, his mind-voice very excited as he chirped to the female. Oddly, it reminded me of a teenager courting his first girlfriend. *Twitch.* I almost missed Belisario motioning me to join him on the ground. Cautiously, I complied.

"The Arrows and guards will both be hiring at the Trials. My advice? Don't bother with the Arrows—you'd hate it anyway. To get into the guard, you only have to be the best of those who try. You need to match Fwen at archery, hold your own with me at hand-to-hand combat, and not get killed against Alala with a blade. Depending on your control of your mount—and with you working in the stables, I'd bet it's damned good or Cavallo'd have killed you by now—you'll be able to hold your own against Rankar in mounted combat." His eyes bored into mine as he willed me to understand. "How hard are you willing to work for it, Kinan? You should have no problem beating the other recruits."

He grinned at me with sharp, white teeth. The son of possibly the most feared Teharan demon—and all Teharan demons were pretty scary—sat across from me on the ground and honest-to-Goddess *grinned* at me.

"Especially if you accept my help."

CHAPTER 8

A WEEK LATER, Rankar pounded on the bathroom door. I groaned as I stepped out of the shower stall just enough to flip the lock before moving back under the stream of scalding hot water. The door opened, and cold air caused me to shiver. After a second, the shower curtain pulled back.

My husband's eyes flashed like sparks coming off a fire as he saw my split and swollen lip. Then his gaze trailed down to the already healing span of bruises that covered me from my shoulder to my thigh. "Son of a... Who the hell did you get in a fight with?"

Hypnos cheeped from the curtain rod, having chased down his bondmate after finding me limping back to the apartment. If the little snitch had waited an hour, my bruises would be completely healed. Instead, I managed a wan smile that only pulled at my lip a little and raised a blue and purple shoulder in a tiny shrug.

"Belisario."

For just a moment, Rankar's eyes rounded. Then he tilted his head as he reached in to turn my face more toward him. Last I had looked, the only signs of the fight on my face were the split lip and a tiny bit of bruising, but bruises tended to become more spectacular as they healed.

When 'Sario had realized that his punch caught me entirely unawares, he'd tried to deflect as I turned my head to avoid a direct hit to the mouth. All in all, I had gotten off easy.

"I'm sorry. Who?"

His extreme calm caused my heartbeat to kick up, and I rushed to explain. "I mean, obviously, we were sparring. Otherwise, I'd be dead."

Rankar's jaw worked a moment. "You were sparring with Belisario? For... fun?"

I snorted. "Nobody thinks training with that demon is fun. Those two things are incompatible. No, he's trying to help me hone my technique. I'm weakest in hand-to-hand and knife fighting. But he wants me to avoid his fists better before he starts coming at me with a blade."

He swallowed and closed his eyes. "That seems... like a plan."

I noticed that he hadn't said it was a *good* plan. Also, the water was cooling. I turned off the shower and opened the curtain the rest of the way. "Wanna help me dry off so I don't have to bend and put pressure on my bruised ribs?"

He exhaled slowly through his nose as his eyes wandered over the rapidly darkening bruises. *"Eirlys..."* His extended pause led me to believe he changed what he planned to say. "Mom sent some liniment last week that should help with the bruises too."

Undoubtedly, he'd had to push down his protective instincts. We'd both agreed long ago to be supportive of the other, though we realized our jobs could be dangerous. During the war, that had been difficult. Yet we'd managed—probably because we rarely saw the other's wounds. This was going to be an adjustment.

I wiped my hands and face on the towel before handing it to him. Then I stepped onto the bath mat and placed my hands on his shoulders while he carefully patted the bruises dry. He paused, placing a hand over the worst discoloration. Heat poured from his palm, somehow not burning.

After a minute, he sighed. "I tried to heal you when you first arrived at the ranch, and it didn't work then either. Worth a shot, though."

I kissed his chin and wrapped the towel around me, opening the bathroom door. "I'll be fully healed in a couple hours. Liniment me, and you can get back to your captain duties. I'm going to take a nap before Leara gets out of class. Today is therapy, and I should maybe not see your sister looking like I've been—albeit truthfully—punched in the face."

He went to the medicine cabinet in the kitchen, and I grabbed an extra towel from the hall closet. Once he finished rubbing in the nwazeh, I pulled on underwear and a tank top then spread the towel on my side of the bed. The clock already had a scheduled alarm to warn us to get ready for Leara's appointment, so I lay down.

"Want company?" he asked, half-in the doorway.

I carefully turned on my side. "I won't stop you from playing hooky."

He closed the door, kicked off his boots, and removed his shirt. I leaned into him as he gently rested his arm on a stretch of unbruised skin. "Would you be angry if I admitted that Hypnos scared me out of my mind earlier?"

I linked my fingers in his. "No. He tends to overreact, like he did today, and it can be terrifying."

"Hypnos wasn't the issue. I haven't seen you injured in

nearly a year, and it's been a good look for you. Knowing you'd been hurt inside the walls of Asez, a place where it's my job to make sure everyone stays safe, threw me hard."

Turning on my back to look up at Rankar more easily, I buried the wince as one of the bruises touched his arm. "I've worked a lot of jobs in my life, Rankar, and I've traveled to a lot of places. The Banded Traveler felt like home to me because Eliecha and Triswon live there. Asez Holding is home to me now. Not just because you and Leara live here, though. There's a pulse under the sand that matches my heartbeat when I walk across the courtyard. The wind caresses my cheek when Pantheon gallops over the training field. And everywhere I look, someone nods or waves or smiles at me—even when I'm grumpy and don't want to see another living soul. I'm ready to take my place as one of Asez's protectors. I want to try out for the guard."

Rankar smiled softly. "Good. That's where you belong."

CHAPTER 9

"SHE'S THE LAST'UN," Davie grumbled as we both eyed the hellbeast from outside the red warning lines. The black Arabian-Deylura mare had only missed my shoulder with her teeth due to a coordinated effort between Hypnos and Davie that nearly ended with both of *them* injured too.

"And this is the first, last, and only time," I added. "If we cannot safely manage her, Rendle needs to tell her owner to do it them-damn-selves."

Davie rubbed a finger along his upper lip, wiping the sweat on his pants. "She's got a bite, alright. I'd rather it not be a hostler she gets ahold of. I'll let Rendle know at shift change." He chuckled. "Never thought we'd stable a bigger ass—" He paused as I raised my eyebrows in his direction. "Well, uh, never thought any horse would be moodier than your Pantheon, but here you have it. Now he's the second most ornery Deylura here."

I shook my head, picking up the food bucket that Davie'd tossed at the horse when she moved in for the kill. "The twins' mounts are worse than mine. Pantheon doesn't try to hurt either of us."

Davie leaned on the shovel and chuckled. "Anymore. You forgot the times before you came home. I'm pretty sure he thought about biting Rendle once, but the beast realized he'd end up with food poisoning and decided against it."

Something twanged in the back of my brain, something from years ago but somehow important. For just a second, it was there. Then gone.

"Rendle says we're gonna lose you soon," Davie grumbled, opening the storage room and taking the bucket from my hand. "You're gonna go to the dark side for the cookies."

I laughed as we moved to the main stable for shift change. "*If* I am accepted, I'm going to miss working with you. Make sure whoever takes my spot keeps your optimism balanced and your skin attached, yeah?"

He carefully patted my shoulder. "If you promise the same."

"That's a big task you want to put on someone. I'm not sure if anyone ran you through my track record before arriving, but I seem to attract injuries."

"I heard a rumor that you went directly to the infirmary when you got here," he admitted, raising his arm in a shrug. "But you've not been hurt once since then."

No one's been shooting at me, though.

Suddenly, I realized I would be exchanging a somewhat safe lifestyle for one significantly less so. Rankar's trepidation made a little more sense in that light. Whether I'd noticed or not, things had been almost… calm. Now my plans would disturb the status quo.

During the meeting, Davie signaled Rendle to stay after, but they both waved me on. Upstairs, I showered and changed before beelining for the main entrance to the gym.

I had about an hour to train with Belisario before Leara joined us.

"Hey! Wait up!" someone called across the courtyard.

A quick glance over my shoulder assured me he hadn't yelled at me. I hadn't ever seen him around Asez before. He was probably one of the early Arrow arrivals to negotiate the upcoming Trials with Keawyn and Rankar.

The light turned green on the scanner, and the door clicked open. As I pulled it, a hand gripped the metal above mine. Suddenly, the demon attached to it loomed over me, crowding me.

The gym strictly enforced the one person per scan rule, and anyone who would be granted entry to the building would never double up. Without thought, I pushed all of my strength against the door to shut it back. Even if he knocked me unconscious after I closed it, the guard monitoring entry would not admit him.

Surprisingly, he released his hold, and I slammed into the door as it closed hard. Turning, I balanced on my heels and prepared to rush him. However, he had backed up at least four feet and had his palms facing me. My eyes moved from his eyes up… and up more. The demon stood a half-foot or more taller than me.

"Holy shit. It's really you!" He dropped his hands and grinned. "I never expected to see you again!"

Shading my eyes against the afternoon sun, I looked closer. The wide shoulders and bright blue eyes—only a little darker than my own—made me feel a little déjà vu, like I'd seen him before and should recognize him. However, faces and names were not my strong suit.

"I'm sorry. I think you have the wrong person."

He snorted. "You're Sarki Kinan. You would need a twin for me to mistake you for someone else."

Fair, I acknowledged, still eyeing him as though it would help jog my memory.

"You were the only mercenary on a trade route willing to take on a human partner. Shit, it was—I don't know?—2004, I think. Only I almost got dead in the middle of an attack." He untucked his shirt and raised it halfway up his abdomen, showing that he stayed in excellent shape and also had been turned to mincemeat by a blade a while back. "You dropped me off on the Elysii Plane at the Banded Traveler with a healer. By the time I healed up enough to track you down to thank you for saving my life, you'd disappeared. The owners at the Banded Traveler were even away."

He raised his eyebrows and tilted his chin at me. "Everyone called me Jet, but you…"

Somehow, the flirty look cinched it. Everything connected in my brain. The caravan had been betrayed by the man charged to handle its protection, and we'd taken incredible losses in that attack. However, I'd killed all the demons in my path when I realized my partner was in trouble. If Eliecha hadn't given me a charm to take me directly to the Banded Traveler if I had grave need, he would have died from his wounds.

"I called you Atkoy." For just a minute, I smiled at him. He'd almost outshot me in the test I put him through, which was quite an accomplishment for anyone. Then it hit me. "That hellbeast in the stables is your murderous she-bitch. Didn't I tell you she was a liability?"

He winced. "You and Venom have a run-in? She didn't

hurt anyone, did she?"

I growled, resisting the urge to punch him as I recalled our narrow escape. "Only through great effort. We've had her put on a no-touch hold. You'll be caring for her during the rest of her stay. And if she bites you, good."

His laugh echoed off the building. "Your concern is touching. However, I'm okay with tending her. I actually didn't expect anyone to try to handle her after they put the sign on her door that warned people away in a dozen languages."

"It's kind of our job. Next time, make sure they put the red X on the door too. It warns the hostlers to stay back."

The surprise on his face caused me to narrow my eyes. My hackles rose, and Hypnos appeared out of nowhere. He landed on my shoulder, sending me a picture of Rankar leaving his office and heading our way at a ground-eating walk. I mentally asked the drakyn a question, and he showed me Rankar answering the phone in his office.

The guard inside the gym must have jumped the gun. The scene probably looked a little concerning in the initial bit.

"You work in the stables? Not as a guard?" he questioned, pointing behind him at the closest barn to emphasize his point.

I gritted my teeth, low-key offended for all of Rendle's employees. "You too good for that kind of work?"

He shook his head. "Okay. I stepped in something there that I didn't intend. What I meant was your skills would be highly sought by the Arrows, and I'm shocked that Asez Holding's captain of the guard hasn't snatched you up."

"I kind of did," Rankar corrected, stepping around

Atkoy to move to my side. "I married her."

Suddenly, any residual anger disappeared. Most people at Asez Holding knew Rankar and I lived together, but we didn't plaster our marital status on the side of the stables. Against all reason, hearing him tell a complete stranger made me feel more comfortable.

"Atkoy, let me introduce my husband... Captain Rankar Sirach. Rankar, this is Jarrett Atkoy."

Rankar extended his hand, and Atkoy clasped his forearm like he'd greeted me that first time. When they let go, they each looked at the other for a long minute. Finally, Atkoy smiled.

"Nice to meet you, Captain. Call me Jet. I'm Commander Montgomery's second, and I'm—uh—here to meet with you and Councilwoman Asez about the arrangements for the upcoming Trials."

Rankar nodded as I reeled at Atkoy's promotion from mercenary to upper echelon of Orion's policing force. "You also, Jet. As for the gym access, we'll need to get you in the system for you to go in. Two people entering on the same scan is never allowed, and we have someone monitoring it twenty-four seven."

For a moment, the information seemed to leave the human speechless. Then he shook his head. "Actually, I was trying to catch up to Kinan. I yelled, but she didn't hear me."

Hypnos chirped, and Rankar chuckled. The darn bird had probably told him I ignored the shout. "Do you two know each other?"

"We worked together," I admitted as Atkoy said, "She saved my life."

"Same assignment that nearly killed me," I continued, pretending Atkoy hadn't spoken.

"Glad you both served at the same time then." Rankar remained silent for a long moment, his hand brushing mine reassuringly. "She killed the man who betrayed you all. She avenged the fallen."

Atkoy froze, his jaw working. Then he nodded. "There were rumors, but I couldn't ever find Abshoc to get the truth."

I swallowed, trying not to go back in my head to the day I executed the demon for his sins. "He confessed, just before he offered me a bribe to let him go."

We stood silent, allowing the Arrow to process the information. Finally, he exhaled and looked from me to Rankar. "Kinan, you need to be doing that work again. Captain, she'd make hell of a guard or Arrow."

Rankar nodded. "She would, but she makes her own decisions."

I linked my fingers in Rankar's. "I'm trying out for the guard. If I don't make it in, then I'll continue to be hell of a hostler."

"Excellent. It was a pleasure seeing you again, Kinan." He glanced at his watch. "Captain, I've been informed that I need to make a quick stop to check my mount, and I'll see you at our scheduled meeting time in thirty minutes."

They shook again before Atkoy jogged toward the stable for guest mounts. When he was far enough away that his human hearing wouldn't catch our conversation, I lifted my chin and looked up at Rankar. "Sorry. If I'd realized who he was, I would have stopped."

Rankar grinned, stepping closer to me. "No, you

wouldn't have."

My lips twitched. "Or I would have walked faster and been inside before he caught me."

He kissed my forehead lightly. *"Eirlys,* I love you. I'm going to go do Captain-y things while you avoid 'Sario beating you up too badly."

I kissed the side of his mouth. We'd moved on to knives, and it was a damn good thing Belisario had insisted we wait for a month of hand-to-hand training. The demon would have definitely killed me, which would have put a pall over his and Rankar's friendship.

"Love you too, but no promises except that I'll try to be mostly healed by the time you get home."

His exhale sounded loud near my ear. "Deal."

TODAY, THE MATS were filled with people wrestling. Belisario walked up and down the rows, correcting postures and stances as he went—some more roughly than others. Alala sat on a stool that she must have brought with her. Upon seeing me, she waved and saluted me with a tub of popcorn. Though she didn't smile, her green eyes looked delighted.

This was the weirdest day.

On the sidelines, I changed to my soft-soled shoes, put on my fingerless gloves that minimized skin-to-skin contact, and stretched. Belisario and I had graduated from using punching gloves before moving on to knife work. In his words, no one we encountered in the outside world was going to stop to glove up before punching me. That didn't stop me from digging out my mouth guard. I really liked my teeth.

"Full house," Treyv observed, plopping down beside me and stretching.

This room hadn't been this packed in... the entire time I'd been working out here, actually.

"Weird," I agreed. "Normally, it is dead in here around this time of day."

He snorted, leaning forward to touch his toes. "Don't be surprised. The choice between kicking your ass or Belisario kicking theirs was not a tough one. All of us could use a free day."

I turned my head in his direction slowly, leaning sideways toward him instead of straight ahead. "I'm sorry. What did you say?"

For just a moment, his eyes widened. "Oh. He... You... Well, this is certainly going to be a surprise for you."

Finished stretching and suddenly full of adrenaline, I hopped to my feet as Belisario stepped over.

"Pick a number between one and eighteen."

"Seventeen?" I asked, caught off guard.

"Seventeen!" he shouted.

The second to last demon from the right stepped off his mat and came toward us.

"The fight is to yield. If you win, they spar with Alala once at a time of her choosing. If they win, they can pass on a single sparring session with me. And each time one of them uses that get out of jail free card, I'm going to kick your ass in their place. Understood?"

I opened my mouth to tell him I never agreed to any of this, but he nodded. "Good. Okay Fighters, match ends at yield. No damage that won't heal before tomorrow's shift.

No weapons. Otherwise, at the whistle."

Adrenaline surged through me as I slipped in the mouth guard and faced the stranger on the mat, bouncing to keep my muscles warm. We stood eye to eye, but his build suggested he worked out heavily. If he'd been human, perhaps that would have affected his speed. However, his energy and heat felt more like a lycanthrope flavor of demon. Fast and strong.

Training is great. Muscle memory can mean life or death. But desperation occasionally turns an underdog into a winner. That's how we'll win the war, Locke's voice reminded me.

I grinned, and the demon's brow wrinkled as the whistle blew. Hands up, I jabbed toward his face as I brought my knee up hard into his side. He blocked the punch. The knee connected, causing him to sidestep.

Belisario growled for him to watch the surprise attacks, and I glanced his way. Whose side was he on anyway?

Movement in my peripheral caused me to sidestep, and I ducked low beneath the swing. He had taken advantage of my inattention, but he didn't adjust his body to accommodate the punch. Off-balance, he entered my ideal range. It might be a trap, or he might have erred.

Adjusting my center of gravity, I came upward from my half-crouch. I gripped his shirt with my left hand to keep him where I needed him. My right fist rose up to catch him under the chin.

His feet left the ground, and I released his shirt. Just as perfectly as in the movie Leara and I watched the other day, his body arched and landed in the middle of two others sparring one mat over. For a long few seconds, he didn't move. I shook out my fist, still bouncing in case he came up fast.

Belisario walked to him, bending down to check his pulse. "That's yield. Pick a different number."

Fuck.

CHAPTER 10

OPENING THE SAFE, I stared inside for a long moment. Though all the weapons were familiar, I hadn't openly carried them since I had arrived at Asez Holding a lifetime ago. So much had changed since then, for the better. Would holstering the weapon in the open somehow jinx our progress?

Over the past few months, life had settled into a routine. We hosted family nights every Friday with Leara's cousin Alera at the apartment. The two of them visited their great-grandparents in the Katataros Sithen twice a month. So far, a day there seemed to be a day here, though time usually passed differently inside the Sithen versus out. Rukchio and the yearlings had begun basic training with Rendle. Belisario and Treyv regularly trounced me in hand-to-hand fighting. Plus, Rankar and Alika had found a therapist, though their first session was still a ways out. Everything came together.

The sword strapped to my hip felt both unusual and familiar, like an old friend I hadn't seen in a while. The weight gave me a measure of strength, something I knew I'd need to get through the next two weeks. Looking down as I slipped my Glock into its underarm holster, I noticed that my hand was shaking. *Lovely*. My 9mm went into another holster at the small of my back, while a compact version of the same gun fit nicely into the top of my boot.

"You're dressing like you're going to war," Leara observed, sitting on the floor with the pups.

Cullyn—the male, named the Irish word for sword master—and Caiftín—the female, named the Irish word for captain—tugged at the rope toy together. Faela had suggested the names, because she thought they helped them fit our warrior family. Their ferocious growls punctuated Leara scooting across the floor on her butt as they worked in concert to pull. As the Rottweilers grew, small differences began to show to help us tell them apart at a glance. Both were intelligent, stubborn, and learned quickly, already having mastered all the basic commands and moving into intermediate ones.

"That's how this feels. While none of the officers want me to fail, it is their jobs to make sure the candidate most fit for the guard is the one accepted. Plus, the other people competing for the spot are going to actively fight against me."

As suspected, the guard only intended to take a single applicant. The Arrows training in the Asez facility boosted the guard numbers significantly, and they were taking almost a dozen more from the Trials. Outside the compound walls, a sea of tents in every imaginable color created a rainbow as far as the eye could see from the watchtowers.

"Wish me luck," I urged, locking the safe back.

The pups noticed I planned to leave and abandoned Leara in an attempt to trip me. We both grinned as she commanded them to come back to her. They hesitated a second before obeying, weighing the consequences of doing what they wanted with the reward of obedience.

"You won't need it. Give them hell—heck."

I winked at her then slipped out of the apartment and dropped to the ground instead of taking the ladder down. Stepping into the courtyard, I hesitated. The lines to sign up as guard and Arrow candidates were long. Luckily, one trait I had in abundance was patience. Ten guards and ten Arrows accepted applications at any given moment and barely made a dent in the lines. Worse, the applicants had been signing up for the past three days. The Goddess only knew how many were applying for the single open position at Asez. Still, I had been waiting on this opportunity for months. I did not intend to let anyone else take the post that I coveted.

If I had to, I'd destroy every person who stood in my way.

At least an hour passed as the line moved slowly forward, the sun position my only indication of time. More people joined behind me, so the line never seemed to become shorter. Finally, though, the single person ahead of me stepped to the side.

"Next!" The timbre of the voice sent chills down my spine, though he didn't raise his eyes from the paper. "Name?" he continued, pen still scrawling information from the last applicant.

If one wants to apply to the guard, I thought, *one might as well apply directly to the captain.*

"Sarki Kinan Sirach, sir. Applying for the Asez Holding guard opening."

By the sudden stillness and tension in his posture, I

knew he had recognized my voice at the first syllable. He glanced up, and I smiled in reply to the grin he gave me.

I love you, I told him silently as I headed toward the practice arenas to see what I was up against.

ON THE FOURTH day of the Trials, they held my interview. I tapped my foot lightly against the floor to relieve some of the pent-up energy. My fingers rested on the heavy, metal table in front of me. The edge almost touched my stomach. I didn't feel like I could draw a weapon or even move free of it quickly if I was attacked. Unfortunately, the panel of witnesses for my interview would probably shoot me if I scooted it forward. Literally. Everyone appeared to be extremely wired, and I had the overwhelming urge to ask them if they were having a bad day. The looks they directed my way left me feeling like the weakest member of a herd being targeted by a pride of lions.

In a half-circle across from me were my interviewers. Sareya Montgomery, Belisario, Rendle, and a mind reading human named Michelle Craig stared at me while I attempted to relax enough for Ms. Craig to make a mental link. Oddly, I didn't sense any energy in the room, though I'd completely dropped my own shields. That meant everyone else in the room shielded like a sonuvabitch.

A demon entered, hurrying toward me. He apologized to the panel for being late as he immediately began affixing the probes for the lie detector test. It took long, quiet minutes, and no one spoke as they waited for the ministrations to be complete. Finally, he nodded and settled in at the table.

Sareya Montgomery calmly watched me, as though trying to place me. I scrutinized the Barcki demon in return. Had she already forgotten Locke too? What about the other men and women she'd lost on the battlefield during the war? Did their faces not haunt her at night like they did me?

"Please state your full name," Rendle urged, his accent in full bloom as he got the process moving. As Keawyn's spymaster, he had spent a lot of time these past few days mingling with the applicants. He read people well, so his presence made perfect sense to me. Plus, his friendly face helped my racing nerves a little.

"Sarki Elayne Kinan Sirach," I annunciated, noticing that Montgomery blinked at my name.

For a second, she turned and looked at the men on either side of her. I thought she might ask Rendle or 'Sario something. But she didn't. Instead, she took over the line of questioning.

"Why do you want to join the Arrows?"

Perhaps the question was standard for all applicants, but the answer I gave her probably wasn't. "I don't want to be in the Arrows; I am here to apply for a position in Asez Holding's guard."

"Why do you want to be in Asez Holding's guard?" Belisario interrupted.

I nodded to him, a way of letting him know I meant him no disrespect. "I want to be in Asez Holding's guard because I'm a fighter. I'm a good fighter, in fact. Montgomery should be able to confirm that I take orders well—even orders I don't like—once I give my allegiance to someone or something. After all, I spent the better part of the war Gating to coordinates she chose and taking out targets she pinpointed."

For a moment, her eyes widened minutely as I confirmed that she *should* know me.

"I'm grateful to have the position in the stables, but others are more suited to it than I am. As I'm more suited to the guard than others will be. If it's my fate, I'll continue to work with Master Cavallo and the Deylura horses. However, I want to protect my home and my friends here at Asez in a more immediate capacity."

Montgomery looked to the mind reader sitting nearby. "Do you detect anything suspicious or that should eliminate the candidate from tryouts?"

Ms. Craig shook her head. "She is married to the captain of the guard and their daughter lives here also. She holds a lot of respect for the councilwoman and many of the ranking residents. I see no red flags."

Her matter-of-fact breakdown of my relationships left me a little unsettled, though she had spoken the truth. I never mentally classified Leara as my daughter, because it felt disrespectful to her biological parents. However, she was as much my child as I was Eliecha and Triswon's. It made sense.

"Do either of you have more questions?" Montgomery asked Belisario and Rendle.

Both of the men shook their heads, and Montgomery nodded at me. "We continue interviews tomorrow. The schedule for tryouts will be posted once we finish."

The male demon unhooked the lie detector probes quickly, wiping them down with alcohol. Obviously dismissed, I stood, rebuilt my shields, and walked toward the door.

TWO DAYS LATER, too many people crowded into the firing range. The first ten aisles, including mine, held demons trying exclusively for the single open position in Asez Holding's guard. All of the other applicants who'd swarmed the grounds wanted to be Arrows, which was just fine with me. In my estimation, nine too many applicants already wanted my spot.

When we'd entered over an hour ago, Atkoy had a line of potential Arrows in the far range and a crew cleaned the middle room and reset it for the next group who waited outside. They planned to move people through pretty quickly, it seemed. However, a number of the Arrows applicants had never fired a gun, which was going to be interesting for them.

Second Lieutenant Fwen Panthrus paced up and down behind us, occasionally stopping to drop a compliment or comment. Rendle was nowhere to be seen, though he had appeared for a short time earlier. Rankar, Belisario, Keawyn, Montgomery, and Alala all huddled together in a little group talking.

Rumors suggested a few spies had been arrested, escorted away by Sareya Montgomery for interrogation. At least fifty had decided that whatever secrets they hid were more important than joining the Arrows. Those men and women had disappeared of their own will, for the moment. All of the guard entrants were still in the game.

Today, I had dismantled and put together a couple tactical semiautomatics. I had cleaned three 9mm handguns, all similar to the one I had holstered at the small of my back. After each exercise, I had been required to fire the weapons to prove they worked. Five "kills" had marked my progress, all headshots. As far as I knew, my direct competitors were doing as well. A couple had taken chest shots, still considered "kills" for the purpose of trials but less certain in the real world with the number of physiological anomalies found across the demon breeds. Also, bulletproof vests could be purchased off the black market right beside cop-killer ammunition.

I'd already reassembled, fired my five shots, and cleared the chamber for this round. As he passed down the line, Fwen's hand rested upon my shoulder for a moment. I wasn't sure whether he tried to keep me upright or show me his support. It did feel like we'd been sitting for hours. Once everyone in the line finished, they'd rank us in order of completion and accuracy before removing the weapons and handing us a covered tray with the pieces of the next one. Luckily, the judges expected the exact same thing regardless of the weapon—clean kills, precision, accuracy, control of the gun, and experience-driven confidence.

"That's all today," Fwen announced, to my surprise. "Be back here at seven a.m. tomorrow."

After a long moment, I stood and stretched. Rolling my neck and shoulders relieved some of the pressure, enough that sitting in Alika's waiting room that night didn't seem so daunting. With nothing else on the Trials schedule for me today, I could even shower!

"As accurate as I remember," Atkoy congratulated from behind me. "I see you still like Robin Hood-ing your shots."

I grinned, recalling the Desert Eagles that were the human's preferred firearm. When he and I had competed, I'd used the holes his bullets had made as my own target—like the famous outlaw of history had done with arrows. "It's easier when the person firing before you uses ammunition that leaves elephant-sized holes," I admitted as I turned.

Fwen stood beside him, the two obviously having bonded over their love of projectiles. "You two know each other?"

"She saved my life on a job off-Plane before the Enlightenment," Atkoy advised before I could head him off.

"We were partnered on a protection detail. It was literally my job to watch his back," I grumbled.

Atkoy raised his eyebrows at me. "You'll never believe who I interviewed yesterday as a potential Arrows recruit... Kitry Abinaleh."

I tried to place the name, but names were really not my forte. "Who?"

He shook his head. "*She* recognized me, which helped my pride recover a bit. If you don't remember her, though, I am back at one hundred percent. She's tall like an Amazon warrior with vibrant red hair," he prodded, but I shrugged. "She was your final partner on that fucking terrible job."

Shock dropped my mouth open. "Goddess bless! She survived?"

Abinaleh and I had realized our forces were falling too fast to beat the attackers. We'd made a last-ditch effort to rescue a group of civilian hostages. Only, the demons guarding them hadn't been enough to hold us back, so they'd called in reinforcements. We'd been engulfed in a fireball, which damaged our shields. Then the hail of arrows containing the anti-energy arrowhead killed my shields. My Deylura mount had created a Gate, but the enemy rushed us. The ground had shaken and dirt and rock rained down as we entered it. Abinaleh never made it through.

"She's also a hell of a storyteller. Last night, over drinks, she filled in the blanks from the day you saved my life. Then she told me about the lives you two saved before everyone fell." He made a gesture I didn't understand. "I let her know that you killed Abshoc."

My brain took a long moment to process. "I need to see if she'd be willing to meet Leara."

Fwen cleared his throat, reminding me he was there. "Is there any reason she wouldn't want to?"

I shook my head then shrugged. "Leara and her parents were in the group we saved, and the girl remembers that rescue vividly. Basically, the same reason that Atkoy telling everyone I saved his life bothers me. It makes me really uncomfortable. However, there's the chance Leara is going to see her around Asez. I don't want either of them blindsided by the other."

Atkoy took out his phone and typed out a text message. A woman paused at the wall, and we all stepped back to give her room to clean up the shells for the next round of recruits. His phone dinged, and he flipped it open. "She says we should have drinks tonight, and she's happy to meet Leara." He checked his watch. "We should finish about eight here. Nine would be good. Where?"

I tried to think of a place safe enough to take Leara that

would have booze. "What do you drink? Our apartment is in the stable on the end, closest to the gym."

Fwen raised his hand, his expression sheepish. "Can I invite myself? I'll bring a couple bottles of brandy."

Rendle and Rankar joined our half-circle. "I have whiskey," the Tulevi demon offered.

I looked at Rankar questioningly, and he smiled ruefully. "Party at our place."

CHAPTER 11

I TOLD ALIKA about the pending introduction so she could discuss it with Leara during their training session. Considering the trauma of the event and the link to her parents, I didn't want to dredge up unhappy memories. As I'd predicted, the teenager desperately wanted to meet Abinaleh. She'd even spent a couple hours in the cafeteria kitchen making appetizers for everyone and had convinced someone there to let us borrow a few chairs.

As the clock approached nine, she grew more fidgety. I reached over the table and patted her hand. She squeezed it back.

"You okay, warrior-girl?"

She grinned. "Thank you for doing this. I know how much you hate gatherings like this."

"Most of these people are family. The rest are friends. It'll be okay."

The dogs came alert, and Hypnos cheeped.

"Rankar," we stated at the same time then laughed.

He knocked three times before typing in the code, signaling that he had people with him. We both stood, and she gripped my hand tighter and pulled me against her side. When the door opened, Cullyn and Caitlin rushed forward until he commanded them to stop. They waited patiently for everyone to enter, their eyes never leaving Rankar as they hoped for the command to release.

Rendle and Fwen entered together, each carrying promised liquor bottles. Then Atkoy and Abinaleh came in, also holding bottles. We'd moved the kitchen table closer to the living room area, and it was already set with alcohol and food. A few buckets of ice sat out, one already holding a bottle of wine.

"Leara, this is Jarrett Atkoy and Kitry Abinaleh. Atkoy, Abinaleh, this is my ward, Leara Sinton."

Atkoy grinned at her. "It's wonderful to meet you, Leara. Please call me Jet."

Abinaleh smiled fondly. "Thank you for letting me visit you, Leara. It is gratifying to see a story of success from an event like we lived through. I am excited to hear the story of how you and Kinan were reunited."

My chest ached, and I held tight to Leara's hand. Suddenly, I realized that Leara hadn't meant I hated crowds, which was true. She'd meant I hated being the topic of conversation. "That's a long story, Abinaleh."

Leara put her other hand over our linked ones. "And I look forward to telling it."

Rendle cracked the seal on his bottle and poured a healthy dose into one of the tumblers. His lips twitched. "Want one?"

I shook my head, reaching for the bottle of wine. "Unfortunately not. I compete in the morning, and I'm not taking any chances. Even if I regret it tonight."

Once everyone had settled, Rankar released the pups from their hold so they could greet each newcomer before settling on the floor between Rankar and my feet. Atkoy's drakyn rested on his lap. Alabaster was better behaved than Venom, at least. Hypnos curled on the couch behind me, and Thanatos lay on the arm beside his bondmate.

Leara sat to my left, her feet crossed beneath her. She held a mug of citrus tea between both hands and nodded to Abinaleh. "I should start the story just a bit earlier, I think. You see, my parents traveled the Planes as merchants, and I loved that life. Dad found gems capable of holding energy and spells, and he did all the negotiating. Mom enchanted the jewelry she made and homeschooled me in the back of the wagon. It was perfect. Everything an adventurous kid like me wanted. Until it wasn't."

She sipped her tea before setting it back on her knee. "The morning had been quiet. Then Dad yelled for Mom to boost the shields. Sounds of fighting outside the wagon came closer. The screams—some battle cries, some death ones. It was awful. Combined with the fear on Mom's face, I knew this was bad.

"Then Dad shouted in pain, and Mom opened the door to check on him. Hands pulled her out. I hid in the corner like she told me, but the man who came in saw me almost immediately. He stopped searching the wagon and took me to where they'd tied Mom and Dad up."

I looked at Abinaleh, and she watched Leara in fascination. In fact, everyone did except me. Rankar had turned to face her better without my noticing, causing Thanatos to crawl onto his lap. Suddenly, I realized he'd never heard this story. He hadn't been there when this happened, and I didn't speak of it. I slipped my hand onto his leg, and he slid his palm beneath mine.

"Most of the guards were dead; only small groups still

fought. The enemies outnumbered them too much. However, the attackers continued to search the wagons, one after another like they looked for something specific."

I turned my attention back to Abinaleh, and she met my gaze. Her expression revealed she caught on to her role in the story long before I had in the camp. Anticipation lit her eyes.

"In front of us, a Gate opened. Two women rode through like Amazons of legend. Abinaleh's Tuatha de red hair streamed behind her like the blood flowing from her scimitar. She slid from the back of her horse, no sign of fear, and ran into the group of demons holding us captive. Her blade found purchase every time, like a beautiful and deadly dance."

Swallowing hard, I tightened my grip on Rankar's hand but focused on Leara. She smiled gently at me before grabbing the hand still on my leg. "Kinan rode a palomino whose white blaze matched her bright hair and pale skin. As she exited the Gate, an arrow hit her directly in the chest. Still, she charged forward without hesitation and dropped to the ground near the line of hostages. One of the demons fired toward her, over and over, until we thought for sure these two women would abandon us and save themselves. But they fought until all the prisoners fled through the Gate. Abinaleh and Kinan saved us all."

The silence in the room felt profound, and I wanted someone else to break it. However, everyone seemed to holding their breath too.

Somehow, Leara recovered first. "Dad joined the recovery effort, returning to the site of the attack to bring the dead back for identification and final rites. He also brought back the wagon, most of the jewelry intact. However, a number of pieces had soaked up the death energy. Mom had to completely cleanse them and start over. We spent a lot of time recuperating, mentally and financially, before going back out. This time, Mom paid a lot of money for a bracelet that would Gate me to Asez Holding if something similar happened again. They had an escape plan."

Her hand flexed around mine, and Hypnos rubbed his cheek against hers. "Six months later, we planned to visit our cousin's family on the Terra Plane. We left our wagon with the caravan where they were overnighting and Gated into their garage. Only, the house was burning. Smoke filled the garage, like the fire started on the other side but definitely planned to engulf it all.

"Mom pushed me out the small door, but Dad opened the one to the main house and yelled for Paul. He wasn't sure if they'd gotten out. But someone grabbed Mom and me as soon as we stepped outside, pulling us apart and moving us toward the road. At first, I think Mom assumed it was emergency personnel trying to get us away from the fire." She shook her head. "It wasn't, though. They'd lit the fire with the family inside. And when the mom fought to go back into the fire to get her youngest boy, the leader shot her. By the time they grabbed us, Dad's cousin Paul sat crying in the grass with his other son."

She paused to sip her tea, hand shaking as she stared into the cup for a second. "Dad found the baby, but he had stopped breathing. When he carried him out, they took Dad and left the two-year-old on the ground. Didn't even put him with his mama. Then we were transported in a van with bags over our heads and handcuffs around our wrists. At some point, they took my bracelet, all of Mom's jewelry, and Dad's wedding ring."

Of the people in the room, I assumed that only Leara and I had been in a camp. Rendle watched with no expression, but Abinaleh's eyes held sympathy. Atkoy and Fwen's held horror. I didn't dare look at Rankar.

"They shuffled us around a lot at first, but we stayed together. Sometimes, the rooms were empty. Other times, they weren't. However, for days, they moved us and moved us until I was disoriented and tired. Then they moved us to a room with only one person."

She shook her head. "Her hair didn't shine as bright, and her eyes were somehow dimmer. But I recognized her immediately. It was the woman who'd rescued us before, and I felt hope even as Mom cried herself to sleep that night. I realized she didn't recognize us, but that was okay."

Atkoy clinked his glass with Abinaleh's, obviously trying to lighten the mood. "Well, there's apparently a club."

Leara did smile. "Don't take it personally. She legitimately has this issue where she thinks it is no big deal to save people. It didn't kill her, so it doesn't matter."

I swatted her leg lightly. "It matters, but I was being paid to do a job. I was *doing my job*."

Leara regripped my hand, shaking her head at me. "The next morning, she tried to give us all the food. But I knew she needed her strength if she were going to save us. I introduced my family to her, and we played games. When the guards came in for any reason, she always tried to run interference when Dad antagonized them. Even when she was powerless, she tried to play the hero."

I snorted. "I'd somehow made it that long. I figured the Goddess had to be watching out for me or something. Turns out, I was half-right. She sent my soulsibling to be one of our guards."

Her eyes looked into mine. "I'm sorry I never met him outside the camp. He definitely saved our lives. If only he'd been there when…"

I shushed her. "He would have loved meeting you too."

For the first time since she started her story, she sniffled. "Kinan has the Gift of Prophecy, and somehow, it pinged even inside the walls. After Mom tucked us down to sleep, I always stayed awake for hours. This particular night, I overheard Kinan warning my dad that terrible things would happen if he tried to protect my mom. She told him that he had to choose—Mom or me.

"When the guards came in during Latin lessons, they were so big. One of them ordered Mom to walk forward, said they were moving her. And Dad told her to listen to them, to go. But she didn't understand. He had protected her my entire life, and she looked terrified… I think that's what caused him to go for her."

Rankar squeezed my hand, and I realized that the rapid breathing was my own. It matched the frantic beating of my heart. As my eyes met his, the only visible emotion was love. Not pity, not disgust, not hatred. Just love. After a long exhale, I forced my body to match his breathing.

"They shot him. Then they shot her. As I rushed forward, they would have shot me if Kinan hadn't grabbed me and pulled me into the corner. By moving away from them and covering me, she seemed less like a threat. Also, one of the soldiers—Aaron Locke—pushed us into the corner like he was restraining us. In hindsight, he placed himself in the line of fire, thinking they'd hesitate to shoot 'one of their own.' And Kinan held me there until they removed the bodies of my parents and hosed out the blood."

Rendle stood up, silently refilling both his and Fwen's glasses with liquor. I hadn't touched my wine, so he poured a shot from the second bottle into a snifter and handed it to me. With a small headshake, I accepted it and tossed it back. "It's just as terrible as I remember," I admitted, not talking about the alcohol.

"Less for me," Leara corrected. "I know how it ends now."

Abinaleh leaned forward, her expression gentle. "Please finish, Leara."

"We'd started a routine, my mother and I. Lessons and games to pass the day. I grasped that hard the next morning. Only, the one thing worse than internment for Kinan was teaching math. Instead, she started teaching me self-defense moves. Her knowledge of languages surpassed even my mom's, so sometimes we learned different ones for fun. And she talked me through the basics of Gating. We couldn't actually practice, because human witches had warded the place against energy-working. However, she made sure I knew the general principle and where to go to—here. She told me every story she knew. Anything to pass the time. Then her Gift showed her the future again, one where she left me unprotected in the worst place on Terra."

I swallowed, losing control of my breathing again.

"Trust me," she murmured in Raspea. "I love you," she continued in English.

Behind me, Rankar scooted closer until I felt the rise and fall of his chest against my back. My hand shook free of his, needing at least one hand free to feel in control. *Too soon. Too much.*

"They removed me from the room, and they attacked her in a group. With nothing but stubbornness, she killed four of them. But they hurt her. When they put me back in the room, her body was gone, but the place smelled of blood and the pallets were both new. The single guard who lived told everyone he killed her, and I didn't learn differently for months."

My throat sounded raw when I interjected. "Locke came back on shift and heard about the attack. He pulled my body from the room and left, blowing months of undercover work. If he'd waited, I would have died, and he knew it would be impossible to find Leara if they'd moved her. They didn't keep records of which prisoner was in what room. Then we went back in during Vengeance, and she was gone, presumed dead."

Leara shook her head. "They rotated people in and out of my cell for weeks. One night, they put another kid in my cell. Also alone. Chaz Haversham's parents were killed, too, but when they were first taken. Two nights later, a man walked through the wall."

She coughed, a half-laugh. "It tripped me out, because I knew the door hadn't opened. We'd definitely been the only two in there when we fell asleep. Then I wake up and there's this guy just there. But he was the boy's uncle—Garth. His wife and kid had revolved around the camp for months as they looked for Chaz. He decided he couldn't just leave me alone, and he took us both back to their cell. Then he carried us all out, one floor at a time, one cell at a time."

Leara rubbed her arms fast, like she was trying to warm them up. "The stone hurt when you went through, like sandpaper. And we couldn't cry in case the guards heard us as we moved. Then we were outside, and his wife Gated us to Albuquerque. Things were chaotic. We holed up for a bit and recovered. Plus, I needed to practice the Gating in a place where energy actually worked."

She squeezed my hand and cleared her throat. "Sorry. I'm running out of steam. I tried repeatedly to Gate to Asez, but I couldn't ever get it right. I built Gates to other places, accidentally leaving the family and unable to get back. I never could get where I needed to go. Then a team of Rankar's siblings and Asez Holding guards appeared. They told me that Kinan had sent them, and I almost lost it. They Gated me to the hospital, where the waiting room was packed with people glad I was safe, and it was really weird. Suddenly, I was meeting all these people I'd heard stories about. People who didn't know me but spent hours every day searching to bring me here. And that's how we got here."

She finished her tea and stood up. "Someone else's turn." Heading to the kitchen, she filled the kettle and put it on the burner.

Abinaleh cleared her throat. "Well, it is neither as long nor as soul-searing, but I witnessed Kinan save Jet during the first attack on the caravan."

As she began telling the story, weaving the elements of

battle so well it almost took me back, I refilled glasses. By the time Leara rejoined us with fresh tea, everyone had a full glass and Abinaleh finished making me sound like the Terminator. "While three of us held the ward to protect the noncombatants, she took down all ten of the demons battering them. We could only watch."

"You're really good at what you do," Leara offered, grinning at me like I had done something magical.

"I do my job. Just like in every walk of life, some people are better at it than others. On a caravan job, our first objective is to protect the merchants. The second is to protect the goods. If we don't watch each other's backs in the process, there won't be enough hired guards to do either one. Double bonus if you kill the bad guys too," I explained.

Abinaleh raised her glass. "To more mercenaries prioritizing like you. A lot fewer friends of mine would be dead."

Atkoy nodded and lifted his beer bottle. "To future Arrows who watch one another's backs like Kinan did mine."

"To family and friends determined to see the best in others," I added.

"To people who save the day, who protect any creature weaker than themselves." Leara lifted her tea cup.

We clinked glasses and took sips. For a long moment, we savored whatever thoughts were in our heads. Then Atkoy finished his drink and stood. "Thank you for the company. We all have early mornings. I'm going to head out."

In short order, everyone made their excuses and left. While Rankar showered, Leara and I put away the leftovers and moved the furniture back. Then she hugged me tight for a long minute. "I love you, Kinan."

"I love you too, warrior-girl. Thank you for choosing us," I whispered, not wanting to let go.

She squeezed tighter before stepping back. The dogs perked up and followed her toward her bedroom. For tonight, she let them in. More than anything, that told me how rough tonight's stories had been on her. Yawning, I sat on the couch and took off my boots.

Soon after, Rankar stepped out of the bathroom. He paused when he saw me sitting alone, looking for Leara.

"Gone to bed," I told him.

After a second, he changed directions and knocked on her bedroom door. She called out, and he went in. Their voices were low enough that I couldn't hear, helped along by the soundproofing wards we reinforced a couple times a week. When he came out, he joined me on the couch.

"She's emotionally exhausted but better than I expected," he murmured.

"We have a strong teenager," I agreed. "Sometimes I forget everything she's been through, things that adults decades older couldn't have survived. Then nights like tonight, I wonder how I could forget."

"Come here?" he asked.

I snagged the throw from the back of the couch and crawled toward him as he lay down as far back as he could go. We fit comfortably with me in front of him, blanket spread over us. The bed would have been better, but we both knew the nightmares would come for me tonight. Too much of the past in the present.

For now, though, the rhythmic sound of his breathing

near my ear lulled me toward sleep. I linked my fingers in his where they rested on my thigh. His lips touched the back of my neck, and I sighed softly. *"Eirlys?"*

"Hmm?"

"She learned that strength from you."

Snuggling closer to him, I hummed softly. "Love you, Ran."

"Love you too."

CHAPTER 12

THE NEXT MORNING, the coffee did not seem to help. Day seven was going to be a long one. However, the first sound of an arrow striking a target brought me alert instantly. Fwen smiled at me, handing the crossbow in his hand to the competitor beside him. Then he continued down the line, testing each one for faults.

Thirty minutes later, bolts sang as they cut through the air, all thudding securely into the targets. Second Lieutenant Fwen nodded his approval to my left as everyone in the line hit the center point on the targets twenty yards out for the tenth straight shot. Of course, crossbows were scarily accurate at less than thirty yards. At thirty yards, bolts dropped twelve inches. I watched closely as each target was moved out an additional ten yards, and I smiled my approval as two nonparticipants measured the distance from the firing line to the edge of the target for all ten of us. Adjustments were made as needed. Then we lined back up.

Adjust your aim up twelve inches, hold steady, and fire at the signal.

I released the bolt, following the trajectory with my eyes even as I pulled the string back to the latching point. To each side of me, the other demons were doing the same. I glanced down and gently adjusted the string so it was centered. Damn. My shot could have easily been yards off target. *Pay attention, Kinan.* Bolts had hit bullseye from the first target to the last. The rat bastards.

But could they calculate it perfectly for ten out of ten? I could and had. And what about at sixty yards when the drop difference was a little over forty-eight inches? Despite the small amount of sleep from the night before, I was secure in the knowledge that this was my forte. No amount of luck could make any of the competition perform as well as I did in all the stages of the archery competition.

Concentrating, I easily hit the point where I was aiming for the remaining nine shots. Again the targets were moved. This time, the first shot left me with a smile on my face. Only three of us had managed to hit the center point—and Fwen was not an official competitor which left Sage Jaxon as my sole competition. I looked at the man who stood on the other side of Fwen and grinned broadly. Jaxon winked back, knowing that I took as much joy from the competition flunking out as he himself did. For a couple demons, it took all ten shots to finally adjust their aim. One down the line was icing his shoulder.

"I can do this all day," Jaxon warned.

"Me too," I admitted as Fwen and the rest of Asez Holding's officers examined the papers.

We waited in amiable silence as the final decision was made. Rankar crumpled paper after paper, leaving three. Neither of us spoke as a caliper was used to measure the diameter of the holes in the bullseye. Murmurs were going through the audience, but the noise level had diminished from the earlier roaring crescendo to a low hum. "The winner for the crossbow competition put all thirty bolts through the same, perfectly centered hole without enlarging the hole with a single shot."

Jaxon eyed me with interest, clapping his hands together lightly in congratulations before the official verdict had been announced.

"The top three competitors—in order from first to third—are Sarki Kinan Sirach, Sage Jaxon, and Cruce Alishion. We will reconvene here for the next stage of the competition in two hours."

Leara ran over to me, wrapping her arms around me in a hug. Before she could speak, he did. "How good are you with a longbow?"

My white-blue eyes met those of my ward, and her smile held even more smugness than mine. "Better than I am with the crossbow, for damn sure."

Jaxon whistled softly. "Shit."

I winked at him before letting Leara lead me away to get lunch.

THE HAND-TO-HAND ELIMINATION tournament started in the room where Belisario, Treyv, and I usually trained as dawn broke on the eighth day. Now dusk approached. Already, I had defeated four of the potential Asez Holding guards and three Arrow potentials. As I bounced in place, waiting for Belisario to tell me what the holdup was, I glared at the hopeful future guard I was supposed to be currently sparring.

The mercenary had chickened out at the last minute. When she drew my name, she threw it back into the jar and demanded another draw. "I'm not fighting her. She's broken or dislocated something on every person she's been up against!"

The judges had led her to the side, but I'd overheard most of the conversation as the crowd had quieted to eavesdrop. Belisario had laughed at the demon's accusation that I didn't fight fair. He ordered her to take the draw or forfeit.

She'd forfeited, swearing she could prove her mettle in the remaining competitions.

I fully intended to make sure the demon couldn't afford even that one appearance of cowardice. That forfeiture would be the first in a long string of them for the quitter. If I had to break more bones to accomplish that, so be it. However, I still maintained that the sixth demon had a medical condition. His ulna should not have broken in three places with one blow. Furthermore, almost all of them had been bigger than me. I had to fight dirty to win. It was a rule… Belisario's.

"Ready for round two?" Fwen inquired, walking up behind me.

I couldn't contain the groan. "Two? I thought this was nine?"

He shook his head, winking at me. "This is round two. We are counting down, not up."

I grinned. "Two? I think I can handle that."

Leara slid under my arm, forcing me to stop moving for a moment. "Holy shi—shivers, Kinan. They are saying the guy whose arm you broke is going to have to wear a cast for a couple days. An actual cast."

Fwen snorted, and I shot him a chiding look for encouraging her. However, Belisario motioned me forward. Slipping the mouth guard back in, I took my position. Rolling my shoulders, I looked around. Impatient, I glanced at Belisario. However, Montgomery's face caught my attention first.

"You've got to be kidding me," Montgomery muttered, watching over my shoulder.

When I turned, I almost repeated the leader of the Arrow's statement. He had to be faster than he looked. *Actually, I sincerely hope he's not,* I corrected myself.

"His last opponent injured him seriously before he took her out. He changed forms to heal," Atkoy informed them emotionlessly, also staring at the seven-and-a-half-foot—and emerald-green—demon. "Either he likes this form better or he can't change back without the injury acting up."

I snorted. "Lovely."

He joined me in the center of the ring. The starting position was standard for the Trials. Each opponent gripped the other just above or just below the elbow. Jolly Green Giant had to almost bend himself in half to manage. I stared up into eyes the color of evergreen, and I plotted the quickest way to bring him down.

As we waited for the whistle, the demon dug his fingers into my biceps. His eyes narrowed, and I grinned up at him. Obviously, he wanted to play. He just didn't realize his games had nothing on mine.

The whistle echoed in the crowded room. Digging my own fingers into his arms, I allowed his grip to hold me up off the ground as I pulled my legs close to my body and shot them back out. Both my feet connected full-force with his right kneecap. He released my arm, so I dropped and rolled out of the way as he fell.

I leapt back to my feet, keeping my feet moving and my fists up. Slowly, my opponent attempted to do the same. As he presented a blindside, I assessed whether I could end the fight with another attack or if he tried to lure me close to avoid more pressure on his bum leg.

By the Goddess, tap out. You are the only thing standing between me and the final match with Belisario.

Apparently, he didn't read minds. He came upright, though his weight rested on his left leg. His right one dragged behind him slightly. To strike at me, he had to bend over due to his height, which would screw his balance more. If he healed that leg, though, he'd be able to use his reach that way.

Lean into the blow, Belisario's voice reminded me.

I ducked in and faked to the left. As he leaned toward me, I moved closer again. His fist struck my shoulder, and my left hand closed around his wrist. My right pulled him forward, toward me. Unbalanced, he fell.

Keeping the grip with my left hand, I moved under his arm and wrenched it backward. His face hit the ground just as I felt the vibrations of the bone snapping. I dropped his arm. Kneeling in the center of his back, I leaned forward with a hand gripping the ankle of his good leg.

"Are you going to stay down or do I take out the other knee?"

"I yield!" he shouted.

The judges accepted his resignation. I nodded to Fwen and Belisario as Leara ran forward with a towel.

Tomorrow. Me and Belisario.

I don't have to win, just do damn well against the master.

ON THE NINTH day of the Trials, I removed my weapons, noticing a few demons in the crowd closely observed exactly where I kept this knife or that gun. It took some doing, but I ignored them as I unbuckled the last weapon on my person and handed my sheathed sword to Leara. Seeing the pile of metal that my ward slowly made disappear onto her person left me feeling completely naked in my unarmed state.

How can I do well fighting hand-to-hand when I don't even feel comfortable thinking of my hands as weapons? I wondered, glancing toward where Belisario was talking to Rankar and his sister, Alala.

Leara finished buckling the sword at her side and glanced up at me. Her expression held serious concern.

"Don't worry. I just need to hold my own," I reassured my ward.

Her glare left me feeling a little singed. "Even though you don't plan to break Belisario's bones, he might accidentally break yours. You don't heal as quickly as most paranormals. A single broken bone could put you out of the Trials," she hissed.

I shrugged. "I'll just have to move faster than he does, won't I?"

Leaning forward, I stretched. Thanks to the hot shower and generous layer of liniment last night, nothing twinged as I touched my toes. I'd have felt more reassured if that thought came before the brief fight between Belisario and the Jolly Green Giant earlier this morning. My fight with the emerald-skinned demon had lasted at least five minutes longer.

"Time," Leara murmured, opening the case for my mouth guard.

I accepted it as I straightened. Looking over, I saw Belisario breaking away from his friends. Leara's sienna eyes followed me toward the center of the mat to meet my friend-turned-adversary. When the sergeant major gripped my arms and I gripped his, I stared into his eyes and kept my breathing even.

He and I had worked together for months, practicing defense and offense, attacks and blocks. Not once had I beat him in a match, but I had gotten better at holding him at bay. After all, we knew one another's favored moves, and we'd learned the best way to counter them. I knew his tells just as well as he knew mine.

I could do this. I just needed to keep him off-balance. Normally, I waited for him to take the offensive. Perhaps I should take the lead this time.

I had followed his advice to the letter in the matches with the other prospects. He'd repeatedly asked me, "What's the use of fighting without a weapon if you aren't going to disable your target? No use at all, is what. You have to be willing to go farther than anyone else, because your enemies aren't going to stop just because you bruised them up a little." And I had seen him smirking on the sidelines after every demon had yielded due to broken bones. Even now, his eyes encouraged me to do my best.

Then the whistle blew, and he struck.

The minutes stretched on with neither of us closer to

victory. I held on longer than I expected to last. That pride made me a second too slow with my punch.

I stepped into Belisario's blow and hissed as the air evacuated my lungs in a rush. I had hoped to get off a headshot of my own, but he anticipated the move. His punch sent me flying—literally—backwards to collide with the ground. Leaping to my feet, I ducked under the Tuveri demon's advance.

That hurt. I rolled my shoulders, feeling the slightest pull.

Soon, Belisario would get my yield. He'd kept me on the defensive most of the fight. As we circled, my breathing sounded more labored than his. My dexterity kept me half a step ahead, able to block or dodge the blows he threw. Unfortunately, I had no advantage over his offensive stance. If I had trained with him for years like Treyv... But I hadn't, and I had no formal hand-to-hand experience predating that.

I spotted the telltale tension in Belisario's muscles. Backpedaling, I brought my hands up too slow. His high kick collided with my right wrist, deflecting his foot from my head to my shoulder. Pain shot down my arm instantly. The pop sounded behind my ears but reverberated through my shoulder, an audible warning.

Fuck.

His footwork pushed me back toward the edge of the mat. He threw a quick jab. A test. I blocked it awkwardly with my left hand. With gritted teeth, I tried to pull up my right hand. It remained waist height.

Last chance, I realized. He had me.

I ducked under his arm and threw my left fist into his

kidney. Completing the rotation, my leg swept out and sent him to the ground. On the balls of my feet, I pushed backwards. Just not quick enough.

Suddenly, I also stared up at the ceiling. By the time the pain finished echoing through my dislocated shoulder, I focused on the demon standing over me.

He'll break my neck before I get up.

Tackling his legs before he could kick me in the face was out of the question. Even if I rolled away, I would still be on the ground and susceptible. I had no choice but to choke out the words.

"I yield."

The pressure in my chest kept me on the mat. I'd known I'd lose against 'Sario, but I had hoped to catch him off guard just once. A couple solid blows or a decent combination before he eliminated me would make me feel more secure in taking first place among the guard recruits. Though no one had beaten him today, I felt as though my chance at the guard was gone.

Belisario nudged my side with his foot, demanding my attention, and I met his eyes. He reached down, offering me a hand up. Exhaling, I placed my left hand in his as he pulled me up. To my surprise, he pulled me in and patted my back gently twice before stepping away. "Great jab at the end," he offered, a hint of pride in his gaze.

"I had an excellent teacher."

He grinned before jogging toward Treyv and Alala. Leara offered me my duffel bag so I could change my shoes. Instead, I slid it over my shoulder. No way could I get on boots one-handed.

Leara glared at me as she slipped the shoulder holster

gingerly up my dead arm before letting me slip my good one through. Though it would be painful to have the Glock bumping that arm, I would rather be armed than not.

"Warrior-girl, it could have been worse. Nothing is broken."

She snorted. "Yeah, you tell yourself that with every step Pantheon takes. We're going to find Rankar and then visit Grandma Elie."

As she stormed toward the exit, I exhaled slowly. I had barely survived Belisario. In two days, I faced Alala with blades.

Maybe we needed to ask Elie and Triswon to just stay over.

CHAPTER 13

D AY TEN OF the Trials started early. I dropped down to the first floor of the stables, landing carefully. The shoulder didn't twinge, the dislocation completely healed by Elie yesterday. I rotated it again, just to be certain. With the first day of blade work starting today, I needed to be top-notch. Which is why I felt relieved that Leara and Triswon had convinced Eliecha to accept Councilwoman Asez's hospitality for the next few days.

Leara had been tasked to bring her adoptive grandparents to the stable while I showered, but only one person stood in the main aisle. A bit shorter than me, her shoulders hunkered forward as though weighed down by the world. Her longish auburn hair had been pulled into a ponytail, which was the only reasonable alternative in the desert for anyone who didn't just cut it short like me.

The stranger stood watching a fenital nursing her kittens in the last stall, not moving to approach the skittish mom or adventuresome babies. At four weeks old, most of them had been spoken for, and I was incredibly grateful that Leara preferred our dogs. Though the warrior-girl did her share in socializing the kittens...

I sighed softly, double-checking my shields in case of attack. She shouldn't be in here. This stable wasn't open to guests without an Asez Holding resident as escort.

"Excuse me," I called, walking toward her. "Ma'am, you need to leave."

Her face turned toward me, and recent tears left her brown eyes reddened and swollen. "Sorry?" she murmured, barely loud enough for my hearing. She cleared her throat and opened her mouth to try again, but I cut her off.

Pitching my voice to be soothing, I interrupted. "Can I help you? Are you okay?"

She choked slightly, waving a hand. "I'm trying to find members of the Eiffel Creek pack? I h-heard a few were trying out here, but there are so many people milling around that I haven't seen a familiar face. I have a list of names and a couple pictures?"

"She's literally the worst person to help with that," Leara murmured from behind the visitor, her voice kind but honest. "Show me, though?"

The teenager had appeared silently in the shadows without a trace of energy to betray her arrival. The slightest movement showed me Triswon. He'd nodded to let me know he had Leara's back. Just in case the woman was more than she appeared, I took a few steps forward myself.

The woman's hand shook as she handed a few photos to Leara; she carefully kept from touching the teenager. She hesitated to release the pictures, but my warrior-girl was patient. After a couple seconds, she let go.

Leara smiled up at her for a second. "He's handsome." The woman chuckled sadly in response, and Leara grinned. She flipped to the next one, then another, and paused. Her brow crinkled. "This one, he's familiar. He's competing in the trials and is in the top ten. I saw him in the hand-to-hand portion two days ago. Vigor? No. Vicar?"

"Miguel survived?" She gestured at the photos. "Anyone else you recognize?"

The look of hope on her face reminded me of seeing Rankar for the first time during the war. Leara pointed at someone. "He looks familiar, but I couldn't say for sure. I'm sorry."

"Thank you, uh…"

"Leara," she volunteered, handing back the photographs. "I'm Leara."

"Karma Delaney," the woman returned. "If you see Miguel or any of them,"—she held up one of the photographs—"please tell him the khan has found a place for us along the Mimbres river. He needs to take I-10 and think of our angel. She'll make sure he takes the right road."

The cryptic message piqued my interest. "Let me see. I can't promise I'd recognize him if he came up to me, but… I'll try," I grumbled, moving closer.

"They're all Lykos of the Eiffel Creek pack. We were separated during the Enlightenment."

I accepted the pictures and flipped through slowly. I concentrated on the demons' eyes before handing them back.

She licked her lips. "Remember—take the interstate near the Mimbres River and trust our angel."

Eliecha stepped from behind Triswon as Leara used her phone to take pictures of the photos. She approached with her husband at her side. He and I both watched closely, prepared to intervene. However, the woman had focused on Leara meticulously documenting each pack member and didn't notice them behind her.

"Miss Delaney, may I see?"

The poor woman jumped half a foot. Obviously startled, she blindly reached behind her to offer the photos—except the one clutched to her chest.

"Goddess bless!" Eliecha murmured, gripping the woman's fingers for a moment.

"Shit," Karma hissed, shaking her fingers like the touch had burned or shocked her. "How did you do that?"

Eliecha looked both concerned and amused. "Oh, child, that wasn't me. But I think you know where to go now to find your pack. And so do I."

The stranger accepted the photographs back with a thoughtful expression. "Someone deserved some insanely good fortune. That was... nothing I've ever had happen."

Eliecha grinned at Karma, snuggling into Triswon. "She sure did."

I studied the two women. "Everyone okay?"

Karma Delaney grinned at me, looking genuinely happy. "They're nearby. The pack is nearby!"

An exhale of relief escaped me on her behalf. "Then find your family and don't let them go again. We lost too many in the war."

Her smile dimmed. "I hope you free him."

My eyes narrowed. "Free who? From where?"

Eliecha's eyes filled with tears. "Snowflake, if she doesn't go, she'll miss her window."

Triswon cleared his throat. "Do you need a ride?"

Karma looked up at him and shook her head. "Not if you have to touch me. My Gift works on contact, whether I will it or not."

His shoulder lifted and fell. "Sorry."

Her eyes met Eliecha's, and my adoptive mother wiped her tears away before nodding. "Goddess bless your journey, Karma Delaney. May the moon guide you."

Karma opened her mouth, closed it, and nodded back before going for the door. As we watched her leave, Leara tucked herself into my side. "That was weird, but hey… your next fight is against a Lykos. His name is Miguel Vicar, and he's apparently part of the Eiffel Creek pack."

I snorted, unable to hold the sound in. "Thank you. How'd you figure that out?"

She squeezed me. "Eavesdropping, obviously."

Eliecha sniffled and wiped her tears. "I believe it is time we head to the ring. Your turn approaches."

Triswon picked his wife up and twirled her. "I'm excited to see Snowflake beat the sh—stuffing—out of people!"

Leara laughed. "As long as you understand that means she is also going to get the shi—ship—beat out of her. It seems to be the only way she knows how to win."

I growled. However, I didn't argue. My time in the ring would test her theory.

HEAD WOUNDS ALWAYS bled the worst, and the stream of blood running down my face barely missed my right eye. If I tilted my head even a millimeter to the left, it might impair my vision. Combining that with the pain shooting into my left shoulder from the arm hanging limply at my side cast a kernel of doubt on how well the blade competition was going. Even though I'd broken the arm of the Lykos fighting me, wolf-flavored lycanthropes healed faster than fae. Even now, he was able to wiggle the fingers of his injured arm. Or maybe it was the nerves twitching?

Please Goddess just let it be the nerves.

"Oomph!" I groaned as Miguel Vicar charged me, planting his shoulder solidly in my chest. Pissed, I instinctively wrapped my legs around his so we'd crash to the ground together.

You godsdamned prick!

Using one's body wasn't frowned upon in blade work, but nothing about his posture had tipped my dazed mind off to his plan. Twisting for a dominant position, my right hand connected with the ground. A stone hit the bone in my wrist, and my grip released. My short sword skittered out of reach. Despite the agony shooting up my left arm, the numbness in my right hand, and the blood burning my eye, I grabbed the knife from my right boot.

Vicar wasn't giving up, though, as he tried to buck me off. His good limb flew at my face, leaving parallel scratches across my cheek from his partial shift.

I growled, my alternate form pissed. Bracing myself, I curled the fingers of my injured arm around his good one above the wrist. My eyes watered as the pain intensified, but the tears washed the blood away. Then a deep swipe of my sharpened blade severed the tendons and muscles that connected his good hand to his arm. Only the bone kept it from falling into the dust beside us.

"Don't worry," I snarled, rolling off him and climbing to my feet. I almost wiped the blood from my face, but now my right hand was just as bloody as my cheek. "You can grow it back."

And he would. He already proven that he was Alpha,

capable of shifting outside the full moon. One good shift and he'd be just like new.

He hissed at me, more like a pissed off house cat than a wolf. My body went cold with anger. He had two useless arms and no way to hold a blade. In hand-to-hand, he may have been able to come up with something. Those competitions were over.

Does he not think I'll kill him just to go rest?

Luckily, someone from the sidelines stepped in and saved his life. "Miguel Vicar loses by default, unable to finish the bout with blades," Sareya Montgomery shouted for all to hear. "Victory belongs to Sarki Kinan Sirach."

I nodded at her, and she nodded back with respect. Leara wrapped an arm around my waist and took some of my weight, causing me to realize I swayed precariously. The blue drakyn draped across her shoulder chirped at me, obviously concerned. I scratched under his chin with my good hand, and he melted against my palm. Leara slapped my hand, and I realized I'd covered Hypnos' head with blood.

"Good news: This was your final battle against guard competitors. Bad news: You have three more fights to finish out the tournament. Worst news: Grandma Elie is going to have to fast heal you. Again. You can't even hold your sword," Leara observed. "If she can't fully heal you, you are *not* continuing with combat. I swear by the gods that I will kill you before you give strangers the chance."

I laughed, no doubt in my head that Eliecha could take care of this injury before my next battle. The flippancy earned me a glare that nearly melted my bones. With a sigh, I gave her more of my weight. "Fine. Please grab my sword so we can head back to the room. Triswon motioned at me before he and Elie disappeared."

When we arrived, my adoptive mother had even found another table somewhere to spread out her supplies, as though our counter wasn't large enough.

Leara snorted. "It's like she knows you."

An hour later, I headed into my next fight—battling to the finish with the Veracruz twin who liked me less.

Death by a thousand cuts.

Alala circled, her steps sure on the rocky ground though her eyes never left mine. She moved like the earth dared not trip her. Knowing who her father was, I couldn't blame it. Also knowing who her father was, I felt damn lucky to still be standing.

I needed stitches in at least three places. Six more nicks would clot over if I stopped pulling the edges apart soon. And I'd only drawn blood once—with the dagger in my right hand—a laceration on the first lieutenant's forehead.

Three forced healings in a row left me irritable and dark, with a bone-deep exhaustion that urged me to sleep for a week. The fight was damn hard with the urge to sit down always just a thought away. However, this would be my final combat for sixteen hours—if I survived it.

Alala, as always, played for keeps and pushed forward. Her Teharan-style rapier looked beautiful in the light, reflecting almost purple. I brought up my own rapier, ready to hold her back. *Block, block, block, block.*

The tip of her dagger slid under my guard as I concentrated on the sword, slicing a line across my thigh. The sting only added to my fatigue. I didn't glance down to see how badly it bled. Instead, I brushed aside her next attack with my sword and darted forward with the dagger. The base of her palm connected with my wrist, preventing it from landing. However, I kept my grip on both my blades as I danced back.

Using her own wrist, she tried to brush the blood away from her eye. However, the quick wipe as she kept her eyes on me missed the main trail. If she didn't clear her vision soon, she would be blind in that eye. It would hinder her depth perception, leaving her more susceptible to missing a block. She needed to wipe her face.

The hitch in her step prepared me. The droplets had moved faster than she expected; she thought she had more time. Again, she moved to brush the trail away with her wrist.

This time, I attacked as she was in the upward arch. Catching her wrist with the hilt of my dagger, I hit hard to stun her fingers into releasing her knife. She tried to drop that nondominant hand to the hilt of the sword to reinforce her grip. Using both rapier and dagger, I forced her blade down before driving my knee into her side to push her back. Twisting with all my strength, I jerked down and toward myself.

The sword came loose from her hand, and I danced back out of range. She stared at me as Belisario called from the sidelines, "Sarki Kinan Sirach wins by disarming."

Swallowing hard, I resheathed my dagger and stepped forward to offer her the hilt of her sword. She accepted it, nodding at me with a twitch of her lips. Then Treyv approached with a towel, and Alala turned to him.

I made it to the edge of the ring before my legs gave out. The soft earth before me sheathed the tip of the rapier, the hilt climbing toward the cloudless sky like a bloodier reenactment of the Sword in the Stone. My forehead rested against the flat of the blade where I knelt, exhausted and unable to stand. In this moment, I felt more Merlin than King Arthur. King Arthur, for all of his skill, was a mortal man. Sorcery ran fierce through my blood for me to have survived this battle. The same blood flowing down the blade, dripping silently into the dirt.

Did I care that the only blood I'd drawn during the battle was the two-inch dagger slice on Alala's forehead? Did it bother me that most fighters would have allowed the first lieutenant to wipe away the blood? Nope. Didn't hurt my feelings at all. If it had been normal training, sure. We could be good sports. Today? I liked Alala fine. I just liked winning more.

"You fight dirty," Rendle chuckled.

When I didn't answer, he gripped me under my arms, careful to keep his skin from contact with mine. If I'd had enough energy, I would have told him I was too tired to have a panic attack. However, that might not be true. Instead, I closed my eyes and stumbled a couple steps with his help.

Rendle snorted, half laughter and half irritation. "How did you beat Alala when you can't even stand?"

He kept moving forward, and I trusted him not to run me into a wall. We paused, and I leaned back against the Tulevi demon with my eyes closed.

"You wanna take her, Captain?"

Arms slipped under my knees and behind my back. I

forced my eyes open as he lifted me. "Hey, *eirlys*. Hypnos and Leara went to Elie already to warn her, and she and Mom are in the apartment waiting for us."

With a sigh, I rested my head against his shoulder and buried my nose against his neck. He smelled delicious, musky with a touch of leather and horse and male. Mostly, he smelled like home.

"Love you, Rankar," I murmured as I dozed, barely opening my eyes when he opened the Gate to the loft.

"I love you too, *eirlys*."

CHAPTER 14

THE TWELFTH DAY of Trials began mounted combat. Jaxon had a spectacular seat, and the horse beneath him was obviously accustomed to the steady hand at her reins. The man held the bō—a wooden staff—with confidence, managing a bow for me before the whistle blew. He attacked, and I blocked. When I attacked, he blocked. The fight appeared almost choreographed as we both moved agilely. Hours later, I would still feel the lash of the wind as Jaxon attempted to behead me with the blunt edge of the wooden weapon. Pantheon's quick response to my signal saved my life as the gelding moved backwards out of range.

The clatter of the wooden staves sounded incessantly, like the hollow percussion of woodpeckers in a redwood forest. Click. Clack. Click. Click. Click. Clack. I was tiring, but Jaxon appeared just as able as before the match begun. His horse, however, didn't have the stamina of the Deylura beneath me. The Friesian faltered, allowing me to drive Jaxon from the back of the ebony mare. Even still, the warhorse was not giving up. She bit at Pantheon, rearing in rage over the injury caused to her rider. Her reaction annoyed Pantheon, and the gelding issued his own challenge. Smaller than the Friesian, the Deylura-Arabian crossbreed used guerilla tactics. He lunged in, reared, then moved back out of range. Only my firm hand kept him from actually harming the mare.

Seeing my opportunity, I intentionally reared Pantheon. A soft whistle caused him to back up two steps on his hind legs. Jaxon, attempting to remount, only realized his danger when he felt the end of the staff gently touch his neck. "You are dead."

Gracefully, the man accepted his defeat. "That I am," he admitted with a self-deriding smile, finishing his motion and grabbing his mare's reins to back her out of the ring.

The next challenger, though, was not nearly as skilled a horseman as Jaxon. Will Allan's mount had no true training, and I wondered who had even approved it for the ring. Two swift blows knocked the demon from his mount, and I prepared to force his yield only to find the man's stallion attempting to take a chunk out of Pantheon. Unlike Jaxon's mare, this effort wasn't out of any training or loyalty to his handler. Pure testosterone.

Pantheon was temperamental on the best of days, and he was already edgy from the earlier fight. Without warning, my gelding lashed out. The untrained mount then backed over his rider, stomping on the man with every step.

His own horse's sharpened hooves decapitated Allan, effectively ending the battle. The demon paid with his life for his and his mount's incompetence.

Afterwards, the other seven contestants refused to fight me.

The air around me crackled with a cold static as I passed straight into pissed... Enraged barely touched it. Mounted combat trials were not tournament style. No one could surrender a match against a specific person before the fight began. That was not proving one's mettle. Forfeiture was a sign of cowardice, neglect, and disrespect. People who walked away from a scheduled match because of fear were likely to walk away from true combat for the same reason.

And I wanted to punch them in their godsdamned faces!

Each of the ten competitors had to compete nine times with one another, plus a final round with the captain of the guard. I snorted, a very disdainful and unladylike sound that held only contempt for everyone who walked the earth that day. The only round I had left to fight was the one against Rankar. However, I had only competed twice. Not nine times.

"Cowards!" I screamed to no one in particular, earning me a dirty look from Cullyn, who tried hard to nap despite the ruckus in the lower portion of the stables. Pantheon barely shifted, despite his skin flickering beneath my hand in irritation. Likely, my rage fed his.

Every rule had been followed! All of the guards watching, even the ones who didn't know me, admitted that the man held his death in his own hands by applying at the Trials with a useless mount. The other contestants apparently disagreed.

"You *are* scary," Rendle informed me as he knocked on the wood of the stall beside Pantheon's. "Just wanted to let you know that you are scheduled to fight your third and final battle in mounted combat an hour and a half from now."

I threw my arm wide, pointing down to where Jaxon was facing off with the cowardly demon who had now forfeited to me twice—once in hand-to-hand and once in mounted combat. "Tell them they can't forfeit!" I yelled.

Rendle grunted. "Yes, let me go tell them they have to let you beat them to a bloody pulp and break their bones, which is not only painful but somewhat inconvenient." I glared over his shoulder, wanting to see Jaxon knock her forcibly to the ground. "Look, Kinan, you win. You won. You meet up with Rankar in a couple hours."

The growl that emerged from my throat would have done a Lykos proud. "I didn't win. They just lost. I see the difference, and so will everyone else."

Rendle shook his head, waving away the hostler who called for him near the entrance. "Don't get distracted from the goal. A win is a win. As long as you don't break rules to make others forfeit, you still get the credit."

I whispered a thank-you as he walked away. After a couple deep breaths, I headed up to the empty apartment. I set my alarm with fingers stiff and frozen in position. Sitting tailor-style, my eyelids dropped over icy blue eyes alive with rage. Then I reached for my center, knowing I couldn't face Rankar like this.

When my eyes opened an hour later, my pupils were pinpricks in the midst of irises the color of a frozen lake on the coldest day in the Antarctic. My movements were precise, holding a fluidity of motion belied by the sternness of my features. Emotions were boxed, controlled, and discarded like ineffective refuse forgotten in an attic for centuries. All unrelated thoughts died, quashed beneath the importance of my goal.

I will win, I thought as I flexed my fingers and headed downstairs to where Leara waited with Pantheon.

She studied me as I finished checking all of the roan's gear. When she handed me the bō, her hands lingered long enough that I met her eyes. "Be careful. I don't want either of you injured. You'd never forgive yourself if you hurt him."

I didn't have to explain to her that I couldn't battle Rankar one on one without the cold, blackness of centering myself to keep the fear of harming him at bay. To keep me from cringing away from any maneuver that might accidentally hurt the man I loved. Hefting myself onto Pantheon's back, I settled the reins loosely around the pommel and guided the horse with my thighs. Both my hands rested on the wooden stave lying across the saddle in front of me as he walked sedately from the stable and out toward the crowd who was waiting to see our battle.

The staff in my hands felt grainy and thick. Pantheon's muscles shifted beneath my legs, his movements in sync with mine. Both the wood and the horse were extensions of my body, weapons to be used. Intentionally, I kept my focus on those two objects and noticed nothing else. Not the breeze against my skin, my earlier rage at the mass forfeiture, the grave expression on Rendle, Leara, and Triswon's faces as they silently watched me ride Pantheon from the stable, or my fear of harming Rankar.

Ahead, the mounted combat arena was blockaded so that noncombatants couldn't enter. Even the entrance had been roped off for the duration of the trials. Pantheon broke into a trot then a gallop. The audience cleared away, and we leapt the barrier. I shifted my weight as his front legs touched the ground and easily stayed in the saddle. Both Belisario and Alala stood inside the large corral, about twenty paces apart. Alala waited at the shoulder of Rankar's mount Shara, next to her captain's leg. Her twin brother nodded to me.

Firmly centered, I could see Rankar and Shara as only an adversary and his mount. Alala approached me as Belisario approached Rankar. The Tuveri demon calmly raised her hand and accepted the staff from me to check it for charms or spells. Then she checked my horse and my person. Belisario was undoubtedly doing the same to Rankar and Shara. It wasn't until the twins were satisfied that neither Rankar nor I had cheated that they stepped away and exited the corral.

From the edge of the clearing, a whistle blew to indicate that the match was to begin. Pantheon immediately leapt forward, obeying my directions. However, only skill kept me in his saddle as the first clash of the staves reverberated down both of my arms. My fingers clutched the wood desperately to keep it in my grip. The second meeting was slower, more practiced. Click. Click. Click. Clack. Click click click.

I WATCHED MY opponent's eyes, staring objectively into their brown depths. The muscles in his upper torso bunched, telling me to block. Pantheon instinctively predicted the movements of Shara. I blocked, defended. I swung, attacked. The timekeeper called out every five minutes to apprise us of how much time had elapsed.

"Five!" ... "Ten!" ... "Twenty-five!" ... "Forty!" The crowd kept cheering, but the sound never reached my ears.

There were things I noticed while centered, though. My arms grew heavy. Lifting them to block blows and attack felt like pushing through taffy, though nothing ached. Sweat soaked my pants where it touched my roan's barrel. His reactions to my commands slowed, a tiny hesitation as his tired muscles responded. My brain analyzed the performance, and it told me that much more exertion would threaten my life, my gelding's, and Shara's. But I couldn't gain ground over Rankar, and he couldn't break through my defense. One of us was going to have to yield.

As we broke away from one another, a wild scheme formed in my mind. The logistics needed to be perfect. Otherwise, I'd be in my current position again. Or worse.

I waited for him to charge and moved to meet him. At the last moment, a signal from me slowed Pantheon. As Shara passed, I raised my staff to block Rankar's swing with one hand and used my other to grip her reins.

As one, the two horses spun while our staves locked together. He rose in his saddle to get more leverage, and I met him. However, I charged Pantheon forward while using the tip of the bō to push him backwards. With my other hand, I pulled Shara toward us—too close for our safety.

Satisfaction filled me as my adversary fell backwards and over the chestnut's rump. Instinctively, Shara wheeled and attacked Pantheon. She tried to push us away from her rider, but she was too late. I coated my weapon with my energy to prevent meddling, and it was already on the downswing. My ice-colored eyes held no acknowledgement of the injury that Shara had caused Pantheon, no recognition that the man on the ground was Rankar, and no sign of the emotions aching to burst forth once everything was over.

The wood barely brushed his skin, and I halted the swing. "You are dead," I stated, cold and calm as I held the staff against my enemy's neck.

The whistle blew from the sidelines. I tossed the staff to Belisario and rode through the open gate of the corral. It wasn't until I entered the stable that I realized I was still firmly centered. My fingers were numb despite it, telling me better than anything that pain would hit me soon.

Gradually, I released my hold on the Void. My eyes blinked rapidly as they adjusted to the dimness of the stable, but I managed to smile at Leara as she ran toward us.

At Pantheon's head, Davie tugged lightly at Pantheon's reins. "I'll take care of the beast," he murmured.

I thanked him as I slid free. The pain in my shoulders was agonizing. I wouldn't have been able to lift the saddle off his back, much less tend the bite marks on his shoulder.

"Good boy, Pan. The best boy," I murmured to him, stroking his muzzle gently as Leara grabbed my free hand and pulled me through a Gate and onto the catwalk.

A moment later, I was curled up in the center of her bed. "I won."

Leara nodded, pulling my boots off and removing my socks. She returned after a moment with the tub of liniment, rubbing it from my shoulders to my hands.

"I beat him."

The words were more of a whimper than anything, and the warrior-girl wrapped her arms around me. My forehead rested against her shoulder, and my whimpers turned to cries which turned to sobs. As the fear and anger that had been buried in my emotionless center worked its way out, my ward stroked her fingers through my hair.

"Kinan, has anyone told you that you fight dirty?" she asked as I cuddled up to her and the puppies who'd climbed into the bed.

"All complaints should be filed with Belisario," I grumbled, nestling deeper into the covers.

CHAPTER 15

I AWOKE HOURS later with only Cullyn and Caiftín on my bed with me. *Damn dogs,* I thought, gently stroking Cullyn's velvety soft ears. He barely twitched, even when I patted him on the head. Carefully, I pulled my legs out from under the cover and crawled from between them. With surprise, I realized that the mutts had trapped me beneath the cover and the feeling of being held down hadn't awakened me. I couldn't remember moving from Leara's bedroom to mine and Rankar's. In fact, I wore only my undergarments, but I didn't recall undressing.

Muscles stretched as I bent from side to side. With a few economical movements, I dressed and stood ready to face the world. The clock said it was nine p.m., so they'd announce the final decision in three hours. The yawn snuck up on me as I climbed from the apartment. Half-asleep, I nearly missed Davie's greeting as he passed. By the time my mind processed it, he was out of sight. I shook my head and sank onto a bale of hay positioned conveniently out of the way of the daily bustle of the hostlers.

Barely half an hour passed before my ward sank down beside me. Hypnos appeared overhead, winging down to my shoulder. He snuggled his head inside the collar of my shirt and exhaled sharply.

I rubbed my finger under his chin. "How's Rankar, 'Nos?"

He cheeped and sent me the image of Rankar sleeping at his desk in his office. I winced, considering going to him to urge him to the bed. He was going to awaken more pained than rested.

"Alala is fighting the Arrow's knife-fighting champion."

I understood her meaning. They'd already chosen Asez Holding's new guard. We just had to wait for the announcement. I shifted, feeling the prickly pieces of dried grass poking the skin of my leg through my soft leather pants. The discomfort gave me an excuse to shift when the quiet became too much to bear, and it also kept me awake. The only things that interrupted the somber watch were the sounds of the horses shifting and calling to each other.

Leara did not move at my side, leaving me impressed with the young fae's potential for lengthy stakeouts. Any other teenager might have kicked her feet idly or cracked her knuckles. My warrior-girl showed an eternal patience and calm most people never achieved. My own gaze was focused forward, watching the Deylura mare in the nearby box nosing through the feed bin for the type of grain she preferred. Somewhere down the line of stalls, Rukchio was likely growing hungry. However, the little bastard refused to consume oats. The young horse and I were having a battle of wills. He could eat the oats or starve.

The next couple hours passed in relative silence. The pups came down from the loft to sleep on either side of us. Their quiet snores and occasional dream movements brought a soft smile to my face. *Goddess, how did I go from a solitary mercenary with no friends to a stable hand with a husband, a ward, two horses, two dogs, and a drakyn?*

She didn't reply, but I wasn't surprised. It wasn't often I heard her voice; mostly I just saw the hand she dealt.

Well, thank you.

Outside, everything went quiet. My eyes burned, and Leara listed to the side. Her head leaned on my shoulder, and her arms wrapped possessively around me. One of her fingers rested casually upon the hilt of my sword, but I didn't move it. I had a knife easily within reach on the other side. Instead, I watched as groups of demons walked by the entrance to the stable. They'd all be gone soon, and the double patrols would end. There'd be fewer horses to tend, and the noise level would diminish to the normal hum.

Rendle passed by the entrance, paused, and then walked toward us. He looked down at Leara with an amused smile before bending to lift her. Though he looked older, the ease with which he lifted her told the true story. The girl barely twitched, even as he walked up the angled ladder to the apartment with the balance of a tightrope walker. The dogs had awakened at his approach, and they followed him up now.

Probably going to beg him to feed them, and he likely will.

When Rendle came back down, he gave me an encouraging smile and a nod. Then he disappeared to complete his rounds.

With no clock, time dragged by. I convinced myself briefly that whoever was to announce it might take a bit to find me, but all four of Asez Holding's officers would know exactly where I'd be waiting. Dread was a ball of lead in my stomach, and I considered going to find Belisario to see if he wanted to practice. Unfortunately, he'd be working tonight in his sergeant major capacity. Everyone had been told to consider themselves on duty twenty-four hours a day for the week of the trials. And in the morning, the exodus of demons leaving for parts unknown would begin.

Laying my head back against the wall, I inhaled. As I did, I heard the clicking of boot heels against the stone at the stable's floor. I peered down the aisle of the stable. Two people strode toward me through the shadows, faces not visible in the dim light but steps timed and strides matched like two people who'd fought together often.

The blue drakyn lifted his head, roused from sleep on my shoulder. He cheeped softly, and Thanatos chirped back. Standing, I waited. My lungs burned as I forgot to breathe. Hypnos felt me tense and crooned ever-so-softly into my ear, the noise barely audible over the horses shifting as they settled into sleep. Belisario and Rankar kept coming until they stopped dead in front of me, expressions serious.

The silence drew out, my heart beating faster every second it lasted. Finally, they took pity on me.

"You're in," Belisario congratulated.

I launched myself at him. My arms wrapped tightly around his shoulders, uncaring that the hairs on the back of my neck stood on end at the contact. He patted my shoulder, winking at me as he stepped back.

I faced Rankar, the nerves in the pit of my stomach aflame until he smiled at me. "It was a unanimous decision. Commander Montgomery might want to steal you, but there was never any doubt you'd be one of the guard," he murmured.

Relief escaped in a sigh. Moving forward, I didn't stop until no space separated us. Even my rapid breaths couldn't slip through as I wrapped my arms low around his waist and pulled him closer. His chin rested on top of my head as I tucked it against his chest. Together, touching, our tense muscles relaxed.

When I opened my eyes, Belisario had disappeared, and Rankar urged me toward the ladder.

"Come on, *eirlys*. Let's grab a nap. You go on duty at ten till three, and it's been a long two weeks."

My lips twitched. "Yes, Captain."

THE RAIN PATTERED lightly against the rubber of the commercial-grade rain poncho. Beneath the waterproof material, my hand gripped my belt loop to keep me from hitting the demon beside me. The sky had already started to lighten, so his ebony poncho was visible. He made an easy target.

Asez Holding used rotating four-man patrols around the compound and grounds. Treyv and I had walked in silence for the majority of the first third of the shift. After two hours, I moved through a Gate to accompany Ries Jacobs while Ilyetik Hoxez went through to Treyv. Ilyetik was a frequent visitor to the stables, and she'd joined the hand-to-hand practice with Belisario a couple times to give tips. Overall, the woman was quiet and spoke only when she had something important to say. We'd gotten along well, and I'd expected my new partner to be the same. Unfortunately, Jacobs didn't believe in companionable silences. In fact, I wasn't sure he believed in silence at all.

"I hear you and the captain are together. And you both wear wedding rings. But he sleeps in his office sometimes, which doesn't make much sense for a married couple. I wasn't here when you first disappeared, but some of the other guards were. Of course, the captain is pretty closedmouthed, except with the other officers, so the people who knew and were willing to talk didn't know much. Part of which was probably total BS. Okay, most of which. But still, they talked. Anyhow, why did you leave?"

I blinked, glaring at him from beneath the hood of my poncho. If the water dripping from the corner diminished the dislike I put into my gaze, he didn't notice either way.

"Okay. You don't want to talk about leaving. Why'd you come back?"

I swallowed hard, twice. My feet kept moving forward, and I wondered how badly they'd penalize me for decking one of my squad members on my first shift.

"Guess that is a no-go too." He was silent for ten seconds, long enough that I was sure he'd gotten the hint. "Do you and the cap'n have a sexual relationship? I mean, I don't need to know whether you actually liked each other or were just fuck buddies. Am just curious as to whether you two… y'know… together."

Beneath the poncho, the gun jerked as my palm clutched it. Carefully, I moved my hand away from the holster under my arm and back to my belt.

"I wouldn't ask—well, I actually probably would anyway but that's beside the point—except that there is this betting pool. Most of the betting pool has to do with the officers. Rankar is a favorite, because he's kind of mysterious. No one even knows what his preference is. Y'know.

Hetero, homo, bi... asexual. And if he'd had sex with you, that would limit it to a couple choices. My odds would be more like fifty-fifty than twenty-five/seventy-five."

Jaw clenched and hand spasming, I kept moving despite the inquisition. Two hours in the grand scheme of things wasn't that bad, I tried to convince myself.

Relief swamped me when Jacobs received the text that it was time to switch off again. When I stepped back through the Gate to join Treyv, it took me a second to realize that Treyv and Ilyetik both stared at me.

"Did you hit him?" the woman asked, her brow raised in question.

My teeth had apparently fused together, and I couldn't get a word out. Instead, I shook my head in denial.

She grinned at me. "Damn." Without shame, she handed Treyv a twenty. "Damn," Ilyetik said again, shaking her head as she entered the Gate.

I blinked, eyes glued to the money my friend folded into his pocket. Two things bothered me. Not that they'd bet on whether I would hit the guy. Gambling was the favorite pastime of soldiers, mercenaries, and guards. First, they'd known before I went with Jacobs that I'd want to deck the demon and they hadn't even mentioned how annoying he was. The second thing, though, was the real kicker. "I was allowed to punch him and you didn't *tell* me?!"

Treyv coughed, trying to hide the smile. He damn sure wasn't trying hard enough, and the impulse to plant my fist against his nose came over me. "No," he managed hastily. "No, you aren't allowed to hit him... or me! But you would only have gotten in a tiny bit of trouble if you had.

Ilyetik beat the shit out of him her first shift, but there were rumors that she was sleeping with Fwen at the time. For the record, she wasn't. They were just friends." He shook his head. "As for me, I was pursuing 'Sario and 'Sario was avoiding the hell out of me when I first patrolled with Jacobs. The books were stacked on whether Belisario would turn me in for sexual harassment or fall into bed with me first. He made a comment about 'Sario that I took amiss, so I gave him a black eye and busted lip."

Unsure whether to laugh or be angry, finally I asked, "How did you know I wouldn't hit him?"

He grinned. "I didn't. Rankar did, though. That's the only reason he would have put you with him for your first shift."

The rest of the shift passed in silence. Occasionally, a shifter would call in the distance that all was clear. I winced each time, knowing how annoying it must be to patrol with wet fur. However, each check-in told me we were closer to the end of my first patrol. The stress from the weeks before and the rain had combined to make me weary. I was doubly glad that Treyv hadn't wanted to hold conversation.

Energy coalesced about ten feet away. "Incoming," I managed to snap as the hairs on my neck tingled.

We both dropped to a knee to make ourselves smaller targets. Glock unholstered, I aimed before the Gate actually appeared. Our relief guards stepped through, greeting Treyv familiarly. I grinned at Gerald Brock, recognizing him from his visits to the stable. A tall hyena lycanthrope with a vampire guard for a lover, the Bouda'd once confided that his girlfriend was more than satisfied that he worked while she slept and vice-versa to give them more time together awake without duties interfering. Both of them were good people, and I empathized with their predicament as Rankar and I would have different schedules now.

The lycanthrope's shift partner, though, despised me. And Ivan Karl had no qualms about letting everyone know. He'd spit on me once in the stables, and Brock had nearly punched him in the teeth. This time, Karl was remarkably silent as Brock patiently held the Gate for me and Treyv to use. I mouthed a silent thank-you as we stepped out near the mess hall.

A glance at my watch showed that Rankar had already gone on shift. Leara had likely already grabbed breakfast and was in her first class. Ooh. Breakfast. *A steaming cup of coffee would be amazing.*

"Want to join me for a drink, Treyv?"

He glanced at me. "I'm having breakfast with my sister-in-law, but you're welcome to join us. She won't bite. Not outside of combat or unless you ask."

I exhaled. "I'm not sure Alala likes me."

Treyv laughed. "She didn't 'accidentally' kill you during combat, did she? That means she likes you just fine."

The laugh escaped before I could stifle it. Mostly because it was true that she could have killed me at least four times during the knife fighting challenge. I doubted she would have murdered me short of outright hate, though, because she liked Rankar well enough. I still understood his point.

"Coffee then."

The cafeteria held about fifty people, only a fifth of its

capacity. The seated groups were spread evenly, but most demons seemed to be grabbing their food to go. Like us, the greatest number of them had probably just finished the morning shift. A sign just inside the entrance reminded everyone to take off their rain gear and leave it in the alcove to keep the floors from becoming drenched.

As we stepped out, Alala waved and Treyv signaled back. "She already has my order, but she wasn't sure what you wanted or could eat. Meet us at the table?"

Today's special was chicken and waffles, so I went with it. I added hash browns and a side of fruit before doctoring a cup of coffee and heading to the table. I slid onto the bench across from Alala and Treyv. He'd also ordered the special, and a double helping of hash browns. Alala appeared to have a bit of every type of protein offered—three kinds of pork, the fried chicken, eggs, and whatever she'd just finished chewing—and then covered all of it with a generous amount of hot sauce.

"Good morning," I greeted before taking a grateful sip of the warm coffee.

"Morning," Alala responded as Treyv finished pouring syrup on his breakfast. "Any trouble on your shift?"

I accepted the syrup Treyv passed over and began adding the sweet, sticky goodness to the waffle. "Only that Jacobs can't keep his mouth shut."

Alala rolled her eyes. "I told you she wouldn't hit him," she reminded Treyv, taking a drink from her travel mug and wincing slightly. "Humiliate him later, maybe; you have that kind of energy, Kinan. But annoying as Jacobs is, he's good enough at walking the line not to get assaulted while he's on shift." She speared a piece of sausage with her fork and popped it into her mouth. "Although if he said anything to you like what he tried with me, I don't know that I'd blame you."

The waffle tasted slightly like sawdust as I finished chewing it. "Mostly he asked about Rankar. Why did I leave him? Why did I come back to him? Are we married to each other? Are we sleeping with one another?"

I ate a large piece of pineapple and stared down at the bowl of fruit as though it had the answer to why those questions—particularly the last one—bothered me so badly. I lived around soldiers and mercenaries my entire life. Drama was their favorite topic.

Alala nodded. "Sounds about right. He asked me if and how often I was fucking 'Sario. The look on his face when I told him we were twins, not married, was fucking priceless."

I felt her staring at me and met her intent green gaze.

"Why do I get the feeling that being asked about Rankar was worse than him asking if my brother and I were having sex?"

Her question rattled me, enough that I wanted to answer it. The voice in my head reminded me that I didn't talk about Rankar, didn't discuss him with other people. Especially not with his friends and coworkers. As I once told Leader Laso, my husband was off-limits. However, this wasn't a Rankar-based problem. Our issues stemmed from a problem with me. My past, my inhibitions, my anxiety.

Picking up my coffee cup, I wrapped the fingers of both hands around it to comfort myself with the heat. "Maybe because you had an answer to his question." I set the cup back down, suddenly needing my hands free. "I, on the other hand, just have a lot of problems I carried home with me from the camp. Problems that cause me to wear gloves to reduce skin-to-skin contact during hand-to-hand fighting practice and leave me wanting to punch Ries Jacobs in the face for not keeping his mouth shut."

Alala stole a bite of Treyv's hash browns before she spoke. "Technically, you also have an answer to Ries's question; your answer can be 'Fuck off' if you're on patrol or a punch in the face if you're off. No one you have to answer to in your chain of command would ask about your sex life. Not while you're at work, anyway; Rankar's still in the chain of command when he's off duty, but you're on equal footing as his wife then."

My lips twitched, mostly because she was right. Not answering him at all had been a response, though not a satisfactory one. If I ever caught him in the stables off-shift, the idea of punching him in the face then had merit. Having trained with Belisario, I had faith I could get in a lesson-worthy tussle before help arrived.

Treyv interrupted my thoughts. "The next time Jacobs gets out of line, remind him that eyebrows are a privilege, not a right."

Alala's smirk hinted there was a story behind the comment, but she didn't otherwise acknowledge Treyv had spoken. She took a slow sip of whatever was in her travel mug while she gathered her thoughts. "If you don't like touching strangers, keep the gloves. It's not like Rankar's a stranger, right?"

"In some ways, he might as well be," I muttered.

The moment the words escaped, horror punched me in

the stomach. I glanced over my shoulder, but the nearest group was too far away for even paranormal hearing to have picked up my words. When I turned back, Treyv eyed me curiously and Alala had raised an eyebrow.

Lowering my voice, I tried again. "I... should not have said that. What I meant was, it is hard to overcome certain relationship fears when the last thing I want to do is disappoint Rankar. He is everything I could ever ask for in a partner and husband, and I hate that I hold us back from being the best we could be."

Alala ate a piece of bacon and followed it with a sip from her travel mug. The silence continued long enough that I wanted to fill it. With what, I wasn't sure. Just before I caved and opened my mouth, Alala set her cup down and looked at me.

"Kinan, has anyone ever talked to you about safewords?"

CHAPTER 16

M Y KNUCKLES RAPPED twice against the door, other hand already turning the knob before I was invited to enter. Stepping through Rankar's ward and into his office, raw nerves prevented the smile I wanted to display. Instead, my teeth chattered beneath tightly compressed lips. I closed the door and leaned against it, trapping my hands between my back and the door. Feeling the lock, I turned it.

"Kinan!" Rankar greeted, sounding surprised to see me. "Everything okay?"

Because you just came off your first shift, and you almost never interrupt his office hours.

My feet carried me halfway to his desk, stopping abruptly when I was within arm's length of the guest chair. "Are you doing anything important?"

Chewing on my lower lip, I noticed him looking me over for injury. The anxiety in my voice caused him to stand.

"Nothing that can't wait." He was obviously torn between walking toward me and allowing me to approach him.

A glance at my hands revealed my fingers fretfully twirling my wedding band. This wasn't what I intended.

No part of my plan had included the tension filling the room as he tried to work out what was wrong, and I attempted to convince myself nothing *was* wrong.

"Good." If, when I met his eyes, there was a pause, blaming it on my throat closing up wouldn't be a lie. "Take off your shirt." I coughed, trying to clear the obstruction. "Please."

His brown eyes bore into mine as he gripped the hem of his shirt and pulled it over his head. Sliding through his fingers, it hit the ground. Swallowing, I pointed at the couch. The tilt of his head as he tried to understand my purpose drew my lips into a shaky smile.

"Sit, Ran. Arms across the back, please."

He returned my smile, just as uncertain, and crossed his office to sit in the middle of the couch. Palms down, he laid his arms just as I'd asked. My gaze traveled from the tips of his fingers to his well-defined shoulders, following the natural V-lines of his body.

Mouth suddenly dry, I licked my lips and sucked in my bottom lip. "Rankar, Alala talked to me about safewords."

"Oh, gods," he groaned, knuckles suddenly white against the darker furniture. I froze, and his fingers relaxed until the blood flow returned to normal there. "Sorry. Please continue. What did Alala have to say about… on the matter?"

I stepped forward, forcing my feet each step until my shins touched his knees. "She said we can use safewords to communicate how we are feeling when it might be otherwise difficult to do so, that sometimes it is easier to express emotions without the actual emotion. Some safewords are used to mean stop, while others can convey a willingness to continue, but at a reduced level of intensity. Red means stop, Rankar. Yellow is slow down. Okay?"

His eager nod caused some of the tension to leave my shoulders. "Green, Kinan. Super green."

The grin that crossed my face eased the trembling in my lips, but my fingers still shook as I leaned forward to place my hands on his shoulders. Warmth radiated off him, easing the cold tightness in my chest as I brought my knees up on either side of his thighs and lowered myself to sit on his lap. For a moment, neither of us breathed.

My left hand rose from his bare shoulder, skimming slowly until my palm rested above the pulse in his throat. It thundered so loudly I should have been able to hear it in the too-quiet space, but a glance at Rankar's face convinced me he was okay. His eyes were closed, lips barely parted. My thumb brushed the corner of his mouth, and he met my gaze. I needed him to know what I intended, to be able to stop it if he did not want this.

Leaning forward, my lips touched opposite my fingers, barely a graze. His exhale caressed my cheek, encouraging me as my hand slid to the back of his neck. My fingers tightened in his hair, firm enough to pull without crossing into pain. Gently, I used the leverage to lift his chin. Then I kissed him.

He let me explore, encouraging me without fully participating. My right hand swept downward, enjoying the feel of his pecs before I rested it on his side. "Kiss me back," I murmured into his mouth, inhaling his moan.

A tilt of his head lined us up perfectly so he could return the nips I'd given him earlier. His teeth tugged my bottom lip, and his tongue greeted mine. All of the oxygen in the room burned away, leaving me panting and hot. My heart beat rapidly, reminding me of an anxiety attack. However, the tightness had moved much lower than my chest.

Walking my fingers upward from his side, my thumb caressed his nipple. His hips bucked, almost dislodging me. "Sorry," he murmured, studying me.

I pulled my shirt over my head in reply, leaving a black sports bra to protect my modesty. No matter, Rankar's gaze traveled unhurriedly from my belt buckle to my face. He smiled as his eyes met mine, and my fingertips caressed his face.

Then I backed off his lap.

For a bare instant, disappointment crossed his expression as I broke contact with him. Then it disappeared, and his encouraging grin returned. "That was fantastic, Kinan." He thought we were done.

You haven't safeworded yet, love.

Using his leg for balance, I knelt in front of him and gripped his left boot with a hand at the heel and the other on top. Pulls and tugs and a single curse word conquered his boots and socks, and I set them side by side at the end of the couch where neither of us would trip over them later. Then I unbuckled his belt, and he lifted his hips, allowing the leather to slide free of the loops. My boots, socks, and belt joined his on the floor.

Eyes closed, my head tilted back. I let my fingers walk up my bare stomach, slipping beneath the elastic of the bra. After a quick movement, the fabric hit the floor. My nipples tightened as cold air swept across them. My thumbs brushed over the hard peaks, flicking gently. A cracking noise startled me into glancing at Rankar, who sheepishly shrugged. Beneath his right hand, the back of the couch looked just a little... off.

"What color are you?" I questioned, crossing my arms over my naked chest nervously. My teeth worried my bottom lip. This was beyond my realm of experience, even before the camp. Had I done something wrong?

"Please don't stop," he begged as he shifted in his seat.

"Color?" The prompt was followed by my foot stepping lightly on his.

"Still green, *cariad*." He used his chin to gesture at me, not moving his hands. "How about you?"

Instead of replying instantly, I considered it for a moment. "Yellowish green. I... Am I doing this wrong?"

His lips twitched. "Definitely not."

I nodded at him, and he returned the gesture encouragingly. My left hand dropped to my side, moving slowly toward the top button at the front of my soft hide pants. "You first. Left hand," I ordered, putting just enough pressure that the waistband pulled but not enough to unsnap.

I followed his left hand as he lowered it to his lap, undoing the button one-handed. He waited for my next direction as I mirrored the movement. "The zipper," I urged, moving my own hand down to the second button.

He winced slightly. "For safety sake, can I use both hands?"

The snort that escaped me was probably inappropriate, but the expression on his face made it impossible to keep in. "Nope. In fact, just put both hands back up."

The distance between us quickly disappeared as I moved to stand between his knees. Balancing against the front of the couch, my legs held me upright as my hands skimmed up his firm thighs. One gripped the zipper, and the other lifted the fabric away from delicate parts. Only, I kept peeling until he sat in boxer briefs, leaving no doubt that he felt attracted to me.

Thank the Goddess.

"My turn?"

His sharp nod agreed. "I think so."

A quick pull opened the other two snaps, and I pushed the pants down my legs and stepped free, leaving only my bikini-cut panties. Goosebumps rose on my skin as the cool air surrounded me.

"Want me to start the fire?"

I shook my head. "Actually, I have a different idea."

A trill of delight shivered through me as my bare skin brushed his. The fine hairs on his body tickled when the inside of my thighs touched the outsides of his. I leaned just a little too far forward, and my nipples scraped against his chest. The moan that escaped my throat reminded me of my next step.

"Rankar, I'm going to... This might... I'm sorry if..." The words tumbled brokenly over one another.

"Yellow."

I paused, meeting his eyes from just inches away, but worried that moving might accelerate him to red.

"*Eirlys*, take a deep breath in." Inhaling at his command, I held it for a moment before releasing it. "Again." We matched our breathing, and my heartrate returned to a normal level of excitement. "What's your color now, love?"

If he hadn't suspended play temporarily, I would have kissed him. However, the rules of each color still left me a little uncertain about limitations. "Green, I think."

"Me, too," he assured me. "Now what were you going to say?"

I swallowed. "I want to escalate this, but I apologize in advance if I have to stop." The sentence sounded so clinical, basically the opposite of my pounding heart and tingling skin.

"I'm yours, Kinan. Say when."

I held up my left hand between us. "Place your right palm facing mine." It had to be my left, because using my dominant hand allowed me more control. This once, his also being left-hand dominant didn't benefit us. However, he never quibbled. "Hold…"

Sliding my hand around until my palm faced the back of his, I clasped his hand. My thumb wrapped around his pinky and my two middle fingers gripped between his thumb and forefinger. Testing, I guided his palm to my lips, placing a kiss in the middle. "When I touch you, the anxiety stands at bay. Even when you slide your hand under mine, initiating but not controlling, I have been okay." Bringing our hands up, my tongue darted out to taste the pulse in his wrist. "When others have touched me, I have panicked, but you've been infinitely patient. You have never pushed my boundaries, so we can only guess whether my trust in you would cancel out the anxiety or send me into madness." Lowering our arms slightly, I waited a moment to gather my thoughts. "By directing your movement, I may be able to work around the triggers… or I may not."

The nervousness that had entered his eyes initially faded, and he nodded his agreement. "Use your safeword if you need to, and I will too."

I grinned, somehow relieved. Then I brought our clasped hands to the side of my face. His callused palm cupped my cheek, and his thumb lightly brushed over my lips. Drawing downward, the feel of his fingertips caressing my skin left me breathless. My collarbone tingled, and something caught in my chest. *Anxiety?* For a second, I waited. Nothing.

Slowly, his wrist then palm then fingers skimmed my eager peak. The gentlest pressure encouraged him to shape his hand under my breast, supporting the weight while his thumb raked across my nipple as my own had earlier. This time, my hips pressed against his erection. We both gasped at the unexpected sensation.

I needed more.

"Other hand," I begged, holding my right palm facing him. He immediately complied, and I adjusted my position to bring his left hand to my aching, lonely breast. "Oh, gods." Somehow, my grip loosened until my fingers rested on his forearms, no longer even pretending control.

The wanting would kill me, I realized as I intentionally rubbed the cloth of my panties against the fabric over his bulge. "Bedroom, Rankar. Please. Please." I whimpered, leaning forward to rake my teeth where his shoulder and neck met. "Bedbedbedbedbed." His shoulder muffled the chant as I sucked the skin my teeth had sensitized moments before.

Beneath me, his muscles bunched as he stood. My legs

wrapped around his waist and a hand on each shoulder kept me from slipping as he strode through the doorway leading to his bedroom. Not until we were falling toward the bed did the panic at being covered, trapped, kick in. Then I landed on top of Rankar, in almost the exact position we'd shared on the couch... except he was lying flat on his back.

Unwilling to move, I gripped the waistband of my panties over my hip with both hands and pulled, repeating the action on the other side. Sliding the fabric from between my legs, I angled my hand upward, arching my hips as the cloth rubbed against my clit.

"Cheater." Amusement warred with arousal in Rankar's voice.

I held my palm to him, and he met it eagerly with his own. Grasping his hand, I scooted forward until he could easily touch me then guided his fingers to the proof of my willingness. His strokes unbalanced me, and my arm shook when I held myself off him. He moved his hand away, allowing me to steal back my arm so I didn't crash against him.

"Roll on your side, *cariad*?"

Anything that might extend this scene sounded blissful, so I obeyed, but first... "Take off your boxer briefs."

His crooked grin caught me unawares. "Can I keep them in one piece?"

I grinned back, sweeping a hand down his abdomen. "Mine are still one piece."

In moments, nothing separated us but space, and he would be able to wear his underwear again sometime.

Hesitantly, my hand caressed his cock, squeezing firmly as I worked my palm up and down the shaft. Somehow, the amount of enjoyment I gained from his pleasure had escaped me. I had forgotten how wet his moans left me, how my nipples tingled as he groaned and tensed.

My inner muscles spasmed, and I inhaled sharply. *Goddess.*

"Rankar?" I breathed.

"Yes. Anything you want," he answered, eyes slitted as he fought to watch me.

My left leg crossed over his right thigh. Guiding his cock to my core, I ignored the shaking in my hand as the tip rubbed against my clit. Small movements left me breathless for entirely good reasons. "Color?" I panted, wanting badly to erase the final distance between us.

"Green." The word was barely recognizable, but it didn't matter. He hadn't said yellow; definitely not red. And I didn't hesitate.

My hips pressed forward, loving the fullness as the stretching began. After a deep inhalation, my hand trailed to his hip and drew him toward me again.

Rankar!

I had forgotten this intense connection, the near-echo of his heartbeat in my head, the warmth destroying the chill that lingered inside me.

Only a couple inches remained, and the muscles of my thighs tensed and drew him closer. His pelvis twitched against mine, involuntary movement that caught my breath. From the corner of my eye, I noticed his hands flexing against the comforter. An invisible fist punched my chest, stealing my oxygen and feeding the sudden panic.

"Stop! Yellow!"

Instantly, Rankar stilled. His hands were fingers spread, palms down, out at his side as he waited for me to do... something. No doubt, he cursed me in his head. This was probably the most inconvenient moment for anxiety to strike. "I'm sorry," I whispered, meticulously inhaling and exhaling.

"*Cariad*, you could stop this now, and I will still be pleased with our progress. Don't push beyond your limits."

I glanced at him, meeting his gaze and seeing the truth of his statement. "Will you put your hands behind your head for me?"

He complied with slow, precise actions. My breathing no longer sounded frantic, but the interruption had definitely damped Rankar's enthusiasm. Careful not to dislodge him, I leaned toward his body. The movement rubbed just right, catching my breath in my lungs.

"If we stop now, neither of us would be *satisfied*. I think the movement of your hands did it. Let's just keep them still for now?"

His nod prompted me to reach toward his torso. My fingernails raked lightly over his nipple, circling then pinching, before deliberately proceeding down his abdomen. His cock noticed, appreciating the attention. Confident he was ready, I rocked against him. *Yes*. Definitely good.

"*Eirlys*, it has been a long time for us, and despite that hiccup, we've been stoking this fire for a bit now."

A chuckle escaped. "I'm close, too."

And I wasn't certain my nerves could take much more.

Transferring my touch from his thigh to my own, I trailed it to my clit. A gentle flick assured me I could find completion. Fingers dancing over the sensitive nub, the familiar tension washed toward me.

"Rankar! Move with me. Come with me."

The tempo of our rhythm increased, and the muscles in my legs trembled uncontrollably. My abdomen clenched. *Goddess,* I hoped he was here, too. His breathing echoed in my head, as though he exhaled near my ear, and the catch in the middle reassured me. Finger and thumb pinching my clit, my forefinger ran over the bundle of nerves. I reveled in the spasms, hips bucking as my entire body tensed. Then I shattered as Rankar shouted my name.

WARM AND LIMP, opening my eyes exhausted my strength. Our legs were still entangled, but we were no longer joined. At some point, Rankar's right arm had draped across my abdomen. His left hand cushioned his cheek. If his breathing was any indication, he slept soundly.

Did I get a wash cloth and clean us up, likely waking Rankar, or curl close to him and sleep until all my muscles reformed? I concentrated momentarily on the sticky annoyance gluing us together, but in the grand scheme of things I had suffered in my life, it didn't even rate. Plus, having a few more moments of normalcy negated any discomfort.

Slipping my leg off his caused him to mumble a protest, but he calmed once I curled my back to his chest. A few tugs unmade the bed, allowing me to pull a third of the blanket over us. His back would still feel a breeze, but no one would glimpse my naked body if they got in.

Fingers on my hip caused me to tense a little as he

settled closer, but I was still too relaxed to feel anything except sated. I linked my fingers with his, and my other fist curled between my breasts. My eyelids drifted closed. Then I slept.

A cell phone rang, but the sound came from far away. I groaned and turned my face into the bedding, tempted to put the pillow over my head until it stopped. Usually, Rankar answered within two rings. He didn't ever let it go to voicemail.

Behind me, the fae in question chuckled and ran his knuckles lightly down my spine. "I hoped you'd sleep through it. I should have known, even with limited rest these past weeks, you'd still wake up."

I scooted back against him, noticing his warmth had seeped under my skin, leaving me refreshed and relaxed. "Morning, Ran."

His lips pressed against my neck, and he smiled into my skin. "Afternoon, *eirlys*. That was Leara's ringtone. I sent Hypnos to her to let her know you're with me. I'm betting she got home and figured you were shanghaied on your first night of patrol."

I snorted, not doubting he was right. She tended to jump to worst-case scenario immediately, instead of working her way there. Therapy had helped some.

Rolling to face him, I rested my thigh over his. A tiny stretch let me kiss him gently on the lips. "'Sario's on shift now?"

"Mmhmm," he agreed, linking our fingers and resting them on my hip. His eyes shone happily as he met my gaze. I'd put that look there. Finally, I did something right.

"Rankar?" I murmured, bringing his palm up to my lips

and kissing the center.

"*Eirlys?*" His fingers brushed my cheek, the caress as light as his breath.

"We need a shower."

His laughter caught me off guard, but I grinned at the sound.

"Hey, Ran?"

He leaned forward, his lips nibbling at mine as he hummed in reply.

"Green."

CHAPTER 17

Our routine changed with my acceptance into the guard, and it took over a month for us to settle into a pattern. Rankar and Leara had breakfast each morning and left the apartment before I came home. I showered and slept until Leara got in from school around three o'clock in the afternoon. We trained together on days she didn't have an appointment with Alika—sometimes working on language lessons and other times working on combat techniques. Her favorite times seemed to be when we used the range and Fwen joined us. The shapeshifter enjoyed mentoring the young fae, and he talked shop with me. Once in a while, he seemed to be testing me.

When Leara's lessons ended, mine began. I would head down to the gym to work out with Belisario, Treyv, or—more rarely—Alala. Usually, Leara accompanied me. However, twice a week, she trained with Rankar to improve her horseback riding technique. She had to be able to ride well before she could learn to fight mounted at all.

We rotated who provided supper. Two nights a week each, we alternated preparing supper to be ready to sit down at seven o'clock. For me, that meant a stop at the cafeteria while Leara had become a crockpot professional and Rankar excelled at stir-fry. On Saturday nights, we

Gated to Mystor to visit Eliecha and Triswon for dinner. Often, Mycal and Karyn joined us. Usually, at least one of the other siblings and their spouse or significant other also attended.

My favorite nights at the Banded Traveler were when Asher and his boyfriend, Damienn, came. The shadows and secrets I'd recognized in Asher's eyes when I first arrived at the Sirach ranch had been erased over the years by Damienn. Lucky how we'd both found the person who could light the dark corners of our soul. How we'd each managed to find support even as our safety straps threatened to snap. And found love just before the world became mired in hate.

Rankar leaned toward me at the long table, refilling my cup with ale. The movement brought his lips near my ear. "What are you thinking? You seem far away."

Gently, I leaned my forehead against his. "The opposite," I murmured. "Just reminded how much I love you, how much this family means to me."

"I love you too, *eirlys*. And the family we've built."

Across the room, Leara bounced Erykah twice and then tossed her in the air. Each time she went airborne, Hypnos squeaked in alarm. I think she did it as much to occupy the toddler as to traumatize the drakyn. Tiernia and Kismet didn't mind, though, only occasionally checking on them before going back to their own whispers.

As the fire died down and the talk quieted, we all hugged one another before heading home. Leara took the dogs out to potty, Rankar moved chicken from the freezer to the refrigerator to thaw, and I transferred a load of towels from the washer to the dryer. Saying goodnight to

Leara, I turned off the lights and followed Rankar to bed.

Burrowing my nose into his chest, I inhaled his comforting scent and slept.

"Bravo!" I cheered as I blocked the beautiful swish then lunge Rankar completed. Picture perfect, exactly as sword masters of old likely taught their noble protégé. Similar to the moves I taught Leara as she became comfortable with the feel of a blade in her hand.

In answer, I tossed my rapier from my left hand to my right and back again while staring into his beautiful brown eyes. I finished by cutting a Zorro-style "S" into the air for Sirach. Rankar saluted me with his sword, grinning as we circled.

"Umm… someone wanna explain why we're having a sword fight in the living room?" Leara questioned, stepping out of her bedroom and freezing.

My husband looked at her sheepishly, but I spun behind him and tapped him on the butt with the flat of my blade. I continued the maneuver until I was out of range.

"Because…" I paused to laugh at the affront on Rankar's face before starting over. "Because if we fooled around like this in the training area, Belisario would punch us in our faces and the other guards would vote us out."

"Hey. The captaincy was not secured with a vote, I'll have you know," Rankar interjected, moving swiftly forward until our blades locked. We each leaned toward the other without a word for a quick kiss before I broke under his guard and danced away.

"Okay. Yes. You're right. You all definitely can't be

doing this in the training room. Jeez," Leara agreed, shaking her head.

"Here," I called. "Show Rankar the pretty moves *you've* been learning."

Waiting until she focused on me, I carefully tossed my sword the fifteen feet to Leara. Her eyes tracked the movement, and her body tensed then relaxed. In a flash of reflexes, she caught the sword by the pommel, adjusted her grip to fit the feel of my sword, and kicked off her house shoes.

Backing up out of the way, I leaned against the kitchen table where Hypnos and Thanatos perched to watch. Leara tested the balance of the rapier, a bit heavier than the blunted practice blades we used in training. However, she charged into the fray without hesitation, reminding me so much of my younger self squaring off against my dad.

Rankar let her attack a couple times before forcing her to retreat. He grinned devilishly at her for a second before intoning, "No man can kill me."

Leara snorted. "I am no man!"

I could only shake my head at how they butchered Tolkien. "No more movie nights for either of you."

She leapt forward again, completely unafraid of defeat. Leara demonstrated her classic stances and executed the attacks with only minor sideline corrections from me. Even in the mock battle, Rankar stayed two moves ahead of her, careful not to hurt her or let her harm him. The teenager had neither the experience nor the control to read her partner like Rankar and I could one another.

After ten minutes, Leara retreated and held up a hand. "Yield. I yield." She switched the sword to her left hand and rotated her right shoulder. "How do you all do this for so long?"

I grinned, stepping forward to take back the rapier. "First, decades more practice. Second, both Rankar and I are ambidextrous in sword work. When one arm gets tired, we can switch. Third, imagine how your arm will feel when you are blocking blows meant to do you harm. You'll tire five times faster. Eventually, you'll build stamina."

Leara handed me the blade hilt first, but she didn't release it. Instead, she tilted her head and studied me for a second. "I've never seen the two of you practice together. Not *really* practice like you do with 'Sario and Treyv in hand-to-hand or blade work."

Rankar walked up behind me, entwining the fingers of his left hand with my right. "Because we haven't since before the Enlightenment."

I squeezed his hand. "After I came back, it didn't help that hostlers couldn't carry swords. Other than to face Alala, my rapier just reminded me that I wasn't where I was best."

Leara raised her eyebrows. "But now you are, and you carry your sword. And look, the captain of the guard is conveniently also armed with a sword!"

One day, her words were going to get her into trouble, but Rankar's half-laugh behind me tickled the back of my neck and won a smile.

"So he is," I agreed.

"To yield?" he asked.

"To yield."

We began, blades crossed and awaiting Leara's signal.

"Two. One. *En garde!*" she cried with such glee that the pups hopped up to investigate. Luckily, her quick hand signal sent them back to their spots before they could trip us.

Rankar and I circled for a long moment, accustoming ourselves to each other's rhythm. His longsword had more weight and length than my rapier, but rapiers were designed for the dexterous, quick motions that suited me best. Our earlier antics fell away, and this dance began to feel familiar.

As the thought crossed my mind, Rankar led. Sparks literally flew as our swords crossed. Leara yelped, but her position was far enough back that she wasn't in any danger. I quickly brought my sword under his, and he parried. The force pushed me back a step. He surged forward, and I dodged to the side. However, he brought the longsword around to brush my opportunistic strike away.

Long minutes went by, our eyes searching for tells to give an advantage. The clash of metal against metal became more furious as we met again and again. Neither of us could disarm the other. Not drawing first blood extended the fight, kept us searching for an opening that wasn't there.

"I yield!" Leara called.

Swords locked, Rankar and I grinned at one another. Slowly, we both eased off.

Our ward came between us, hugging us both. "My heart is beating a million miles a minute." She moved the hand from my waist and put it over her chest. "You were moving so fast I'd lose track of you both until your swords met. That was crazy!"

When she put her arm back around me, I completed the circle by resting my head on Rankar's sweat-soaked shoulder. "We weren't in danger, warrior-girl. I could hear his heart beating with mine, like an improvisational dance where we read each other's minds."

"Kinan, that sounded almost romantic." Leara squeezed us both one last time then gestured to release the dogs from their hold. She headed back to slip on her house shoes before going to the door. "You two need a shower. I'm going to take the dogs down to play in the stables. Send Hypnos for me when you all stop being all gross and are ready for lunch."

She shut the door behind her, but neither Rankar nor I moved for a long moment.

"I love you, *eirlys*."

"I love you too, Rankar."

I looked up at him, preparing to ask if he wanted to share the shower. However, his eyes sparkled at me so mischievously it took my breath away for a second. "Ran, what exactly are you thinking?"

His grin stole my thought, and I smiled back. Then he leaned close. "I was just wondering… what's your favorite color?"

CHAPTER 18

"C'MON, LEARA! BREAK his wrist!"

Belisario oomphed as both Treyv and Alala hit him in the stomach. However, I grinned at 'Sario's bloodthirsty encouragement. It reminded me of Uncle Dukon shouting helpfully when my father and I had trained.

Sitting on the top rung of the corral as Rankar and Leara crossed blunted practice swords, I looked around at the eclectic family gathered at the Sirach ranch for Leara's fifteenth birthday. Hypnos and Thanatos both rested in my lap. Beside me, Eliecha also chuckled at the Tuveri demon's shout. Triswon leaned back against the fence between her legs, his arms wrapped around her calves to hold her steady. She looked completely comfortable with a throw hanging over her shoulders and her hands resting against her husband's neck. Mycal murmured something to his soulsibling low enough that I couldn't hear, causing Elie to swat Triswon's arm and shake her head with a grin. Alala, Belisario, and Treyv sat on the fence, too, 'Sario's arms around their shoulders and theirs around his waist. The twins were bundled in hoodies against the recent temperature drop, but Treyv still wore a t-shirt and shorts.

Most of the United States had a blizzard advisory for

the weekend. Luckily, the weather-workers employed by Orion's council had managed to push the snow away from our borders. We'd lost our eighty-degree March heat after a fifteen-degree plummet. However, sixty-five degrees didn't feel bad when our Texas neighbors to the east reportedly expected more than six inches of snow.

Leara grunted as the practice sword caught her in the side. Rankar backed off as she caught her breath. "Sword up. Don't fall for feints," he warned her.

The frustration building on her face told me the match would be over soon. She and Treyv had started by demonstrating what she had learned the past few months with him in kickboxing. Afterwards, she'd fought admirably against me with blades before yielding. Now her emotions were going to lead her to a mistake that gave Rankar advantage.

Keawyn and Rendle approached from the barn, having stepped away to check on the Asez Holding mares inside. One of the lucky ladies was under consideration as a breeding match for Keawyn's prized Deylura stallion. The two stopped talking animal husbandry as they came within earshot and looked toward the main show. Keawyn rested her arm on the rung beside me and posted her hip against the center rail. "Who's winning?" Keawyn asked, watching the two with a grin.

Rendle snorted softly, his accent harder to understand when he spoke quietly to keep Leara from hearing. "He'll disarm her in the next minute. She's leaving too many openings for him to ignore."

I nodded, agreeing with his assessment. "And then we get to eat cake! Well, the delicious meal Karyn is currently finishing and then the cake Eliecha's cook baked. Are you staying for dinner?"

Keawyn grimaced, glancing toward the house yearningly. "I wish. I need to go back to Asez shortly to collect my personal guard. Then I have to join the other council members at the Fortress at sundown. If I skipped getting Fwen's unit before the meeting, I could have the dinner as a last meal before Rankar killed me for being too careless."

Rendle chuckled, and I shook my head, not certain whether she was joking. "I'll ask Karyn to make you a plate. Rankar can have one of your suite guards place it in your fridge when we get home."

Her eyes lit up, and she grinned. "Thank you! That gives me something to look forward to after this meeting." Standing up straight, she glanced at her watch and sighed. "I need to go, but… Kinan?"

"Hmm?" I asked, my eyes already back on Rankar and Leara.

"Cake too?" The wistfulness in Keawyn's voice couldn't be resisted.

"Of course!"

"Yes!" she cheered.

My laughter unfortunately startled Leara and gave Rankar the opening he needed. Her sword flew to the left, landing in the rocky dirt. Keawyn winced, her expression guilty. "Oops. Time for me to go." Raising her voice, she yelled to the disgruntled teenager. "Happy birthday, Leara! Have a good rest of your evening!"

Rendle raised his eyebrow at me as Keawyn opened her Gate. I waved him on. "Yes, yes. You too," I promised, knowing he'd prefer not to miss out on either Karyn's homecooked meals or sweet treats from the Banded Traveler.

Jumping down from the fence after sending the drakyn into the air, I jogged across the distance as Rankar went to retrieve her sword. Leara stood with her hands on her hips, displeasure obvious. With enthusiasm, I came up behind her, picked her up, and spun her in circles. After two circuits, she let her feet fly out and laughed.

"Fine. Fine. Put me down! I'm done pouting."

I set her down and kissed the top of her head. "You did great, warrior-girl. Every single day, your stances improve and your attacks are tighter. Just remember, we have decades of practice over you. You'll catch up."

Alala nodded. "I agree with Kinan. You're better every time I see you."

Leara grinned, baring her teeth in an Alala expression. "When do I start training with you?"

I interrupted. "As Belisario once advised me, you should be able to avoid bare-handed blows before trying to avoid ones with a knife edge."

Leara's grin widened. "Then when do I get to train with Belisario?"

Treyv stepped in this time. "Once I think you are ready. You still have a lot to learn with me before we introduce other fighting styles."

Relieved, I let them all say their goodbyes as I leaned back against Rankar. "Nice deflection," he murmured, resting his chin on my head.

"Saved by Treyv," I allowed, laughing. "P.S. Do not let us leave tonight without plates of food for Keawyn and Rendle. Otherwise, we might both be fired come morning."

His hand found mine, linking our fingers as Leara finished hugging the trio. "Mom wouldn't let us forget. I promised Fwen one too for switching shifts with us all today so we had time off together. He'll send Jeannie with Keawyn tonight for the meeting while he gets some rest."

"Dinner's ready," Mycal announced, herding all of us back toward the house, his arm across Leara's shoulders as she walked between him and Triswon.

Rankar and I fell behind the group, following slowly. My arm wrapped around his back as I leaned into his side and trapped his right arm between us. The heat radiating off him made my long-sleeved shirt less necessary, and I enjoyed the moment of peace. Then the wards buzzed, warning of an incoming Gate.

"Tier," Rankar reassured me as I lifted my head from his shoulder and moved to look around. "Of course, he times it perfectly so he doesn't miss the food."

Footsteps ran to catch up. "Have you eaten the Sithen food? No comparison. If time weren't wonky there, I'd show up every night."

The two hugged, both radiating happiness at seeing one another. As Rankar stepped back, I moved forward to—much more cautiously—hug Tier. He grinned at me. "Good to see you, Kinan. I'm sorry I missed you getting married."

I laughed, stepping back. "I nearly missed it myself. Luckily, no one seemed upset about the abruptness of the ceremony, not even Leara."

He handed me a folder and a binder. "These are for you, for the lawsuit against the State of California to get your money back. You'll need to take these certification pages to Italy to be notarized. Since that is where 'Sara Nichols' is currently living, it would raise the fewest questions. The binder is yours to review when you have time."

Flipping it open, I peered inside. The top page contained questions he'd received from the defense attorneys with the answers I sent him last month. A number had lines drawn through them.

"I filed objections on some of those." He pointed to the first marked-out question. "That's irrelevant. This one is overly broad and unduly burdensome." With a snort, he continued, "That's protected by work-product doctrine, and those three are attorney-client privileged, but without waiving our objection, we submitted much more limited answers."

I nodded, though his lawyerese was not a language I spoke. Instead, I flipped to the pages farther back. "I know a *notaio* in Italy who will meet with me as Sara. And I brought Sara's passport and things you requested."

He nodded. "If you can get those signed this weekend, we can file on Monday."

I did the mental math. "I'll prepare everything before my shift tonight, starch Sara's suit and style her wig, and then I'll visit my *notaio* buddy tomorrow after I'm off. That should put me there right before he closes up."

Rankar opened the little gate in front of the house, allowing us both to go through. "When do you think the trial will be?"

Tier waited for him to close it back. "Too soon to tell. Suing the State of California will take time and patience.

I've already put it out there that this is going to be my final trial before I retire and that I have nothing but time to cram motions to compel down their throats if things go awry."

My lips twitched. "If I knew what those were, I would probably feel a little sympathy for them. However, if Sara Nichols is going to sue California for taking her money while she lived in Italy waiting on the Enlightenment chaos to calm down, she would have no one but the best at her side. And if the best had already spent years making California's life hell for what they did to innocent families, she'd pay him extra to take her case."

A look passed between Rankar and Tier, and I couldn't read it. However, neither of them appeared happy. This case would be difficult and dangerous. We'd have to perfect being human, not paranormal, in front of the world—while unable to lie due to Tier's Gift of Truth. I wanted to reassure them, but I wasn't sure how. After a moment, though, Rankar smiled softly. "Come on. Let's cut through to the patio, and you can finally meet your niece."

Leara and Tier hit it off, each delighted to meet the other. Once in a while, the remnants of his Scottish accent caused her to ask him to repeat himself. Goddess. I felt so proud of my warrior-girl as she wrapped her family around her finger.

As the meal wound down, Rankar and I volunteered to clean the kitchen as Eliecha and Karyn discussed herbs and poultices. Triswon began a game of chess with Leara, Tier encouraging her while Mycal criticized his soulsibling. We carried the empty dishes inside, clearing the table to make more room.

As I ran water in the sink and pulled a washcloth out of the drawer, Rankar separated the dishes that were dishwasher safe with those we needed to handwash. Sticking my hand down into the bubbles, I pulled it out quickly, assured the water was quite warm enough.

"And we didn't break anything," Rankar murmured, stepping in behind me as I turned off the water. "Yet."

His hands rubbed from my shoulder to elbow, knowing the cool air outside had left me chilled. After a moment, I turned into him and glanced to the side at the granite countertop. I raised sudsy fingers and touched his jaw before peeking a glance at the empty doorway.

"You once wrote that my telling you to kiss me was the hottest thing to happen to you. Well, Rankar… Kiss me."

He groaned, picking me up. Our lips clashed as my legs wrapped around his hips. After wiping my wet hand on the back of his shirt, I buried my fingers in his hair and tugged. Rankar devoured me, his teeth tugging at my bottom lip as my other hand reached under his arm down to grip his ass.

On top of the fridge, Thanatos and Hypnos both cheeped in alarm. ::Inside!:: Hypnos warned.

Rankar let me slide to the ground and stepped up to the side of the sink with water. He began scrubbing a pot, his chin bowed as he studied the dish. Heat crept into my cheeks, and I moved to accept the pot and turn on the water to rinse as he handed it over.

"Damn. It's warm in here," Tier commented casually.

I peeked back to see him standing with his shoulder leaning against the doorjamb. He grinned at me, the mirth sparkling in his eyes. Embarrassed, I leaned my forehead against Ran's shoulder. Rankar turned to look at his soulsibling before glancing pointedly at me.

"Did I ever tell you how Tier developed a complex about Fabuloso cleaning spray?"

Tier guffawed. "Don't you dare—"

Rankar winked at me, and I bit my lip. "Hmm? I'm sorry. Were you saying something, Tier?"

"Well, I came in to let you know Leara fell asleep during the chess game. Mycal put her to bed in the downstairs guest room. They'll bring her home in the morning, they said. But Karyn says not to forget the plates in the fridge. Aunt Elie left your suit bag and the boxes you'll need tomorrow outside the apartment door on their way here. I'll finish dishes before heading out, and I'll drop by tomorrow at lunch with the trial stuff. Why don't you two go home—alone—for the night?"

"What cleaning spray?" Rankar mumbled, quickly pulling the plates out of the fridge.

He opened a Gate right there in the kitchen and motioned me through. I waved at Tier before stepping inside and coming out in our bedroom. When Rankar stepped out, I'd already removed my boots. We raced to see who could undress the fastest.

We both won... But the meals were delivered a long time later.

CHAPTER 19

"Yield," I croaked on an exhale, unable to draw breath into my lungs. Belisario's hit had literally sent me flying, the first time in six months that he'd caught me so distracted. Lying on my back, I closed my eyes and concentrated on remembering how to breathe.

"She taking a break?" Fwen called from somewhere across the room. He definitely hadn't been here a minute ago.

Alala snorted from her position near the wall. While she did not often watch our sparring matches, she sometimes dropped in for a minute or two. Usually with snacks. Today, she hung around after Leara started a discussion about Teharan metallurgy. "She might be broken."

Leara spoke, her mouth full of—I assumed—Alala's popcorn. "He really caught her off guard with that kick. Like, it's almost cheating to do actual taekwondo when he's told her all this time to never do competition moves."

I inhaled, but the sound was a wheeze. *Another minute.*

"You okay, *eirlys*?"

I forced my eyes open to look up at Rankar. Though his voice had been calm, almost neutral, his warm brown eyes held a tinge of concern.

While not breathing wouldn't kill me, oxygen was required to speak. I completed the Raspea gesture that usually accompanied a statement for good health before remembering that my husband spoke many languages, just not Raspea.

"The hand gestures are intended to accompany spoken dialogue, but I think she said she's fine," Leara observed.

Finally, my chest rose and fell with my efforts to breathe. Whatever damage Belisario's blow had caused had healed. Another breath left me somewhat confident I could stand, and I held a hand up to Rankar.

He accepted with a tilt of his lips, urging me to pull myself up to keep from causing further injury. His fingers held my elbow, allowing me to press my forearm into his until my equilibrium was restored enough that I didn't sway. A second later, the room stopped swimming. Still, he didn't release me until my gaze met his.

Belisario, to my left, also stood from his crouch. I hadn't even noticed him beside me when I'd been healing. However, now I realized that all of the officers, Rendle, and Keawyn had joined us.

"Everything okay?" I murmured, looking around the worried faces near the wall.

Fwen snorted. "It is now that we know Belisario didn't kill our new second lieutenant of the guard before she could even start her first shift."

I half-turned my head to Belisario, curiosity eating at me. "Who did you almost kill?"

He cocked an eyebrow. "He means you."

The laugh slipped free. "You didn't alm. "

Leara's scream echoed from one wall to the other,

even the pads not effectively capturing the high-pitched screech. I caught her, easily holding her weight as she launched herself at me. She squirmed, and I lowered her feet to touch the ground. Still, her arm stayed firmly linked with mine as she beamed up at me. "You're being promoted!"

"I'm what?" Then the conversation finally caught up to me. "Wait."

Fwen shrugged. "It's taken a while for someone to come along with both leadership ability and aptitude with projectiles. After your performance at the Trials, we've all been watching you closely. Your actions in the months since your acceptance cemented our impression. When I asked around for references from demons you'd served with in the war, I received recommendations and commendations from dozens of people from a variety of Planes."

Keawyn raised her hand and waved her fingers. "My favorite said something like, 'Kinan is the most stubborn, closedmouthed, professional demon I've ever served with. She saved a dozen people in a single attack, not that she'd ever admit it. You're all idiots if you don't hire her.' It isn't often that people call me an idiot anymore—especially if they are signing their name to the paper. I was impressed."

My heart raced. "I'm not ready for an officer position. Belisario literally just wiped the floor with me in front of all of you!"

Fwen shrugged. "If beating Belisario at hand-to-hand were a requirement for my position, we'd have to make one of the twins do double duty. Besides, neither of them could beat you with rifles. Asez's officer duties were organized to make sure the compound has leadership that excels on multiple fronts—not a single person who can perfectly do all four things."

I looked to Belisario, searching for a lifeline. "Then he should be second lieutenant."

Belisario grinned and shrugged. "I'm good. Thanks."

Fwen grunted, his voice turning to a feline growl. "I've tried that four times now. He refuses."

Rendle offered me a flask he magicked out of thin air, and I accepted, swigging the whisky without smelling the fumes first. As the liquid fire touched the back of my tongue, he clicked his tongue comfortingly and spoke, his accent fully engaged. "It won't be so bad. Instead of training Leara daily, you'll just be training two dozen Arrow greenies who may or may not have ever held a gun in their life. You'll have to carry a phone for emergencies and have office hours for any questions or complaints. But other than that, really nothing changes."

I choked as the burn hit my throat. "You are not very nice. I thought you *wanted* me to take this position?"

Rendle snorted, his brogue deepening again. "I'd rather you were back in the stable as my second, but this job suits you better. I'm resigned."

Keawyn clapped twice. "Well, that settles that. Congratulations, Second Lieutenant Kinan, on your promotion. Fwen, I look forward to having you as the head of my security team full-time. I have a meeting in thirty minutes. I'm going to go grab a snack and then meet everyone in my office to Gate out."

"He wasn't joking about the phone, I guess." The candy bar shaped phone fit in the palm of my hand, though I held it out like I expected it to transform into a venomous snake and bite me.

Leara snorted, dropping onto the couch with a plop. "Rendle doesn't joke much." She rubbed her hand across the leather. "But isn't it weird how Fwen cleaned the office out before you even accepted? Did you have a choice? If you didn't accept, would they just kill you?"

"It sounds like Belisario has turned down a promotion more than once, so probably not."

Opening the top center drawer on the desk, I found various sizes of paper, pens, pencils, and assorted office supplies all organized in little plastic bins. I chose an oversized sticky note and a blue ink pen. It took a second for the ink to catch. Then I penned a quick note and thought Hypnos's name loudly.

By the time I put the pen back and closed the drawer, he'd arrived, and I handed the note off.

"You know, you could have just sent Rankar a text. His number is preprogrammed into the phone. I checked," Leara chided.

Raising an eyebrow at her, I deliberately dropped the phone into the empty right drawer. "It's not the same."

She popped up from the couch and opened the door across from it. "Bathroom," she observed. "You've got a small closet, shower, and toilet. How come Rankar has an entire bedroom but you don't?"

I finished checking the rest of the drawers, but they were all empty. "Well, before he moved in with us, he was living in his office. Fwen has his own suite in the main building, so he didn't need a bedroom in here. Also, Rankar is the captain. He has rank. Plus, I'm absolutely okay napping on the couch. If I'm going to sleep, though, I want to be in our apartment."

Leara closed the door to the bathroom and studied the empty walls. She undoubtedly planned to raid the stores for artwork, and I had no issues letting her. Her and Rankar's picks for the apartment had been perfect, and I had no doubt she would choose something appropriate for me.

"We need to get you a safe in here for important documents and extra weapons," she observed, still staring at the wall. She shook her head and slid her hand into her pocket. "And I'll leave you for an hour or two so you can start weaving your wards."

I locked the door behind her and moved the couch and cabinet away from the wall. Closing my eyes, I opened the door to my center and felt the cold darkness fall into place. I pushed that cold out from my fingertips, trailing my fingers along the wall as I walked clockwise around the rectangular shape over and over. Time flowed differently while centered, and both seconds and eternity passed before I felt the ward snap into place.

Exhaling, I opened my eyes and enjoyed the peace a moment. Still more needed to be done, though. Sinking to my knees in the middle of the room, I placed my still-chilled right hand against the floor. The energy I sunk into the walls reached for my touch, spreading the safeguards slowly down the wall and across the floor until it found my hand. Inhaling deeply, I pushed more energy out to reinforce the ward. The cold pulsed under my knees as it flowed back out toward the walls.

A wave of dizziness hit me as I stood. Carefully, I moved toward the couch and stood on it. Balancing with my thigh against the back as I tiptoed on the arm, I placed my palm against the ceiling. Reflecting how tired I felt, the energy slowly crawled up the walls this time toward my touch. Then the chill caressed my palm as the ward snapped fully into place, a solid box of protections.

Sitting on the back of the couch, I mentally explored the fortifications. Though the layers were thin, no point felt weaker than another. Tomorrow, I would walk the room again. Then the wards would be thick enough to push into the bathroom and closet. Perhaps Rankar would have time later on to add his own energy to mine.

Feeling marginally safer, I pushed the furniture back against the walls and looked around. On the desk, the note I sent to Rankar had been returned. "'Your real duties begin tomorrow, Second Lieutenant. Get some rest before your shift tonight, and meet me during my office hours tomorrow. We'll work on your schedule,'" I read aloud.

With a glance around the office, I decided to take Rankar's advice and sneak home for a nap.

CHAPTER 20

*T*HWICK. *THWICK*. *THWICK*. Half of the arrows hit target, almost in concert. Walking behind each stall, I paused to adjust stances and postures. After a month in the position, training the mix of Arrows and guard demons, I determined that guard recruits in general took direction better and retained the information longer. Perhaps because the guard accepted fewer people twice a year—only the best who wanted to continue being the best—while the Arrows took significantly more people with less discernment.

Patience had never been my strong suit. Being placed in a teaching position hadn't improved that. In fact, at this rate, I would start beating my trainees in full Belisario-style by next week if karma didn't step in first.

For example, Arrow recruit Kiss Yleva was quite well endowed in the chest area. She preferred to wear shirts that enhanced her assets until it distracted anyone attracted to breasts in a half-mile radius. That was fine. Firing from horseback during a battle had lots of distractions. Except I had warned her multiple times that she might lose a pound of flesh if she didn't bind herself while using a longbow. While I refused to believe Amazons cut off their left breasts to make themselves better archers, I didn't doubt at all that they restrained them to keep from falling off their horse mid-battle over a relocated nipple.

On the other hand, Arrow recruit Killian Winstead was a plant. He used every weapon at least passably, he never took a single step out of line, and he studied everything like he gave a nightly report. I couldn't prove it. I couldn't even voice it aloud without sounding crazy, and I wasn't certain myself whose side he played. However, he definitely had a long game. And Rendle needed to know.

"Pull. Aim. Fire," I ordered, stopping to congratulate a young demon on his bullseye. "Pull. Aim... Hold." Moving down the line, I checked each demon's form quickly. While the other demons would have no issue holding the stance for an hour, the lone human in this group didn't have such luxury. "Fire."

The scream truly sounded musical with the backbeat of dozens of arrows hitting the targets. Walking quickly to the end of the line, I squatted beside Recruit Yleva. Keeping my voice neutral was difficult with amusement, sympathy, and satisfaction all warring for a stage. "Deep breaths. You are going to pass out."

The words she half-screamed in Ferente didn't even translate to a proper sentence, a garbled, "Your mother's penis is a rotting whore."

"Graver, Winstead, please escort Yleva to the infirmary. I'll open the Gate. Once they take her to a room, Graver come back to let me know she is being cared for. Winstead, please stay in the waiting room until they let you know she's been released."

None of the three looked pleased, but no one argued, either. When I opened the Gate, Yleva limped through under her own power, her arm wrapped tightly over the injured area. I counted to ten before closing it and turning back to the remaining class. "And pull."

The next half hour passed in quiet, only the typical sounds of archery and my corrections filling the firing range.

It was perfect.

My wards tingled, followed immediately by two firm knocks. The wards recognized Rendle, so I didn't place my hand on the gun under my desk before inviting him to enter. Instead, I scooted the chair back and came to my feet.

"If you wanted to be my first office-hours complaint, you are about twenty minutes too late. Apparently, mundane weapons are pointless. Guns are stupid. Bows are antiquated. And the only 'training' Asez Holding should require is how to strengthen the Gifts of the trainees." By the time I finished reiterating the Kirian demon's message, my back teeth clenched.

Rendle sank into the chair across from my desk, crossing his ankle over his leg. His eyes shone with amusement as he raised a brow at me. "And how did you handle this official complaint?"

Guilt filled me, but what's done was done. "I shot him."

His foot hit the floor, and he leaned toward me. Rendle stared at me intently, as though he wouldn't misunderstand what I said a second time. "You did what?"

Opening my mouth, I closed it and shrugged a shoulder nonchalantly. "I shot him. Point blank. With my Glock."

The Tulevi demon roared, his laughter overfilling the room. I tried to explain, but I doubted he could hear me over his own amusement. "It was just a flesh wound! But it proved my point that a single close-range projectile can take down a shield in a millisecond while a Gift might take hours to penetrate!"

"You shot him," Rendle repeated, placing his hand over his eyes, "for disagreeing with you."

Affronted, I sat on the edge of the desk. "Absolutely not! I did it to prove a point."

This time, he leaned forward with his elbows on his knees as though he was half-heartedly trying not to pass out. "You can't kill people who don't appreciate Terran weapons."

"Rendle," I chided, "I didn't kill him. It was a through and through, and I made him sit here and put pressure on it until he healed."

The demon pulled a flask out of somewhere, but he stopped before taking a drink to chuckle. "You made him wait fifteen minutes like he was a kid getting a shot at the infirmary."

My lips twitched. I could see the humor in that. "And we spent the time wisely. I explained to him that the larger the caliber of the bullet the more quickly it can puncture a shield. Honestly, he acted quite excited for our next practice session."

"He probably thought you'd shoot him again if he didn't." Finally taking a drink from his flask, he paused then took another sip before putting it away. "I stopped by because rumor had it that your friends from the Elysii Plane sent a blackberry pie as congratulations for your recent promotion, but this visit turned out better than I expected."

I snorted, moving to the table in the corner. "I'm glad I could help." Grabbing one of the plates Eliecha had added to basket, I cut a piece of the pie and carefully scooped it out. I stuck the fork in the top of the slice, perhaps a little more forcefully than necessary, and passed it across to Rendle.

I'd already hidden a generous piece for Leara in the refrigerator at the apartment. Rankar and I would share a piece, because he didn't enjoy sweets. At most, he'd take a bite or two after dinner. *Which basically makes him perfect for me, because I could eat the entire pie alone.*

As Rendle savored the slice of pie, we discussed the lot of two-year-old Deylura going up to auction soon. A few of them were being held aside for guards interested in bonding a second mount or replacing an aging one. Since the war, interest in owning an Asez-bred Deylura had quadrupled now that fewer demons worried about exposure when visiting Orion versus the United States. Plus, a number of horse connoisseurs needed to begin their lines again. Most had escaped only with a prized stallion or mare. Even more with just their lives.

I remembered to mention the Arrow trainee, Killian Winstead. He chewed the last bite for a long moment as I finished relating my suspicions. Then he nodded. He scraped the last of the filling onto his spoon then moved to the bathroom to wash the plate. When he handed it to me, he held on until I met his eyes.

"You planning on shooting anyone else today?"

I tugged harder. "No." The tone sounded petulant, even to me. "I'm going to bed in ten minutes. I won't have time."

He let go to hold the corner of the desk as his eyes literally held tears. "I adore you, *lrakavi*. Sleep well, and thank you for the pie."

"I love you too. And you're welcome," I murmured as he left.

With a sigh, I grabbed the rest of the pie, turned off the light, and locked the office door from the inside before Gating to the landing outside the apartment. With a chirp, Hypnos landed on my shoulder and offered me a scrap of paper with Rankar's seal.

Did you really shoot him? –R.

Grumbling, I opened the door and shooed Hypnos away. I placed the pie in the refrigerator, packed most of my weapons into the safe, and headed to the shower. His response could wait…

RIES JACOBS PRACTICALLY vibrated as soon as Treyv switched places with him. "Yes, I shot him. Belisario says my new goal is to shoot one guard a day until people stop saying stupid stuff to me." I paused and then looked at him. "It's a little early for me to hit my goals, don't you agree?"

A solid hour of watch passed before Ries couldn't resist speaking. First, he held up his hand in surrender. "I actually have something I need to talk to you about, as the second lieutenant."

Cullyn was keeping pace, occasionally scenting the air but otherwise showing no sign of concern. The phone in my pocket hadn't vibrated since watch began, and the shifters on the border had checked in at regular intervals.

"Lucky for you, she's at your disposal for at least another hour. *And* she has office hours today," I congratulated him. A quick glance his way revealed a serious expression. Was this the same demon who'd asked me if I slept my way into the position—with Fwen—the first night after my promotion?

"No. Really, Kinan.

I exhaled, bracing myself for whatever idiocy he might throw my way and knowing I really couldn't shoot my shift partner. A dozen guards would descend on us at the noise if I did. "Okay. What is it?"

He scuffed his foot, the sound odd in the darkness. "I've heard some pretty disturbing rumors about the Arrows greenies. A couple people brought it to my attention, though I don't think they were worried about the situation so much as pissed off that anyone would be that stupid and be allowed to stay at Asez." He paused, and I glanced at him to see him chewing on his bottom lip. Worry filled me. Anything capable of reducing Ries to speechlessness was likely to send me into a cold fury.

"Spill it," I ordered, eyes scanning the area in front of us. The sand crunched silently beneath our feet, and Cullyn scouted about ten yards ahead of us. The border here was completely silent.

"Delta Barracks has been"—he paused as though searching for the right word—"lax. They have been *lax* in their duties as a unit, as members of the Arrows and guard. Let's just say, if a group of nutjobs decided they wanted to take out an entire barracks of soldiers who are reported to be the best trained on the Terra Plane, they would choose Delta Barracks."

Ries was grim, a first for him. Obviously, this was something he took as a deadly breach in security. I ran my tongue over the edge of my teeth, pressing harder on my canine teeth and enjoying the jab of pain. These kids were guys I worked with day in and day out. Belisario, Alala, and Rankar all trained them, as well. We preached to them about the importance of guarding one another's backs, even when they weren't on patrol. The entire first month of their training at Asez Holding had been on setting fireguards, creating wards and shields, and detecting attacks. Now someone I trusted was hinting that the time we'd spent with them had been wasted.

"Just so we are clear," I started, enunciating clearly, "are you saying they aren't taking the off-duty precautions required for their personal safety, as well as Asez's?"

Ries nodded, though I felt more than saw the movement. "That's exactly what I'm saying. I even did a walk-by myself in case the information wasn't accurate. Didn't detect a single ward on the doors or windows."

Neither of us spoke for a long hour. In my mind, I was running names. Five-man teams would be best. Five-person groups were small enough to pass unnoticed while being large enough to get results. *Alala, Belisario, Treyv, Ilyetik, Ries, myself, Leara, Jeannitra, Brock, and maybe Rankar.*

I paused. "Ries, why didn't you take this breach to the captain?"

He glanced at me, but his eyes quickly shifted focus somewhere in the distance. "Uhm, well," he cleared his throat, and I grabbed his shirt to pull him to a stop. When he looked in my eyes, I raised my eyebrows at him and gestured for him to continue. "If I told the captain, he'd have to *officially* reprimand them. That's his job. Kind of like it is my job to report the matter to *someone* of rank and follow that person's orders on the best course of action."

My lips twitched, but the smile stayed hidden by sheer dent of will. "Are you telling me that you figured I knew just the group of nutjobs to train them properly?" When he shot me a glance, I saw that he was holding back his own grin. "Unsurprisingly, I do. Why don't you consider the issue reported and not mention it again until you hear from me?"

Damn him, though. He was right. This was one that Rankar would have to sit out in case we were caught. Marcul Zuhavi, then. He would keep his mouth shut but enjoy the hell out of the exercise. "Ries, text our coordinates. Time to switch up again." A few minutes later, the Gate opened and Ilyetik stepped through. As she crouched next to Ries, I went through to signal Treyv.

The shifter took one look at me and whistled. "Uh-oh. You look happy — what's going on?"

I winked at him, petting Caiftín as she waited patiently for me to join them. Cullyn would stay with Ries and Ilyetik then meet me in the stables after shift. "We are going to attack Asez, but first, we need to get our hands on some artillery rounds." The laughter bubbled out as his jaw dropped. "Don't worry, Treyv. It's for the greater good, and the only thing hurt will be the pride of Delta Barracks."

He winced, and I patted him on the shoulder before outlining the tentative plan I'd come up with during the patrol with Ries.

"First, you shot a greenie. Now this... I assume you are going to invite Alala and 'Sario to the party? Otherwise, he'll pout for months and she'll beat the shit out of you," he finally asked.

Somewhere near the interior of Asez Holding grounds, a shifter called. Three others answered only seconds later. "Those two, our team of four, Leara, Jeannitra, Brock, and Zuhavi. Two five-man teams. We'll take them in three days when we patrol as non-essentials."

"Just for the sake of argument, why the last three?" He was still scanning the horizon, easier to see now that the sun was rising.

Everything was clear for miles around. Quickly but methodically, I scanned the area for any trace of energy. No wards or shields showed up anywhere in range. "I figure our team of four can split up in pairs. Two per group, so when we fall back during the confusion, we are already paired. As primary for Keawyn's personal guard, Jeannitra and Zuhavi can Gate directly and together because it isn't unusual for them to be doing after-hours training. Everyone knows Alala and Belisario are batshit crazy anyway, and the rest of the world are scared of them. No one will think to question their whereabouts, even if they did the mission in their native forms. Then Leara is always a wildcard. And Brock would be getting ready for his next shift."

Treyv and I dropped to a knee as Brock and Karl stepped through a Gate. "Sounds like a good end to the shift then. I'll let 'Sario and Alala know about your plan. You can tell the others."

I nodded, calling Caiftín to follow us through the Gate.

"Five after nine," Treyv murmured, watching as Cullyn and Caiftín played together. The duo acted like they'd been separated for days, instead of hours. If they were going to act like this all day, I'd have to leave them in the office during training. Rankar would be on patrol until three in the afternoon, and Leara would be in class until her break at noon. Right now, it was time for food and office hours. A couple hours of training with Delta Barracks, and then I might be able to convince Rankar to renege on his duties for an hour.

"I'll see you in eighteen hours!" I promised, patting his shoulder.

Asez Holding consisted of thousands of individual parts working as a whole. Each individual stable was guarded by trained civilian stable workers, as well as a team—trained soldiers from Asez's guard. The barracks housed all the off-duty trained soldiers, and they were responsible for setting their own fire guard rotation to be sure the proper number of off-duty guards protected their sleeping comrades from both attack and carelessness. The main compound was patrolled by four-man squads broken into a couple of two-man teams, working together to ensure the safety of the non-guard residents. Other military-trained personnel resided across the Asez Holding territory where their prized animals were housed with civilians' horses.

At a little after three in the morning, the guard's shifts

had already changed; the window of opportunity opened. With a hand signal, I directed the other members of the two five-man units to move toward our objective. Each person dressed in camouflage similar to the ACUs used in the Middle Eastern wars, designed specifically to blend against the sand. In addition, they had covered their faces and painted exposed skin black to protect their identities. All of us were equipped with the hearing protection to pick up and amplify ambient sounds while shielding against harmful noise levels of gun and grenade fire and enabling radio contact between the two teams. Eight of the ten carried assault shotguns armed with less-than-lethal rounds while the point man of each squad was armed with weapons capable of blowing the doors and specialties designed to protect their comrades as well as subdue the men inside the building.

Our eyes scanned the rooftops and the shadows, as we moved like we'd trained together since birth. Twice, the point man used a closed fist to order us to freeze as he caught movement. Quickly, the signal was passed until everyone stilled and waited to see whether our actions had been spotted. Only after the threat had moved on did we receive the signal to begin again.

My eyes carefully monitored the actions of everyone, especially keen when I scanned over the smallest figure in the group. No one stepped out of line. Then I gave the signal. Team B returned the signal, moving around the building to tackle the first entrance. As leader of this mission, I observed them from a position in the middle of Team A. Each demon remained six inches from the wall, ducking low to avoid the barred windows that might alert the guards inside to their presence. My group silently moved toward the second entrance, confidant that their companions would guard the other entrance from anyone wanting to enter or exit.

Without a word, the five of us stacked up to the left of the door. The point man stared straight ahead, while the man behind him stood behind and slightly to the right. I scanned the rooftops, and Treyv stood behind me and to the left. The fifth and final person—noticeably different due to her smaller size—was positioned to watch our backs. Silently, though each man had a radio in his ear, the point man tapped the demon behind him who tapped my shoulder. I tapped Treyv who passed it to Leara who returned it. The lead demon scanned the door for wards or less magical booby traps. Ries shook his head at the arrogance of the guardsmen inside when he found none, eyes meeting my angry ones.

After a deep breath, I spoke into the radio, quietly but firmly. "Go."

Ries blew the lock and busted in the door. The sounds were echoed from the other end of the barracks at the second door. In a smooth motion, he threw a flash grenade into the barracks.

As he stepped to the right, eyes diverted from the interior of the room where the bang bang/flash bang did its job, he secured his now-empty live weapon and accepted my extra assault weapon in the three-second wait before the grenade exploded. *BANGBANGBANG*. He fell to the rear as the remaining four of us entered the large room.

"Down on the ground. Drop your weapons. Down on the ground!" We all shouted in unison, our individual voices indistinct.

Ilyetik, second in the stack, entered first, taking the path of least resistance. She carefully aimed and fired on anyone she felt gathering energy. Then I moved along the opposite path, firing on anyone attempting to move toward weapons. Treyv shot anyone we missed as the youngest member of Team A quickly and effectively drew and threw wards at anyone trying to escape. Ries crouched in the door, his weapon aimed out to prevent anyone entering behind us. From the signal to infiltrate to securing the room took less than a minute, despite the number of shots that had to be fired at the ineffectual prisoner-soldiers. "Clear," I murmured into the radio.

Immediately, four demons from the other team entered and began securing the prisoners with standard issue, warded zip ties as they checked for serious injuries. The flexible baton rounds had been aimed with care at the prisoners' thighs, and all fifty men inside the barracks were secured with only temporary hearing loss, sight loss, and—in some cases—loss of muscle control. Only then did Leara lift her own wards to leave the prisoners' hands and feet bound with the standard issue wards. "Mission accomplished. Retreat and regroup," I announced into my head piece, voice intentionally low and gruff.

Both teams regrouped, each exiting the way they entered but going separate ways. Though only three minutes had passed since the flash bang grenades had been deployed, the other guard barracks would have already awakened and be arming themselves. We had estimated six minutes before the arrival of the first nonessential, trained personnel—the soldier-guards allowed to desert their stations to move toward the conflict during an attack. With only three minutes remaining, our chances of avoiding capture were better if we separated.

The nerves of the demons had to be on edge as we found ourselves ducking for cover five times as often as when we'd been entering the center of the compound. Finally, though, we arrived at the rally point. "Team A reporting. All members accounted for. Changing out," I notified the others. The silence became tense as we removed our ACUs and face paint, redressing in our normal uniforms while waiting for our comrades to reply. Treyv and I exchanged a worried glance. Finally, Alala's voice reported into the tense silence, "Team B reporting. All members accounted for. Changing out."

I grinned. "Five minutes to wake-up. On your mark. Then infiltrate the crowd." The group waited without a twitch as our fellow soldiers changed their gear and stowed it for later retrieval. Thirty seconds passed until the Tuveri demon warned, "Team B, ready for wake-up. Three, two, one, detonate!"

At the final mark, Treyv and I fired simulation artillery rounds over the main compound as Alala and Jeannitra did the same from Team B's position.

"Detonate!" I ordered over the coms. And again. The shrill whistling was the only warning the people on the ground had to take cover before the resulting noise sent them to their knees. "Infiltrate the crowds! Move move move!" In unison, our two groups split into our normal, smaller teams and ran toward the confusion.

Treyv, Ries, Ilyetik, and I had been assigned as nonessential personnel to the outer edge of the Asez Holding compound for our shift. Checking the clock, I noted that I'd still be patrolling with Treyv. Grabbing his sleeve, he and I veered away from our partners silently. All heavily armed, we were running hell-for-leather toward the source of the explosion as the voices in our radio became increasingly frantic. Jeannitra's voice came over the line, calm and firm. "Primary secured."

I sighed in relief. Jeannitra, Zuhavi, and the members of her unit must have Gated directly to Keawyn to join Fwen's unit and move the councilwoman to safety. That would be one less worry for Rankar, and two fewer members of our group that could be caught. My fingers easily dialed the two keys on my phone that patched me through to Rankar, who should by all rights be sleeping. However, I seriously doubted he could sleep through the discharge of artillery rounds.

"No injuries," I muttered to Treyv as we ran.

Then my lover's voice came over the radio, and I hung up the ringing cell phone. Obviously, he was awake and mobile. "Captain, the disturbance appears to be at the Delta Barracks. No craters or damage from the artillery rounds. Probably simulation rounds. Earlier reports from Echo Barracks over the com were about detonation of two flash-bang grenades near Delta Barracks. All nonessential personnel have been deployed to that area, according to procedure. Over," I reported.

After a brief pause, his voice replied. "Copy."

Seconds later, we arrived at the door of Delta Barracks. I literally had to push my way through the crowd, but the sight that greeted me was so worth it. Even when Rankar found out and was pissed that we hadn't invited him to join the fun, this would be worth his ire. My lips twitched, and I didn't dare glance at Treyv. If his expression was even near my own, we'd both be on the floor laughing hysterically in seconds. Unfortunately, as second lieutenant, I had to seem a bit more dignified than rolling around on the floor clutching my stomach would portray me.

"Anyone injured?" I asked the medic who'd been checking the men and women. She shook her head, eyes dancing in amusement. *Dammit, Doctor Lyksva. You are going to make me laugh.* "Anyone missing?" I managed to choke out. A couple blank stares were turned my way. "Did the people who did this kidnap anyone?" I repeated slowly.

One of the guys near my feet shook his head. A chorus of negatives followed from the "prisoners." I shook my head in disapproval.

"Who was the fire guard?" I questioned, narrowing my eyes menacingly. I dared them to lie to me, but no one in the room moved. "*Was* there a team watching the perimeter?" Again, silence. I growled, a perfect echo of my alternate form's. "Who set the wards on the doors? Didn't you feel someone tearing them down?" By this point, even the crowd behind me had stilled. "No sentry. No wards. Someone just walked in here and tied you guys up! Did you even have a chance to open your eyes?"

A man near the center of the room called out, squirming in his bonds, "I counted ten."

I stalked toward him silently. From the corner of my eye, I saw Leara peek out from behind my patrol partner. Relief filled me when Treyv tapped the girl's shoulder and motioned for her to leave.

"Excuse me?" I murmured.

"Second Lieutenant, I counted ten armed men." His eyes were straight ahead, and this time he was wise enough to address me by my rank. "They startled us with flash bangs, and anyone who resisted was shot with baton rounds."

Impatient with the idiocy, I decided to embrace technology for once. Searching the crowd, I found one of the senior guards that I recognized. "You, sir. Go get me a camera." I raised my voice to be heard through the crowd. "Fifty of our guards-in-training were subdued without fight or injury by *ten men* armed with *less-than-lethal rounds*. Fifty," I repeated, my tone deepened with anger, "of our best and brightest were too ineffectual to get a single shot off." My stomach was nauseated at the thought. "Congratulations, ladies and gentlemen. I think you have won a month in hell." As the demon returned with the camera, I motioned for him to take pictures of the bound prisoners. "Make them good, sir. These photos are going to be with these men and women for the rest of their professional lives, a perfect addition for their files. And perhaps after their month in hell, they won't ever be caught unawares again."

My eyes sought Treyv and Belisario, now standing in the doorway together. I didn't know what to tell them about the incompetence of soldiers who *should have been* nearing the end of their training, but I hoped they were as disappointed in the resistance we'd faced as I felt. "When the captain and first lieutenant arrive, ask them whether you should be released. Looking at them makes me ill, Sergeant. They are all yours." I strode toward the door. "Everyone else, back to your stations. I want ten nonessential teams to search for any sign of Delta Barracks' visitors. The rest of us, be extra watchful on your shifts. Give a full report to your relief shifts. And listen closely to radio communication as your captain may have something to say when the situation is fully disclosed to him." Pausing, I glanced back at the group of people still sitting on the ground. "And I hope the rest of you realize that wards and fire guards are for your own protection. Every person over there could be dead instead of humiliated."

I barely made it a dozen steps before Treyv was at my side. "Do you think any of them learned a lesson?" he asked aloud, glancing back toward the crowd gathered at the barracks.

The laughter I'd been holding back leaked out, causing me to snort slightly. "No. I don't think they learned a damn thing, honestly. But give them one month of absolute misery then three months of extra duties—most of which will probably deal with chores they consider are beneath them—and another six months of every other person at Asez Holding digging them in the ribs and making rude jokes at their expense. We'll probably lose about half of them, the half that doesn't want to work twice as hard to regain the respect they lost. The other half, the demons who are going to bust their asses twenty-four seven for the next ten years, are the ones we did this for to begin with."

Treyv mimicked my snort. "You know, as much as you say you only took the position to not disappoint the captain, you just sounded like a leader."

I grinned, knowing he could see it despite the dark. "Well, I left a bit out of my assessment. Like the fact that we probably don't want to meet up with that lazy bunch in a dark alley anytime in their lifetime. Or that we also did it because we thought it would be funny as hell."

"And it was," he snickered.

"Yes, yes, it was."

CHAPTER 21

THE SAND WARMED my stomach through the blanket, but my eyes slowly scanned the horizon through the scope. Leara lay beside me, her elbows resting on a rolled-up pad, and she stared through high-resolution binoculars. Gently, I slid my finger into the trigger guard and fired. The camouflaged clay exploded with a puff of orange dust.

"Six," Leara murmured, confirming. With our hearing protection, I saw her lips move more than heard the word, though she helpfully included the Raspea gesture.

She and Rankar had come out here this morning to hide and ward ten discs. Alika had begun training Leara in different types of wards now that she could proficiently Gate and maintain her personal shields. This month, she learned mirroring. Properly done, it created a reflective shield that showed the casual observer the surroundings instead of the object. In a carefully chosen hiding place in the desert, mirroring basically rendered a demon invisible, though it would be useless in a crowded room. However, a patient person could eventually pinpoint the energy signature used to create the ward to narrow down the hiding spot and then check for discrepancies in that—I caressed the trigger again and another orange puff rose into the air—area.

"Seven," Leara confirmed.

The last three fell more quickly as I found a pattern in the wards that helped me trace the energy back. "You did great," I congratulated Leara after removing my hearing protection. I started breaking down and packing my rifle back into the case to clean at the apartment. Sand destroyed the small working parts if not handled.

Mentally, I tallied a list of observations to discuss with Alika. She'd be able to help Leara vary the weave of her wards to prevent another demon using the weakness I'd discovered. I folded my blanket and rolled my firing pad before stuffing it in my backpack. As I finished, Leara moved to a crouch and stared toward the firing range.

"Ready?"

She glanced up at me. "What did I do wrong?"

I grinned. "You didn't do *anything* wrong. If I had only been searching for one or two discs, I never would have found the last ones as quickly. However, Alika will show you how to keep it from happening next time. And after your Friday session, we'll come back out and go again. This was excellent practice for both of us."

Leara nodded, her shoulders relaxing as she smiled back. "We should make it a competition. I'll come out and hide them. You and Rankar see which of you can find the most first. Loser does dishes for a week."

I slipped her hearing protection and rolled yoga mat into my backpack. Sliding my arms through, I put it on before shouldering my rifle bag. "We are going to start limiting your time with the other guards, especially Treyv. You are too young to develop a gambling habit."

Her happy snort as she offered to create the Gate into

the guard entrance tickled me. "First of all, I wouldn't be betting. I would be enabling you and Rankar and the entire Asez Holding guard to put money on the books. Second, Treyv would never encourage a minor to gamble. He is just teaching me all the things I need to know to properly shark someone at billiards and poker once I come of age."

I finished inspecting her Gate, proud of how steady and focused the energy was. "He's so fired."

Exactly as we'd trained, she fell into step behind me where my shields also protected her when we walked through since Gates pulled large amounts of energy from the creator. Her shallower reserves needed time to grow and develop before she could hold both effectively at the same time, and even as an adult, she'd have to be careful in battle.

The thought caused me to half-step as the door to my Gift of Prophecy forcibly opened. In an instant, Leara stood beside me. My hand found her shoulder as I concentrated on the details of the vision to recount later. The attack was definitely happening in the near future. We only had a few days to prepare Asez before they struck.

"You okay?" Leara asked.

"Let's get through the Gate before it drains you," I urged, waiting until she stepped behind me before we headed through.

As soon as we were on the other side, she dropped it and raised an eyebrow at me. "Foresight. There's an attack coming soon. Nothing to worry about today, though."

She hesitated, her worry obvious, before linking her arm through mine as we crossed from the Golf Barracks toward the stables. Once we arrived safely at the apartment, I would send a request for an officer meeting before cleaning my rifle. If Keawyn already had meetings scheduled today, the officer meeting might be tomorrow. However, telling Rankar would help ease the anxiety building in my chest.

In the distance, Rendle walked with two strangers and two guards toward the corrals. With the increased traffic for the bonding presales, a number of veteran guards were volunteering for overtime to act as escorts—not that the Tulevi demon needed protection. If neither group changed our direction or speed, we'd be close to meeting up in front of the infirmary stables. Leara would notice if I changed my pace to miss them, though, and the last thing I wanted was to worry her.

Brock—who had revealed to me that he was saving for a ring and honeymoon and intended to take every minute of possible bonus money—gestured "hello" in Raspea. I gestured a greeting back. Technically, Raspea's gestures were never meant to be used without the verbal components, but in the past few months, a number of guards had taken to using only the hand movements in certain situations. While a few motions could mean more than one thing without the word to clue the "listener" in, I'd found it effective overall.

The Chegori would hate it.

"You're going to get banned from Elysii," Leara warned.

I glanced down at her before moving back to watching my surroundings. "What? Why?"

She gestured a greeting to Rendle, who motioned back without looking away from his guests. "Because you've butchered their prized language."

"I certainly did not."

She snickered. "Don't sound offended. You definitely did. The day you were promoted, you told us you were okay when you couldn't speak. The guard monitoring the cameras—Zuhavi, by the way, who was pretty freaked out by Belisario almost killing you—saw what you did. So he started doing it inside his unit, because all of them speak Raspea. And it spread like a bad bet."

I clenched my back teeth, refusing to respond as we were in hearing range of the group. Holding a hand out to slow Leara down for them to pass first, I considered her observation. "All languages evolve with time," I challenged, whispering for her ears only.

Her startled laugh echoed off the stable, and the entire group paused and glanced at us. With a shrug, I waved and nodded. One of the men did a double take, which caused me to look closer at him.

"Kinan?"

"Bretinoc!" I returned, shocked to see him alive after our trip to the Kansas Camp together. Relief at knowing he survived and impatience to warn the officers of the attack on Asez warred within me. For a second, relief won. "How are you?"

His lips tightened, and the grief filled his eyes like the rising tide of the ocean. "I am rebuilding. It's hard, but I have support." He placed a protective hand on the shoulder of the man beside him. "Kinan, this is Ulvin Xavic. We were cellmates. Xavic, this is my friend, Kinan."

I nodded to the man, noting his eyes held fondness for Bretinoc and the two seemed close. "Pleasure to make your acquaintance, Xavic. This is my ward, Leara."

She waved to them. "We were cellmates too."

Motioning to Rendle and the guards, I used the movement to resettle the rifle bag and release the building tension. "We don't want to hold up Master Cavallo, but you are both welcome to join my husband and us tonight at the Banded Traveler on Elysii. We have a dinner date there at eight o'clock Orion time. Just tell the hostess you are looking for me if you decide to come."

We all said our goodbyes, and I watched them continue toward where the young Deylura played as we walked to the stable. Bretinoc glanced over his shoulder, and our eyes met. I hoped we saw them tonight.

As I opened the apartment door, Leara broke the silence. "He was the one whose entire family died in the Enlightenment. The one who owned the land where you were captured."

I nodded, stopping at my phone on the table to send a message to Rankar. He'd contact the other officers and check in with Keawyn and Rendle. I hit send then headed toward the cabinets to grab my cleaning kit. "He is."

She watched me set up at the table, finally sliding onto the chair across from me. "Did you know he survived?"

Lining up the pieces, I concentrated on putting everything in order. "I did not." Meeting her eyes, I reminded her, "But I didn't know you lived for months afterwards. The Goddess had to send me a vision before I even suspected after I couldn't find you during Vengeance."

She patted my hand. "Well, I'm glad he did. Now I'm going to go shower. I have sand in inappropriate places."

I gripped her fingers and squeezed lightly. "I'm glad

too."

My phone vibrated with a return message minutes after I heard the shower start.

TWO HOURS LATER, the three other officers, Keawyn, and I gathered around a detailed map of Asez Holding. Using the table markers, I had set up the details I remembered from the vision of the attack for everyone to study.

Belisario used a red wet erase marker to circle the probable targets. Alala nodded in agreement, and she drew her finger across the map. "We strengthen the wards everywhere except this area, so when they break through, they come in here. It's farthest from all prime targets, and it funnels the greatest number into a chokepoint."

I tapped the building in the middle, which was two stories high and a soft target. Nothing of import would be in danger once we moved the civilians out. "I'll take our best snipers up there. If I station them on all four sides, we can provide overwatch. We'll try to mitigate any casualties and watch for demons pushing toward the potential targets."

Rankar tapped two of the stables. "These roofs also have good positioning."

Looking it over, I nodded. "I can set up three longbowmen in each. Then they can alternate shots."

Keawyn shook her head. "No. I'll take position on the central roof. And when they all come through, I'll drop them."

Instantly, Rankar's shoulders stiffened. "That is not an option."

Standing straighter, Keawyn's shoulders went back. She raised her eyebrow at him. "I said, I'll handle this attack. They forget who I am. If they need a reminder, I'll give them one."

For the first time in the months since my promotion, I saw the captain and the councilwoman standing toe to toe. Most of the time, the two seemed to be on the same page—interacting more like siblings than anything else. Rarely did a disagreement put them both into professional mode.

"Perhaps they *do* remember who you are. They throw five hundred demons at us and you drop them all—which we know you can do—and then you collapse—which happened before—but you don't survive the challenge that follows. The only thing that proves is that training and maintaining your own private military is pointless. You have hundreds of guards who have spent years training for an opportunity to prove their skill. Let us do our jobs."

The tension in the room kept me locked in place. Two predators were facing off, and I suddenly felt like the rabbit in the grass hoping they didn't notice me. Belisario and Alala, though, simply stood at parade rest, waiting for them to come to a determination. *Gods*, I cursed. *How the hell do they do that?*

"So you are telling me I should use my people as cannon fodder just in case some mastermind has this foolproof plan to lead me into a challenge?"

I cleared my throat, immediately forgetting what big cats did to rabbits in face of my outrage. "We're not cannon fodder. By definition, that would mean we are poorly trained and expendable. I've been trained by these people, and I've trained the guards. We're soldiers who have been led to believe Asez Holding needs our expertise, but our boss—our councilwoman—thinks we are incompetent? That's disappointing."

Her lips tightened, and she turned her ire toward me. "I never said anyone was incompetent."

Rankar snorted, falling back into sibling-mode as her attention focused away from him. "Just that you can do it better."

She rolled her eyes, still facing me. "Okay. Fine. Big Bad Motherfucker sends his minions, thinking it will weaken us. My extremely competent and well-trained private army funnels the attackers into the center of the compound, like so." She gestured at the map we'd marked up. "Are we evacuating the civilians? What if they rush the stables?"

"Then the gods will have no mercy on them," Belisario muttered causing Alala to bare her teeth in a grin.

I nodded in agreement. "Master Cavallo and his definitely unarmed hostlers will be a terrible surprise for them."

"And you and your private guard will be in the main compound with the civilians. If the attackers make it through us and through Fwen's people, they are all yours."

Belisario changed colors and notated a couple more things on the map, and we all pored over it. A couple small changes satisfied everyone, except Keawyn.

"You aren't going to let me do anything," she complained, exhaling softly in frustration.

Rankar wrapped his fingers in mine for a moment before checking the map one last time. Satisfied, he turned to look Keawyn in the eye. "Actually, you have the most important task to me. You're the last line of defense we have for Leara."

A small tendril of fear filled me at the thought of Leara in danger. However, as I reminded Keawyn, we were highly trained soldiers. To break through all of us, they'd need a military force equal or greater. To defeat Keawyn after, they'd need an ally like Queen Athanasia Serei.

Leara would be safe.

CHAPTER 22

THE GUARDS AND Arrows were in position, waiting for the signal to press forward. Most were hidden by illusion or the buildings. As planned, the hostlers were divided among the stables to protect the Deylura inside. All noncombatants were inside the main compound with the councilwoman and her protection—not that she couldn't handle herself but reinforcements would keep her strong enough to withstand a challenge if that was the ultimate goal of this attack.

On the rooftop, archers and snipers awaited my signal. Each pair had a quadrant to watch and defend. The quadrants overlapped to cover as much ground as possible. I lay on the edge of the roof, scanning slowly through the scope on my H&K in the area where the vision implied the heaviest conflict would occur. Though the disabled alarms in the courtyard were silent, the developing energy alerted us that it was go-time.

The invaders' Gates opened about five feet apart in a semi-circle just outside the main compound building, the wards on the building itself keeping them out. "Ready," I ordered, choosing my target. A silhouette appeared in the portal as I waited. "Aim." The demon stepped out. "Fire." I pulled the trigger twice. The first bullet stopped him in his tracks. The second pushed him backward. The demon coming through behind him shoved his limp body out. I fired two more rounds, hitting him twice in the same spot. He fell forward, allowing the third demon through.

"Someone is carrying their Gates on the other side. Alternate firing and reloading to stop them getting through!" I ordered into my radio, noticing that the two demons beside me had both expended their rounds at the same time. "Let the guards on the ground cover the Gates we can't! Bottleneck the points of entry."

"L-T! Over here!" Zuhavi growled.

Standing, I grabbed my rifle and moved to the opposite rooftop. A mob had managed to push back a cluster of the guard, pinning them down. "Gerin, Mab—Charles will reload for you. Ising, come back up Zuhavi and Keem." I dropped to my stomach after checking my ammunition store. Adjusting my trajectory, I began picking off the demons who didn't have weapons in their hands. Likely, those were the ones using Gifts to push our fighters back.

After four energy-workers fell, the guards managed to shove forward. I took down two more of the attackers before scanning the skirmishes for any other problems. A bullet here or there to take down a shield gave one of our people the advantage, but most seemed to be using their training well. "Anyone need an extra push?" I called then fired twice more.

None responded, which I took as a good sign. When my magazine clicked empty, I stood to change positions as I reloaded. At the back of my mind, my Gift tingled, and I stepped away from the edge before opening the door to my Prophecy.

The second shot broke Rankar's shield. The third, fourth, and fifth clustered his heart. For a moment, Rankar stood still. Then his knees gave, and he collapsed. The searing agony as a piece of my soul ripped away told me more than the sense of dread that at least one of the bullets had pierced his heart, a fatal shot.

Clutching my chest where the soul pain radiated out after the Goddess's vision faded, I moved to the northeast edge where Rankar had taken his position. I frantically scanned the grounds. "Sandhill, there's a sniper on the ground between the infirmary stable and the Golf Barracks. Flush them out."

I quickly spotted Rankar wielding his Gift with a phalanx of guards fighting with swords, guns, and magic. I drew energy, reinforcing my shields and starting a Gate just off the rooftop. "The rest of you... Kill them all," I ordered, opening a Gate to Rankar.

The step off the edge into the Gate gave me time to sling my rifle over my shoulder and pull the Glocks from the shoulder holsters. Then I stepped out, directly in front of Rankar. The falling motion upon my exit sent me to my knees, but I stood easily. Rankar's warm hand touched my shoulder, letting me know he recognized my energy, before he turned his back to me—trusting me to protect it.

"Sniper at two o'clock," I warned, pushing the Gate energy into reinforcing my shields as I searched the open ground for any sign of an energy signature.

Spiderweb cracks burst across my chest, the first bullet hitting center mass. As I had during the war, I poured energy over the damage. A second and third bullet pushed me backwards, my right shoulder hitting Rankar's. For a moment, that touch bolstered my shields as I took aim toward the darkness where the sniper hid. In quick succession, I fired three shots.

The shadowed spot lightened as the illusion faded with its caster. The demon slumped over his rifle, and I fired one shot directly into his skull to make sure he was dead. Scanning the alley, I stepped forward a foot and checked for any other threats.

"Second sniper!" Sandhill's panicked voice reached me through the radio just as a bullet pierced my shield direct center of the earlier damage. Large caliber bullet. Demon hadn't adjusted with the direction I'd turned, so it caught my right shoulder—missing my lung. The hard burn warned of iron. No good.

As I pulled energy from my center hand over fist to reinforce my shield, I felt the entire thing snap as two more shots penetrated near my stomach. Then Rankar's fire burned around me, his wards encapsulating and protecting me as I aimed toward the muzzle flash. I emptied the last of the Glock's magazine into the area, growling as it clicked empty before the illusion dropped.

Ahead of me, the spot lightened as the shadows fell away. Sandhill had sighted the second sniper and finished him. "Good job, Sandhill," I murmured into the radio. Sliding the Glock in my right hand into the holster, I used that hand to cover my burning abdomen.

"*Eirlys*, you with me?" Rankar asked over my shoulder, his voice loud in the sudden quiet as the fighting and firing faded away. Around us, the enemy combatants were either dead or contained. Overwatch occasionally fired a round to prevent the escape of a demon who had broken free. All in all, our men did well.

"Mostl—," I paused, unable to finish the word. My frown followed the hesitation.

"Kinan?!"

Unexpectedly, my knees gave way. His warm hand gripped my upper arm, slowing my descent. I leaned forward and vomited, setting my weapon down and placing my left hand flat on the ground to keep from faceplanting. "Fucking iron."

"Medic!" His voice cracked, probably from the pain as he dropped to his knees beside me. "Kinan, focus on me. Look at me."

Startled by his vehemence, I glanced up at him. The concern in his warm brown eyes gave me strength to lean back and wrap my left hand around his. Instantly, my teeth unclenched as his warmth soothed the iron burn. "Hey. Hey, Ran. I'm okay." A smile tugged at the corner of my mouth. "I can probably even walk to the infirmary if we leave soon."

"Medic! Medic to the captain and second lieutenant! Center courtyard!" someone called, their voice unnaturally loud.

Hypnos appeared overhead, his screech of distress drawing a wince from me. A second later, Thanatos joined him. Rankar must have told them not to land, because their erratic flight showed how desperately they wanted to be with us on the ground.

It's okay, 'Nos. I pushed reassurance to him then Thanatos. I released Rankar's hand to put the second Glock back into the holster. I wiped the back of my wrist across my forehead. Already the iron sweats coated my skin.

However, this outcome was much easier to bear than

the one the Goddess had initially sent me.

::Hurt. Pain. N'okay.::

Well, he wasn't wrong. *I'm sorry, buddy.*

"Ready?" Rankar asked, sliding his arm around my waist.

Swallowing hard, I nodded, and we rose together. We'd only made it two steps when two demons stepped out of a Gate beside us. The first one, a nurse I recognized from my initial arrival at Asez last year, nodded and approached me. The second hesitated. "Captain, Second Lieutenant, the infirmary is full. Doctor Lyksva wants any further injuries transported to Albuquerque City Medical."

The effort it took to swallow my argument almost drained me. A voice reminded me that both my friend Damienn and Rankar's sister, Alika, worked at ACMC, and they were each damn good at their jobs. It spoke highly of the hospital, whether I liked the idea of leaving Asez or not.

"Rankar will Gate me there. I'm sure the infirmary needs you back."

The nurse appeared reluctant to leave, her eyes watching the trembling of my hand over my abdomen. Her partner, though, opened a Gate and pulled her behind him. Rankar's arm tightened around me, and I sighed in relief as he took more of the weight off my legs.

Multiple Gates opened around us, and familiar faces came through. "Anything we can do to help?" someone asked, but they were farther back in the crowd where I couldn't see who'd spoken.

"Start cleanup," Alala ordered, her ground-eating walk bringing her through the crowd in seconds. She looked at me then Rankar. "I'll square things away here. Do you need me to open the Gate?"

In answer, Rankar's energy flared directly in front of us. With him touching me and my shields a mess, I felt the Gate he built as he brought it to life. We didn't speak as we stepped through together into the emergency room.

"I'm Renfri. What seems to..." The Ferente demon paused, shook her head, and continued, "Right over here."

Her gesture urged us to an empty bed only a few feet away. Rankar lifted me onto the edge of it before I could work up the nerve to hop up myself. Renfri ignored us, closing the curtain to block out the other sights though doing nothing to muffle the sounds. She shooed Rankar to the opposite side of the bed, and when I glanced over to track his progress, I spotted Hypnos clinging to the top of the IV pole.

"Let's get this shirt off of you," she murmured, hitting a button on the wall before pulling a pair of scissors out of her pocket. The blades cut through the fabric like water, and suddenly, I waited in my sports bra.

"Anything we can't see?" she asked, her gloved hands—*when did she put on gloves?*—guiding me to lie back.

Rankar cleared his throat. "Iron bullets. She's highly allergic to iron."

Renfri tsked as she hooked up the blood pressure cuff and put a little plastic thing over my finger. "We'll need to get those out then. Lucky for you, Dr. Laoch is here tonight." She winked at me, which seemed twice as weird with her standing over me. "He's a looker, too, that one. Not that you don't already have your fill of handsome. Although, is there really such thing as too much eye candy?"

"Renfri, you paged?" a voice outside the curtain asked.

The speaker sounded tired, but when she pulled back the fabric to let him in, he immediately focused on me. A vibrating calm surrounded him as he stepped forward to take the Ferente demon's spot. This time, I tracked where the gloves came from as he put them on. "I'm Devon Laoch. You are?"

"Kinan. And that's my husband, Rankar."

"Nice to meet you. Tuatha de Danaan?"

At my nod, he pressed slightly on my abdomen. The pain caused me to levitate for a moment, and I saw blackness with white spots for long seconds. Then my vision cleared to see Rankar's pale face. Both his hands gripped my right one.

"Kinan, did you hear what I said?" Dr. Laoch asked, drawing my focus to him.

"No. I'm sorry."

He nodded, as though he'd expected my answer. "We are taking you into surgery. Your abdominal cavity has filled with blood, and because the bullet was iron, you aren't healing. That wound alone could kill you, but we also need to get the iron out. Do you understand?"

Dread filled me then panic. "I understand, but I need to see Leara. She'll never forgive me if I don't see her first."

Rankar's grip tightened, and he kissed my fingers. "*Eirlys*, Thanatos went to get her. She'll be here soon."

The doctor looked from Rankar to me and then back. "You have five minutes. Then we have to go. I'll tell them to prep an operating room."

He stepped outside the curtain, closing it behind him. The moment I heard his footsteps retreat, I used my left leg to turn slightly toward Rankar. Daggers stabbed into my stomach, higher than the previous pain had been.

"Stop. Hey, lie still," Rankar murmured, leaning closer to me and eliminating the distance between us.

"Rankar, I love you. And I'm sorry it happened like this, but I couldn't live with that pain She showed me. I couldn't live without you. And I Saw how good you and Leara are together." I touched my forehead to his. "You two are going to be okay. No matter what. Okay?"

Rankar pulled back, his eyes searching mine. "What? What do you—?"

"Kinan? Kinan!" Leara's voice echoed through the emergency room.

Above my head, still on the pole, Hypnos creened loud enough to wake the dead. However, it brought Leara through the curtain. She froze in her tracks.

"Why do you all look like that?" she whispered, not moving closer.

I tried a smile, but nothing happened. Instead, I reached my fingers toward her. "Leara, I have to go into surgery, and I need to know that you and Rankar are going to take care of each other while I'm gone."

Ignoring my outstretched hand, she moved to the side of the bed where Rankar stood and set her hand over ours. "Of course we will. And Davie, Treyv, and Alala are in the waiting room already. They'll stay with us while we wait too."

"Kinan," Rankar started again, something twinging in his tone.

However, a feeling of light headedness washed over me as an alarm went off.

The curtain flew open, letting in too much artificial light. "Time's up," the doctor murmured. Then he tore away my warmth, and the ground began to shake under me.

Leara's scream followed me into darkness.

Tick. Tick. Tick. Tick. Tick.

The only light in the room shone from an open door, so I walked toward it. As my eyes adjusted, other doors became visible. The room actually seemed like a hallway. Each end had a locked door—like padlocked. Also, each side of the obvious exit was a door.

Who says I can't take the easy way once in a while? I half-joked, pausing at the doorframe.

Inside the well-lit room, my friends and family gathered. Alika sat beside Leara, holding her hand and murmuring to her. Alala and Treyv sat together, each holding a cup of something. For breakfast, the chaos demon drank an orange juice and coffee mixture, and I rather hoped that Treyv hadn't resorted to that too. Rankar and Asher sat side by side, Rankar's elbows propped on his knees and his head in his hands. Both drakyn crowded into his lap, neither moving at all.

Gods, what a morose bunch. Who'd die—?

Damienn walked through me, entering the room with a purposeful step.

What the hell? As quickly as the alarm filled me, it drained away. Somehow, this room seemed peaceful... if a little melancholy.

Most of the people in the room came to their feet

when he entered. Asher moved across the room to Damienn, touching his hip but not blocking the room's view of him. Hypnos and Thanatos perched on the back of a nearby chair. I wiggled my fingers at Hypnos, hoping he'd come to me. Instead, he hyper-focused on Rankar.

"Does anyone know her clan? We need a blood donor." Damienn sounded tired, maybe a little sad. The man needed to go home, get some rest. Instead, who knew how many more hours he had here?

"Kinatnya," Leara blurted.

Rankar pulled out his phone, still not having seen me. Instead, he pressed a couple buttons and brought it to his ear. I half-expected mine to ring, but the room remained absolutely silent in the seconds that passed.

I opened my mouth to ask what had happened, but Rankar interrupted. "I need you at the ACMC to give blood to your sister-in-law." He nodded. "See you in a minute."

As he hung up, Asher cleared his throat. "Tier?"

"He's on his way."

A drakyn popped into the room then back out. It happened too quickly for me to identify it. Then a Gate opened, and Tier stepped out.

Damienn appeared to deflate slightly, relief on his face. "This way."

Leara bolted toward door. "Wait. Damienn, what is going on? How is she? It's been *hours*. Is she okay?"

The young Katataros opened his mouth, closed it, and then looked at everyone in the room except me. "All the bullets are out. However, they did a lot of damage on their way in. Her shields are amazing, but the bullets we took out were custom. Even with most of their power spent taking out her shields, they did what they were meant to do." He exhaled softly, his hand snaking around his boyfriend's. "If the bullets hadn't been iron, she'd be out of surgery and in recovery, but Dr. Laoch is still trying to stop the bleeding because the iron is hitting her hard—which makes sense with her being from the Ghouski Sithen. Entire lot of them are iron susceptible."

Leara broke across the room, throwing herself into Rankar's arms. He hugged her back. As touching as the scene was, though, I looked back out through the door. The scene froze, no one moving or speaking.

Finally, I understood.

My Gift of Prophecy led me here. This was obviously a vision. However, I couldn't tell whether I was being shown the past, present, or future. Was I going into surgery, in surgery, or out of it as I watched this?

I swallowed, studying each of the people I loved. Hopefully, this wasn't the Goddess giving me a last look. If it were, though, I wouldn't waste it. My hand brushed each person's shoulder, and I wrapped my arms around Rankar and Leara as they comforted one another.

After a long moment, I stepped back into the hallway and closed the door.

A SINGLE LIGHT shone above me, though the room was still mostly dark. Slowly, which seemed to be my new speed, I turned my head. A metal door blocked most of the light from the next room, though a sliver peeked through the crack. An IV ran out of my arm, and I recognized the machine designed to pull iron from my blood. Perhaps that and the clear liquid pumping into me explained why I shivered in cold.

Moving my head the other way, the only movement I had enough energy to complete, I exhaled upon spotting Leara sleeping in a recliner. The two drakyn had nested half under the covers, obviously taking advantage of her body heat. Rankar, on the other hand, used the remaining chairs to stretch out. He scooted them up against the bed, as though trying to be as close to me as possible. However, at some point, he had crossed his arms over his chest and dozed.

Damn, I thought, looking at how the top of his hair stood in every direction. He'd obviously had a rough night.

Concentrating, I reached for the swatch of visible skin on the back of his arm. My finger barely twitched, and the exertion caused me to yawn. As I opened my eyes again and closed my mouth, the chills sent my teeth to chattering.

"Kinan," Rankar whispered, his relief washing over me in the single word.

"Love you," I managed, each syllable enhanced by the clicking of my teeth.

He hit the call button, dropping his feet to the floor and wrapping his hand around mine in a fluid motion. "I love you, too, *eirlys*. We'll get you some more blankets, yeah?"

His touch alone eased the cold enough that I could concentrate on something other than not biting off my tongue. My eyes closed in relief. Startled, I blinked.

"Tired. Cold," I agreed, realizing I'd drifted off for a second. The fluttering as Rankar added two hospital blankets to the bed had woken me up. In the corner, one of the drakyn—I couldn't see which from this angle—seemed to be crawling out. "You okay?" I tried, wanting to smooth away the worry around his eyes.

"Better now. This one was really bad, Kinan. A half-dozen people are in a private waiting room—because apparently our friends and family make other people nervous—hoping for news. Mom and Asez's new steward stocked us with snacks and coffee and warm drinks. Lucienn brought leftovers from the restaurant after they closed when he came to check on Alika—who has stopped in at least once an hour all day." Something cracked in his voice as he acknowledged his sister's presence, and I wished I could hug him. However, he continued on without much of a pause. "Dad's gone to find Uncle Triswon and Aunt Elie. He said something about a one-way Gift being as useful as a powerless hobo before he Gated to the Bhinj Sithen. And... both Dr. Laoch and Damienn say you have a long way to go. We're all going to have to be patient."

"Tier?" The word squeezed out, but I had to confirm the earlier vision.

"He came to donate blood. His mom sent a couple others from the Sithen to donate also, just in case you need more."

I'd never met Tier's mom, but Rankar had told me once that she had probably known my parents. I squeezed my husband's hand, barely a fluttering of my fingers against his. *Goddess, I'm weak.*

"Kinan? You're awake!" Leara appeared like magic beside Rankar. Thanatos landed on his shoulder, and

Hypnos stood in her arms.

"Love you, warrior-girl." Words came so hard I didn't want to waste any.

"I love you too." Her hand rested on the covers above my leg. "How are you feeling?"

Rankar met my eyes and nodded slightly, seeing my frustration. "She's cold and tired." His forehead wrinkled, and he looked me over. "Any pain, *eirlys*?"

The answer evaded me, somewhere between no and yes. I didn't hurt like I'd been shot multiple times by armor-piercing rounds, but the cold made my muscles tense and ache. The IV lines burned, both coming and going. Plus, a familiar but dreaded feeling of anxiety crushed my chest.

He squeezed my hand. "Do we need to ask for more pain medication?"

Ah. That I could answer. "No."

I opened my eyes. Though both Rankar and Leara still sat at the edge of the bed, they held a whispered conversation without me. Obviously, I had fallen asleep again. However, with Rankar holding my hand, Leara touching my leg, and the drakyn lying on my feet, some of the chill had retreated.

"It's okay, Mom. The doctors say you need rest. We aren't going anywhere," Leara assured.

I smiled softly as I gave in to sleep.

CHAPTER 23

"THIS IS RIDICULOUS," I cursed into the empty hallway, spinning in a circle.

This time, no doors opened, and no light shone anywhere. With a hand stretched out in front of me, I walked toward the wall until my fingertips touched it. I closed my eyes to better picture the room's setup from the last time I'd been here. Two large steps to the right brought my fingers in contact with a doorframe. Feeling around, I found the doorknob. I turned it, the door opened, but the room was just as dark. Closing it back, I stepped down again. Same result. The third door opened, and the abrupt light flooding the hallway caused me to wince.

Inside, I recognized the private waiting room. A table rested against one wall with a variety of snacks and foods laid out. Two carafes on the end presumably held coffee and tea respectively. Someone had brought in two liters of soda, which didn't appear opened. The chairs that had been on that wall and another were stacked in a corner, and a couple cots graced the opposite wall.

Treyv and Belisario stretched out together on one of the cots, such a tight fit for the one-person bed that they'd undoubtedly tip over if either of them moved. Rendle sat in the chair closest to the door, his back straight and his eyes staring off into nothing. Asher and Damienn sat together across the room from him. My brother-in-law's arm wrapped around his soulmate, and the doctor's cheek rested on his lover's shoulder. I couldn't hear what they were saying from the door because an announcement over the hospital's speakers drowned out all sound for a moment.

Unable to resist, I walked toward the couple. Damienn had been crying, which explained the protective hold Asher had on him. "*Cariad*, you haven't failed her," the older fae murmured. "That would mean you didn't care what happened to her, that you gave up on her. Failing her would be blaming yourself for her death when she isn't dead."

"Healing is my Gift, Ash. I should be able to do something."

"You are. Fighting for her matters, Dam." Asher pressed his lips to the top of Damienn's head, the only place he could reach with how they sat. His hand rubbed from the top of his shoulder to where their hands were joined. "It matters."

Stepping forward, I sat down beside Damienn and pressed my hand to his shoulder. "It really does, Damienn. I am thankful to have you both as friends."

"It isn't enough," he argued, tightening his hold on Asher's hand.

"It is for me," I whispered.

"I know it doesn't feel like it, *cariad*, but you can only…"

He paused as Damienn's pager beeped. When Damienn looked at the screen, he cursed and jumped to his feet. "It's Kinan." Both Asher and I stood too, watching as he rushed out of the room.

The light faded, and the room grew dark. "Nope. Uh-uh. You are not just stopping there," I grumped, walking carefully back into the hallway, shutting the door, and then opening it again.

Damienn's back appeared ahead of me as he pushed his way into a hospital room. Leara had her arms wrapped around Alika just outside the room, her face buried in the fae's shirt. Rankar stood staring toward the room like he could will himself inside, Thanatos curled around his neck like a scarf.

Reluctantly, I followed Damienn into the room. A nurse and Doctor Laoch stood together, both showing signs of an adrenaline dump. "What happened?"

I lay on the bed, appearing peaceful. From here, my skin appeared almost translucent. If they needed another IV, they'd have no trouble finding a vein. However, my body was unnaturally still. Even with Rankar beside me, I never rested *that* peacefully. More than anything, that proved I wasn't sleeping.

"The family hit the call button because she coughed up blood. By the time I paged the doctor and made it inside, she was mid-seizure," the nurse explained.

"I ordered bloodwork. She may need another transfusion, and we have to figure out why she is getting worse." He handed Damienn a penlight and motioned toward the bed.

Opening one eyelid and then the other, Damienn's shoulders slumped. "Her pupils aren't reactive. Is she in a coma?"

Doctor Laoch bowed his head as someone outside the room screamed. Then the room went dark.

"I do not find this amusing. What in the name of the gods is happening?" I yelled into the dark, the haunting sound of Leara's scream still echoing inside my head.

Surrounded by black, my eyes detected the light in the hallway more easily. "How do I know which door is past, present, and future? Do I get to open this door and watch myself die? You do realize that is about the shittiest thing my Gift could do, right?"

Silence answered, telling me nothing. So I grabbed the doorknob and pushed. Nothing happened. Growling, I moved over and slammed the other door shut. Then I tried again.

I was wrong. My Gift could show me worse things.

"Sir, I really need you to calm down," the nurse held a hand toward Rankar as though trying to placate him. However, he looked as calm as a fire tornado headed toward fresh tinder.

"Ma'am, I don't think he wants to calm down," Belisario informed the nurse, his tone conversational. However, the tension in his forearms and his shoulders warned that he only hid his emotions better than my husband. "I don't think the rest of us want to calm down, either. Now you can tell us what's going on and hope that shuts us up or you can continue ignoring our not-unreasonable questions and have to deal with all of us being rather upset with you at once. Truth be told, I could really use a good argument right now, and you're a terribly convenient target."

Rankar stepped forward, his stance warning he itched for a weapon, for an enemy he could slay to make the world right again. Unfortunately, I'd learned from experience that some enemies weren't easily destroyed. Some ate away at you until you hated who you became. I never wanted that for him.

"Something is wrong. The doctors obviously don't know what it is. If they did, they would have already fixed it by now! And why in the name of the Goddess's bloody hells hasn't Dad returned with Aunt Elie by now?"

Treyv interrupted. "Look, Captain, we all understand that you're upset. The rest of us aren't happy about this either, but yelling isn't going to make Kinan better."

Rankar turned toward him slowly, which seemed to snap Belisario out of his own head. "Stop. Treyv's walked more perimeters with Kinan than either of them remembers. I've worked her ass off day in and day out training her. Kinan's apparently the first person who knew about your brother and his soulmate, and she encouraged them to make it work. Leara needs Kinan to teach her how to be a badass, stubborn soldier. And you aren't making this any easier for any of us. You're not making things easier for the healers, yourself, or even Kinan. I get why you're pissed, but you need to shut the fuck up and let them do their job."

Belisario motioned for Treyv to take a seat, and Alika urged Leara to do the same. My warrior-girl looked shell-shocked, and I didn't know how to help. Asher dropped down onto the seat behind him and gestured to Rankar to do the same. "Sit there and make nice, or we'll send you home," Asher threatened. "You know how to behave toward a healer. Mom certainly drilled that through your thick skull. Stop throwing that lesson out the window when it suits you, and the rest of us might actually get some information on what the hell is going on."

Once everyone except the nurse sat, Belisario joined Treyv. He nodded to the woman standing near the door like she might run any moment, and she exhaled shakily. "Mrs. Sirach had—"

Leara interrupted, "Kinan. Call her Kinan, please."

Rankar's lips twitched, as though against his will. "Mrs. Sirach is my mother. She'd much rather you call her Kinan."

The nurse licked her lips, glancing toward Belisario. When he gestured for her to continue, she took a deep breath. "Kinan had a seizure. We're running tests to determine what caused it, and Doctor Laoch believes she may need another transfusion. We should still have enough in reserve from her clan's donations. However, it wouldn't hurt to see if one of them would mind coming back today or tomorrow to give a little more."

Asher nodded, humming quietly to himself. Likely, he was trying to bring the emotions in the room down to a more manageable level before the woman bolted. Behind her, Doctor Laoch stepped forward. Relief filled the woman, and she ducked around the doctor to leave.

"Doctor Katataros stayed with her, but I'm sure you all will want to see her. Unfortunately, we are at twenty-one hours post-injury, and she is not showing improvement. Her red blood cells are critically low, so we ordered up two pints from her reserve. Her bloodwork indicates that her iron levels are still extremely high, somehow higher than last night. We're going to put her back on blood dialysis as we suspect that may have caused the seizure and her coma-like state."

Treyv shook his head. "How is that possible?"

The fae doctor opened his hand and closed it, perhaps grasping for answers. "Her case isn't at all usual, and there aren't any documented precedents. However, Doctor Katataros and I believe her organs may have retained higher levels of iron than anticipated due to the amount in her blood during the surgery. Once dialysis removed it from her bloodstream, her organs triaged themselves by releasing what had been retained. However, we'd already tested her iron and found it to be close to normal levels before then and stopped the treatment for iron poisoning."

Asher raised his hand, and the doctor looked at him. "That's good, though, right?"

"It is, mostly. If the iron had destroyed her organs, this would be much worse. Her body *is* trying to heal the damage, and though our Gifts and regular scientific medicine don't seem to work on her as effectively as on most others, we do see small improvements each time. We just need her to keep fighting until we get there."

"I will," I promised everyone after the room darkened. I stepped back into the hallway and closed the door. This time, none of the doors opened. After an eternity passed, I sat down with my back against the wall and closed my eyes.

Somehow, in this place I assumed was my center, I slept. When I woke up, the temperature had dropped. Light shone under the far door, and it allowed me to see my breath fog the air as I exhaled. Rubbing my palms against the opposite arms, I tried friction to get my blood pumping. Then I stood and moved to the door. Leaning my head against it for a long moment, I tried to convince myself to go inside.

I felt no fear, no pain, no anxiety, but also no motivation, no fight, no push. As it always did for me, my center culled the emotions. Objectively, I knew I loved these people. I knew I wanted to get better, to hug them, to reassure them. How did I press through, though, to *feel* that again?

Maybe by opening the door.

I snorted, settling my hand on the cold knob and turning before something stopped me. This time, my hospital room was behind the door. Leara walked into the room behind me, a cover draped over her shoulder like a cape and balancing two steaming paper cups. She set them both on the hospital tray beside the recliner where Rankar slept, one closer to him. Then she tugged the blanket more tightly around her.

I sighed softly as she sat beside the bed, her small hands wrapping around my still one. The body in the bed didn't react as the teenager cried silently, not loud enough to be heard over the beeping of the monitors. Glancing at the screens, I noticed that I had a fever now. My blood pressure seemed a little higher than normal. Nothing else on the monitor indicated anything was wrong, besides how insanely motionless my body laid in the bed. Except that I didn't react to my ward, my precious warrior-girl sobbing at my side.

Everything, *everything* was wrong.

Abruptly, Leara dropped my hand and moved to where Rankar slept in the chair. She carefully crawled on the chair as close to the arm as she could. His eyes opened, battle-ready until he saw Leara. Without a word, he scooted the opposite way to give her room beside him. However, she followed until she curled up at his side. Her head buried in his shoulder, and her crying was no longer silent.

Sitting up for a better angle, Rankar wrapped his arm around her. Her body on top of his covers trapped him from moving much, but neither of them seemed to care in the long minutes that followed. From the back of the recliner, Hypnos and Thanatos creened softly—a high pitched sound of sadness.

Overwhelmed, I sat in the chair Leara had vacated and watched the four of them mourn. A small noise caught my attention. Glancing at the door, I spotted Alika and Asher standing there. They hesitated a moment then disappeared, giving them their space.

Goddess, why are you showing me this? Are you punishing me? Are you punishing them? I don't understand.

"She was right, you know?" Leara whispered, the tears still coating her voice. "When we were in the camp, she would hold me like this and talk to me if I couldn't sleep. At first, she had a hard time thinking of things that didn't involve fighting or violence. She figured I'd seen enough of that to last me. Finally, though, she realized that stories about good guys winning reassured me, so she started talking about you, your family, Hypnos and Thanatos, Pantheon, and Asez. Mostly, though, she liked to talk about you. She told me how you saved her after the attack where she freed my family. You made her feel appreciated and loved. She promised, once we got free and went to Asez, that you'd see me as more than some silly little girl who wanted to play with guns. And she was right."

She tugged her blanket closer, and Rankar flipped the edge of one of his covers back over her. His eyes stared through me to the body on the bed, as though he needed answers. However, neither she nor I—no, me. Both were me—could answer.

"When I told you all about her saving me in the camp, I left out that she wanted nothing to do with us. But she watched us intently during the Latin and Raspea lessons, and I figured out that was the way to pull her from her shell. She's really, really good with languages. Last time she listed off the ones she speaks to me, it was upwards of twenty-five. Sometimes, she forgets what languages she speaks until she needs to use it. She just compartmentalizes them all until a situation pops up."

Rankar cleared his throat. "Most people who are multilingual compartmentalize their languages."

Leara nodded, though she never raised her head. Her voice sounded a little steadier. "She explained to me that she has a language in her head she automatically speaks with someone. Most people, she speaks English. But with Rezqwa, she usually speaks Raspea. It sounded so complicated, how she does it. Like she specifically learned Welsh because it was your language, but I've never seen her speak to you in it. She even started teaching me Welsh, because she wanted me to have that connection with you."

Rankar's eyebrows raised slightly. Then his expression softened. His hand continued to rub her back gently.

Leara barreled on. "But… I guess she's right. I speak to you in English. It never occurred to me to even practice Welsh with you."

"I would be happy to practice with you, daughter,"

Rankar assured Leara in Welsh, looking down at the top of her head.

She lifted her head and smiled at him. "She loves you so much, you know? In the camp, it kept her going. It kept *me* going. Just knowing you were out there in the world somewhere—probably at Asez Holding—and that you'd be there for us once we escaped. When Asez's guards found me, you were everything I expected you to be. Good and strong and smart and fair. And I knew you had loved the Kinan who'd entered the camp by how you looked when you said her name, especially when you told me you wore Kinan's ring. Then when she first came back to Asez, I was terrified. I was terrified that you weren't going to love the person she had become because of the camp. That you would blame her like she blamed herself, even though I knew it wasn't her fault. *It wasn't her fault.*"

Rankar opened his mouth to say something, but she talked over him. "But she wouldn't talk to you about the camp. She wouldn't explain why she needed time to heal, and I just *knew* you wouldn't stick around. Every night, she had nightmares. And after that first week, you started only staying over once a week. Kinan told me you all wanted to give me structure, but... I thought the worst. And I knew that when you stopped staying at all, it would destroy her. And I'd lose her all over again.

"Nothing I did helped. Even the night Rendle plied her with whisky until she literally could not stand, she dreamt of the camp. During the worst nights, when she needed to talk as she drank Grandma Ryn's teas, she told me that she'd never have been in the camp if she hadn't run. She regretted leaving the moment she stepped into the Gate, but she was too terrified of being trapped in the Void to turn around. She meant to go straight back to you, but the mob grabbed her as soon as she stepped out. And I knew if she just *told* you you'd keep loving her. But she wouldn't, and I was too scared to lose both of you to tell you instead. And now I feel like I still might, and I don't know what to do."

I stood, walking over to the recliner. "Shh, Leara. Stop. It's okay."

Rankar also shushed her. "You aren't going to lose us, Leara. We love you."

"But maybe you shouldn't. Because you don't really know. No one ever told you."

An emotion had finally punctured my center. Panic. "Leara, please..." But she didn't hear me, even when I placed my hand on her back. I put my finger over her lips. Then I knelt on the ground beside the chair as she kept talking.

"I'm sorry that she left you, Rankar. But then I'm not. If she hadn't been in the camp, the guards would have killed me like they did my mom and dad. Or they would have hurt me like they did Kinan. She wouldn't have been there to protect me, to show me how to protect myself, or how to get back to Asez. But if she hadn't been there to protect me, they couldn't have raped her. They wouldn't have almost killed her. And I'm scared that makes me a bad person. I'm scared it makes me a bad person because no matter how hard I try, I cannot wish she hadn't been there with me in the camp."

Unable to cry but wishing I could, I concentrated on Rankar's hand against Leara's back. Nothing could have forced me to look at my husband's face in that moment.

"You are the best of me, Leara. I'm glad I was there for you," I whispered into the silence. "I'm sorry I'm not here for you now."

My heart hurt so badly I couldn't breathe, but I pushed myself to my feet. As I walked to the door, I heard Rankar whisper to Leara in Welsh. However, the ringing in my ears drowned out his words as I stepped into the hallway and shut the door behind me.

"Whoever you are," I told the darkness, "Goddess or gods or other, fuck you and rot in the Void. That wasn't what I meant. And I'm not going to stay here while you screw with the people I love. I'm done."

With intent, I strode toward the door at the far end of the hallway. At some point, the padlock had fallen off. It opened into another lightless room. I strode forward with my hand in front of me and a nightmare full of fight.

Time for me to wake up.

CHAPTER 24

THE FARTHER I wandered from the trio of doors, the colder the air became. Hours passed, and the silence reminded me of the soundlessness of the Void. Had I pushed beyond the past, present, and future into... nothing?

While breathing onto my chilled fingertips, I ran into a wall. My grunt of pain sounded loud, echoing back at me in the darkness. Touching the wall, I followed it to a corner. This time, as I continued around the room, I counted the steps. Fifteen. Another corner. Fifteen more steps. A third corner. Between step six and seven, I encountered a door.

"Sure. Might as well," I told whatever monster kept me here, leading me crumb by crumb to the fate it desired for me. Turning the handle, I stepped inside to more darkness. "Hey. How about some light?" I asked, not planning to move until something happened.

Gradually, the lights came on in the hospital room. Rankar, Leara, and Rendle stood in the back of the room, out of the way of the doctors and nurses around the bed.

Doctor Laoch blocked my view of the bed, but his voice sounded resigned. "I've treated wounds from demon fights, burns from energy bolts, and gashes from unimaginable weapons. I've never seen anything like this."

Damienn ran his finger down my arm, and I shuddered, suddenly glad the me on the bed was unconscious. "Her fever dropped from 105.2 degrees to 103 degrees in an hour." He rubbed his finger and thumb together. "Ice crystals? She turned her sweat to frost on her skin, and it's brought her temperature down when pumping her full of antibiotics and medications did nothing."

The nurse behind Damienn murmured, "Doctor, she's still in a coma. She couldn't have done this."

Another nurse entered, handing a stack of papers to Doctor Laoch. He didn't leave as the doctor flipped through them then handed them to Damienn. When Damienn looked up, the two locked eyes a moment, and I could see the shock on my friend's face.

"Has Kinan ever shown a proclivity for a Gift dealing with cold or ice or... anything?" Doctor Laoch asked, turning toward the three family members in the back.

Rendle nodded. "When she gets angry or upset, the temperature in the room tends to drop. And her adopted parents call her 'Snowflake.' But I've never seen her actively use a Gift for it."

Stepping around Leara, Rankar moved forward. "She's from the Kinatnya clan of the Ghouski Sithen. They lean toward Gifts of Cold, Weather-working, and the like. Plus, she found out this past year that her parents had bound a Gift manifested when she was a baby. While the binding was damaged, the fae she spoke with advised that it would probably never fully manifest."

Doctor Laoch nodded. "And that fae would have probably been correct if Kinan hadn't been on the verge of dying due to a high fever. Often, Gifts of that kind will only become active during extreme circumstances. In this case, the energy inside her determined that the heat was a threat and began to offset it."

"It's turning the water in her blood to ice," Damienn whispered.

"What?" Leara cried.

Damienn didn't continue, so Doctor Laoch did. "Her temperature dropped too fast for it to just be condensation on her skin. Her temperature is falling from the inside out. Already, her heartbeat has slowed, though not dangerously so. But being as this was a latent Gift, it may not know when or how to stop. The danger could swing entirely in the opposite direction."

"She might freeze to death?" Leara asked.

Doctor Laoch rubbed his face and turned to the nurse. "Record her temperature every five minutes. When it drops to one hundred degrees, notify us. Also, prepare some hot compresses in case we need them."

Damienn placed his hand on my shoulder. "Kinan, please wake up. This will be easier to fix if you are conscious."

I stepped into one of the empty spaces around the bed. After a deep breath, I slapped my body's face. However, my hand passed through her.

That was new. I interacted with people this entire time. Concerned, I reached out to Damienn. Again, my finger went into his chest like I was a ghost in a movie.

"That's a bad sign," I whispered, but the words only played in my head, like I hadn't spoken out loud.

Walking to the back of the room, I tried to put my hand on Rankar's arm. I had touched him most with no issue. Until now.

"If you'll send a message out to the echelon of healers, I'll go let the rest of the family know what is happening," Damienn advised Doctor Laoch, who nodded.

Unable to remain in the room any longer, I followed Damienn out. When we stepped out, Damienn disappeared. The light faded. And I stood in the cold darkness of my center once again. Stepping forward, I immediately ran into a door. I turned the handle and stepped inside before the thought that I shouldn't fully processed.

Leara stared at Damienn, her eyes wide as she shook her head. Rankar's back was to us, his head bowed. The heart monitor beat slowly, so sluggishly it drew my attention from the two people I loved most in the world to the screen beside the bed. Thirty-two. Thirty-two beats per minute.

My lips had turned blue, and a layer of ice coated my arm like frost burn. The temperature on the monitor, which had been 103 degrees last time, had dropped to 52.2 degrees. While a low body temperature wouldn't kill me, I couldn't imagine such a low temperature spoke well of their efforts to keep my blood from freezing in my veins. That... that would definitely kill me.

Damienn wiped his eyes. "We've exhausted all our options. We tried making the room warmer and used hot compresses, and her temperature dropped faster as her body offset our attempts. We dropped the room temperature to the lowest setting, and her body still cooled, just more slowly. We've tried medicines, we've brought in healers, and somehow, we've still ended up here." He used the back of the chair to steady himself. "I sent word to a few of the Sithens where I have friends, family, or favors, begging for anyone who might be able to help. No one has responded yet. We need… shit, we need Eliecha Bhinj. But she doesn't seem to be anywhere in the world."

Leara whispered into the tense silence. "She and Triswon will never forgive themselves."

Damienn dropped his hand to his side and looked back at my body. "They aren't the only ones."

Knowing it wouldn't work, I still tried to touch Damienn's arm. "This isn't your fault, my friend. My choice. My consequences. While I only knew that I was saving Rankar by my actions, I'd never trade his life for mine. Especially since I see Leara will be safe and cherished."

Rankar moved forward to the bed, kneeling beside the bed and bending his head over my hand as though praying. Leara stood behind him, her hand on his shoulder. Feeling her touch, he slipped his arm around her and pulled her to his side. The two comforted one another the only way they could. Hypnos creened, the sound so high pitched that I flinched. Thanatos landed on Rankar's shoulder, head bowed. Damienn watched them for a moment before stripping off his white coat and dropping it over the end of the bed.

"No," I argued, trying to grab the coat and hand it back to him. However, my hand passed through it. At a run, I followed him out of the room and into the hallway. Somehow, this time, I trailed behind him until he stopped two doors down and knocked once. He stepped inside, and I entered behind him.

Most of my family waited in the room. They all looked

toward the door when it opened. Damienn paused to wipe his eyes and square his shoulders. "Give Rankar and Leara a few minutes. We probably have an hour to say our goodbyes."

Karyn Sirach fiddled with the table of refreshments, though she didn't seem to be paying attention to what she was doing. I would have died ages ago if she hadn't forced her son and husband to bring the stranger who fell onto their land inside for healing. Gods, the embarrassment I'd felt when she looked me straight in the eye and told me—in her subtle way—that she knew Rankar and I had had sex in her kitchen. And the confusion and joy that filled me when she told me she couldn't have found a better person for her son.

Alika stood beside her mom, offering her quiet support. She had been quite the surprise. From that initial Yule celebration with the Sirach family when we met for the first time to her standing up for Leara—and me—in front of a few of the most powerful beings on the Terra Plane, she'd shown me what an amazing woman she was. That Leara would continue to have her for support and friendship granted me immeasurable relief now. More, I saw these past days that she and Rankar would eventually mend the rift between them. Not today, definitely not tomorrow, but someday, they would no longer tiptoe around the other. And perhaps her presence here would go toward knocking decades off that timeline.

Asher had silently rooted for me, not-so-quietly defended me, and trusted me with his most-protected secret. He challenged me to do more than I should but less than I could. In return, I found my first brother. We'd literally run into fire together, and we'd both walked out different. Better. Closer.

Tier had given his blood—more than once—in my hours of need. His was the last friendly face I'd seen before entering the camp. He'd literally welcomed me into the family with open arms at Yule. His approval had never wavered, even after my absence hurt his soulsibling desperately and when I requested he go back to the United States with me to sue them. Especially then. And now I knew he was blood kin. The closest in my life since my parents passed.

Belisario, heir to the scariest Teharan ever born, considered me friend and ally. He offered me friendship when I had nothing of import to give in return. Bruises, blood, and aches exchanged for knowledge no one else in the world could impart. We drank together, played together, and fought together. He even taught me the dirty trick that allowed me—once, but that was all I needed—to defeat his sister at the Trials.

Treyv had reached out first, had urged me to try out for the guard. He saw my skills and wanted the best for his people. But he'd also seen the best in me and chosen me as friend. He kept me out of trouble and got me into trouble equally, a gamble that I'd been willing to take to keep him as friend and partner. I trusted him without doubt at my back. Thus, I believed he would continue to treat Leara as a protective older brother.

Fuck. Rendle. The demon looked older, like the past two days had caused his illusion to gray more. His skin turned ashen after Damicim's words, and the lines around his eyes appeared deeper. From the first moment we met, I had trusted the chaos demon. Some of the emotion came from how much Rankar respected him, but he reminded me of Uncle Dukon in almost every way. I hoped he found a way to save Pantheon once I passed. If anyone knew how to handle a Deylura who'd bonded as tightly to me as Pan had, it would be Rendle. And if anyone could keep Rankar and Leara too busy to self-destruct, that was probably Rendle too. He had done that for me, and I'd been much farther gone.

I turned my attention back to Damienn, who stood in front of Asher's chair. The first time saw the fae, he'd stepped out of a Gate just outside the fence around the main house. Karyn and Mycal were both gone, but Asher had stopped in that morning for a visit. Leading Pantheon out of the barn to the corral for training, I'd paused when the ward went off. The poor guy had been so startled to see me that he'd stuttered. The relief on his face when Asher opened the front door had left no doubt they cared for one another. I had excused myself for a few hours, taking Pantheon to the outskirts of the fenced ranchland. By the time I returned, Asher had dinner made, and he'd formally introduced me to his boyfriend. Damienn had been an unfailing friend since, and he made Asher blessedly happy.

Gods, we were supposed to be immortal. Yet my death threatened the happiness of so many people, people I never expected to have in my life or care for this much. How had it happened? I walked through years of my life with no attachments, no one to mourn me if I misstepped. And here we were.

Into the quiet, Rendle whispered, "That's the thing

about family. Sometimes you get no say in who they are, and you aren't allowed to tell them that they can't love you."

I moved beside him, uncaring that my hand would pass through his leg when I tried to touch him. "The first time you told me that, I didn't truly understand. I learned, though. You all taught me. And a few balls of metal are going to take it all away."

Rendle looked away from me, toward Asher and Damienn, and I realized that Damienn had dropped to his knee in front of his boyfriend. "I have known since our first date that you were the man I wanted to marry, to spend the rest of my life with. I want to be with you for as long as the Goddess gives me, whether to tomorrow or eternity. And if destiny is determined to separate us, I pray she takes me first. I don't want to be left behind without you. Especially not after today. And I meant to do this in an insanely romantic ceremony that Kinan and I have planned for months, but I know I won't be able to go through with it—not if she isn't going to be there. But we're here, and she's still here too."

Asher rubbed his knuckles across Damienn's cheek, gently wiping away the tears there though he had his own. "Now is perfect, *cariad*."

Nodding, Damienn grasped Asher's hand, kissing the wet knuckles. Then he began speaking in Welsh, slowly but without hesitation. "I love you. I love you not only for who you are but for the person I become when I am with you. As we grow older together, as we continue to change and evolve with age, there is one constant you can always rely upon. I will always be falling in love with you. Each day, I love you more. Today more than yesterday but less than tomorrow. As I stand here today with these people as my witness, I pledge to you my undying, everlasting, and immortal love. I will stand beside you as your partner; I will stand before you as your protector; I will stand behind you as your solace. Please spend your immortal life with me."

I applauded, proud. Despite the emotion of the day and of the moment, he flawlessly said the words we'd practiced—he'd chosen the speech; I'd only translated and coached him—for him to use after an upcoming performance at the recital hall where they'd met.

"Bravo," I whispered as Asher brushed his thumb across Damienn's bottom lip.

"Damienn, shut up," he whispered fondly, leaning forward to kiss his waiting love. He cupped his lover's face in both hands and pressed their foreheads together. Neither looked away as Asher recited back to him Sir Philip Sidney's "My True Love Hath My Heart." As he spoke the final line, he smiled. "'My true love hath my heart and I have his.' And if you have any more doubts, I think I might know more poetry. Most of it is Welsh and Turkish, though. But I want your love for always, because I need *you* all the time."

Asher rested his cheek against Damienn's for a moment, his eyes closed but a smile on his lips. "The answer is yes, in case you weren't sure. The answer will always be yes when the question is whether I love you, want you, need you, want to spend the rest of my life with you."

Damienn slid a thin band onto Asher's left ring finger. "You can choose mine, and if you hate this one, we can return it. I... just wanted you to have a physical symbol of my promise, and Kinan suggested we buy two thin, identical bands for each of us. Then we could fuse one of each together for the wedding, each unique part coming together to create an identical symbol of our love for the other."

"It's perfect, *cariad*," Asher whispered, pulling Damienn up and into his arms for a hug.

"Be happy together. You deserve it," I urged them, wishing the tears in my eyes would fall. Exhaling softly, I walked toward the door. I should go now, let them grieve in peace. They had each other, all of them.

The room went dark behind me, and the door slammed the moment I crossed the threshold. The room or hallway or wherever I was now held a darkness so complete I couldn't see my hand in front of my face. Suddenly, exhaustion washed over me. So tired. My heartbeat slowed, reminding me of the reduced rhythm on the room's monitor, and my limbs felt heavy. However, Leara's voice echoed from somewhere close. Unlike the other times, there wasn't a visible door or a light shining. This was different.

"Rankar, how does healing with your Fire Gift work?"

"Leara!" I shouted, though the sound came out of my lips as an exhale of snowflakes. The words scraped my throat like a razor. Hand to my neck, I coughed and tried again. "Leara?" Just another frosted breath graced the air.

Forcing my legs to carry me forward through the blackness, I listened for more sound. Moving felt like pushing through pudding, and I wondered if this cold, dark place was Hell. Had I moved beyond my center into something worse? I'd always feared being trapped in the Void, and I imagined that was something like this.

"Fire healing burns the infection away. I have to push the warmth and healing out of my aura and into hers via my hands. I put my hands on her head and her chest, try and burn the poisoned blood away from her heart and brain, and I pray to any gods who'll listen that it heals her. If it works, it leaves healthy cells behind. But I've tried it on her before, when she and I first met... and it didn't. Don't know if it'll work this time, but if it doesn't, then by the time I've given up that plan, maybe you'll have thought of one or I'll have a better one."

Ahead and to the left, a red glow pierced the darkness. Two spots of color shone behind a thick layer of ice. Gritting my teeth, I forced myself into a fast walk. Finally, my hands touched the ice. Around the palm-sized flames, water dripped. "Rankar! Rankar, I'm here! I'm here."

A gust of air—like a winter breeze off a frozen lake—came out instead of words.

Frustration and fear warred as I beat my fists against the wall of ice, wishing for something to chip away from this side. Using my short fingernails, I tried to scratch the ice. Over and over, I clawed at it, needing to break through to my family on the other side. If not now, I'd never be with them again. Not until reincarnation brought me back.

Suddenly, the fire extinguished.

After a long moment, I cradled my bleeding, frost-burned fingers to my chest. *Rankar, don't leave me. Please.*

No point forming the words aloud. He'd never hear anyway. They'd never know that I had wandered, fought, and clawed toward home, to them, only to lose them behind a cascade of ice.

Weaponless. Helpless. Useless.

Again.

Turning, I leaned back against the wall and slid to the ground.

Goddess, if this is the price for the life of the man I love, I accept it. I hate it, but I would not change my choice and lose him. He'll be a good protector for Leara. He'll love her and never let harm come to her. He'll surround her with family and friends and hope. He'll teach her to care for Pantheon and Rukchio, maybe easing the loss of Pan's first bond. They will live on, so I do not regret this sacrifice.

The drip of water stopped as the cold refroze the wall. I exhaled shallowly, deeper breaths beginning to constrict my chest as though my lungs slowly froze. A tiny crystal formed on the knuckle of my finger. Another interlaced with it. I watched in fascination as my skin glowed a soft blue, highlighting the gradual spread of ice up the back of my hand. When I tried to wiggle the covered fingers, they didn't move.

Behind me, Rankar's sad, even voice broke through my panic. "We weren't held in an internment camp; none of us were. No one was going to put the family of a United States Senator into one of those hells. But that didn't protect us from everyone. People—frightened, angry people—came to the ranch one night. You were there. I'd gone to Asez to protect Keawyn and our people. And you protected my family. I'm not sure if I ever thanked you for that. I think I was too relieved you were alive to realize how grateful I was that you had been there… that the humans didn't have a chance to hurt anyone because you were there, and you kept them safe when I couldn't."

Closing my eyes, I felt the tear escape down my cheek. My left hand cradled my slowly freezing right. Less and less air entered my lungs as breathing became more difficult.

Please keep talking, my love. If I am to go, I want your voice to be the last sound I hear.

He continued. "I mean, you were the most stubborn creature I've seen in a century of life... and I grew up with Kismet and Alika and Mom, so you know the kind of stubbornness I've been up against. The damned demons shot you in the leg with a barbed arrow, and you hauled yourself back to your mount and went through a Gate, and when you came out in the courtyard, we thought for sure that you'd die. Mom never told you that, but she wasn't sure she could patch you up. When I stayed at your bedside... I was waiting there to keep Mom from having to see you leave the pain behind. She could never stand to lose a patient, and I could never stand to see her cry. So I waited with you.

"I stepped away for just a moment. Guess I was too tired myself to watch a good soldier die. And when I came back, you weren't there. I didn't know what to think. You were hurt, delirious, dehydrated, and basically in piss-poor shape, but you managed to get away from the house and onto your mount in order to protect us. Dammit, if I wouldn't let those demons give you a quick end, I sure as hell won't let you die like this, Kinan!"

His voice cracked and broke on my name. I bowed my head, letting my own tears fall. *You'll be okay,* I told him with a thought. *You'll have Leara, Hypnos, and Thanatos. You'll be okay. And I'll see you in the next life. I promise.*

"But you came back. And after that morning, I thought if you could survive that, you could survive anything." He paused, and I begged him to keep talking. The ice crystals had covered my wrist now, and Goddess, the pain was worse than the time the grenade hit me. His voice gave me something to concentrate on besides the frozen joints.

"That night—the night before you left—that was the worst night of my life. I went to Asez, hoping to prevent something like that from happening to the people of the Holding, not believing it might happen to my family. I wanted to take you with me, knew you'd watch my back, but I didn't want to risk you. I thought you'd be safe at my parents' home, behind the wards. And I was wrong. By the time I arrived, the barn was engulfed in flames, and there was Tier, dragging Asher away from where the roof of the barn had collapsed. He just barely made it out."

I had never seen Tier or Asher in those moments. To think, I'd been worried about the two horses, and I almost lost someone who had become one of my best friends.

"My kid brother walked into hell and barely made it out intact. But when I saw him, all I could think was that if he made it out and you didn't, I was going to make sure he didn't survive the next fire."

Oh, Ran.

"That night was the first night I hated fire. Before, it always meant safety and warmth, and it wasn't to be feared. But when I thought that it might have taken you away, the burning and smoke and ash just filled me with dread. At the time, I referred to it as my blood being replaced with ice water."

Again, his voice hitched. "I thought I was so strong, so

smart before you. But I never knew strength until I saw you teach yourself to walk without leaning on crutches. I never knew stubbornness until I watched you train Pantheon, until I watched you work yourself beyond endurance to get your old skill back. I never knew fear until I came home to hear that you'd gone into a burning barn after a bunch of animals. I never knew love until the day I woke up with you in my arms. And I never knew pain until I woke up without you in them."

My heart ached.

"Please, *eirlys*. There are people here who love you, and they deserve more time with you. They should get to see you happy for centuries to come. Leara needs a family who won't give up, so that she can learn how to be just as stubborn and dedicated as you. Asher deserves the friend who's kept his secrets, and Hypnos deserves the friend who always loved him even when he was a little bastard. Treyv, 'Sario, they and the rest of the guard need an officer who'll never give up on them, no matter what happens; who'll stand and watch the backs of the ones who don't necessarily like her. Rendle needs you, because having you here helped him face the memories of the wife and daughter he lost. I need you here, because I love you so much I think I'll die if you leave again."

I'm sorry, Rankar. The sob choked me, and I realized in terror that my lungs no longer worked. Lifting my left hand to my chest to press down, I tried to breathe, but nothing happened. My logical brain reminded me that I didn't need air. My heart just had to beat.

The light blue halo around my frozen appendages seemed brighter in the darkness as Rankar's voice faded away. Now, my other fingers grew stiff. The cold seemed more confident, as though it sensed the fire retreating.

I love you, Rankar. I love you, my warrior girl. I never wanted to leave either of you, but I'm glad you have one another. Be strong. Be safe. Live for me.

"There is too much ice!" Leara screamed, and my heart stuttered the first beat. The glow in my chest seemed to be spreading, moving upward as it brightened below. "Ice cancels out fire. Fire cancels out ice. But to cancel each other out, there needs to be an equal or greater amount. You can't produce enough fire just by touching her with your hands. But if you pushed your aura into hers, like merged the two together—which you could theoretically do if you are soulmates like Grandma Elie thinks—you could maybe get everything equalized. So fix her!"

Ah, my pushy little ward.

"Asher? A little help?" Rankar called, suddenly louder than before.

The answer was prompt and confident, though much farther away. "Yeah, I heard her. Listen: if you're actually soulmates, then you'll be able to merge your auras."

Wait. Soulmates?

"Never had a soulmate before, *hychydig brawd*, and I don't exactly have the time for the extended description. I need the abbreviated version of 'How to Save Your Soulmate Before Her New Gift Kills Her.'"

Suddenly, I remembered. This was supposedly my latent Gift. Turning my head slowly, I reassessed the wall of ice. If this was my Gift, I should be able to stop it. *If I had trained.*

Asher's irritation made him sound louder, though not

closer. "Drop your shields and bring as much of your body into contact with hers as possible. I'm usually naked at that point, so that might be key or it might not."

Using my legs, I pushed myself up to my feet and turned back toward the wall. My shoulder hit it hard when my heart stuttered, stopping for more than four seconds before beating again. Another long pause then a single beat.

"Stay with me by the fire, Kinan, please," Rankar begged.

I leaned against the ice as a red glow turned the entire doorway purple. The melting ice puddled on the floor at my feet, and I tried to find my center. I concentrated on pulling the cold back into it, away from my physical body and back to the spiritual place where my Gifts resided.

I want to be warmed by your fire, Rankar.

My finger twitched, and I reached for the door's handle. Though the metal burned like an intense icy-hot balm, I forced my thawing fingers to hold tight and turn. The handle moved, but the door itself did not.

"Please, Kinan," Leara cried.

I'm coming.

Throwing my body against the door, I felt something crack in my chest. However, the pain could be ignored. Instead, I kept my hand on the knob and took two large steps back. Rushing forward, I hit the door with my shoulder and still frozen hand.

I fell. The fire engulfed me. Then darkness took me.

I promise I tried.

CHAPTER 25

*G*ODSDAMNIT, DID ONE *of Alala's hellbeasts get loose and trample me?*

Lying still to avoid damaging anything worse, I groaned softly as pain radiated from my toes up my spine. I noticed then that a hand held my ankle, only because it tightened before straightening my leg carefully and setting it back on the mattress.

"Kinan?" a voice asked from the end of the bed, and my brain tried to identify the familiar sound. Whoever it was, I knew him. I just couldn't remember.

I concentrated on opening my eyes. For some reason, my eyelids felt glued shut. Finally, though, I stared upwards through a watery haze at a blurred white ceiling. A humming in the background interspersed with a consistent beeping noise.

Blinking slowly, I tried to clear the residual haze. Movement to my left caused me to tense, the dark blur stopping halfway up the bed. "Close your eyes, Kinan. I'm going to wipe them."

I obeyed, trying not to clench them shut in anticipation. "Dam'n?" I asked, coughing slightly.

"It's me. You normally have a full house in here, but the nurse just finished your bath, and I was doing some physical therapy. I kicked everyone out to shower and eat." He snorted softly as something cool pressed against my left eye. Another against my right. "They're gonna be so pissed." After a few, long seconds, he wiped them. "Wait a second before you open your eyes."

"Hospital?" I asked, vague memories twirling in the back of my mind. Bullets and ice and fire and all the crying.

"You're at Albuquerque City Medical. You were shot, and you had to have surgery. Kinan, you nearly died."

"Long?" I asked, finding words terribly difficult. Between the weakness that prevented me from raising my hand and the burning down my throat, the effort to form a full sentence overwhelmed me to the point of tears.

"Seventy-four hours. The weakness you're feeling, that's normal. Your body is exhausted from healing. It'll get better. You'll be better soon," he promised. "Try opening your eyes now."

I did, able to see the olive-complexioned fae staring down at me with worry in his eyes. "Hi."

He smiled. "Hey."

Filing back through snippets of broken memories, I frowned as I tried to pull the scenes together. "Engaged?"

Damienn laughed. "How did you know? He said yes."

I mentally snorted, this time borrowing one of Leara's words. "Duh."

Pulling a chair from the corner, Damienn sat at my side. "Kinan, can I hold your hand?"

"Try," I offered, unsure if the weakness would prohibit an anxiety response but suddenly desperately needing touch.

He carefully slipped his hand over mine, only his

thumb on my palm applying any pressure. "Think about Hypnos. I don't want to leave you, but everyone is so worried…"

Where are you, 'Nos? I thought loudly, a feat much easier than speaking. I pictured the blue drakyn in my mind and willed him to come to me.

A happy trill filled the air, and my eyes caught a glimpse of the blue blur as he winged down to me. Landing near my shoulder, he rubbed his face against my cheek. "'Nos," I murmured, relieved that my brush with death hadn't severed our bond.

Damienn chuckled. "Hypnos, get Rankar. Then you can come back."

The drakyn grumbled but moved to the safety railing before winging into the air. He disappeared then reappeared almost instantly. I snorted. *Silly bird.*

::Coming,:: he argued, which technically meant he had followed the instructions exactly. He crawled back up to the pillow, carefully curling up against my neck and crooning reassuringly.

A half-second later, a Gate opened. As promised, Rankar stepped out. His hair still dripped from the shower, and his shirt sported a couple damp spots where he hadn't dried off before putting it on. He dropped the boots in his hand on the floor, but he hadn't even put on socks.

His hand touched mine. "*Eirlys,*" he whispered.

I twitched my finger, and he tightened his hold. "Love."

"I love you too. Leara is in therapy with Alika. Hypnos, go get her?"

Hypnos hissed, scooting closer to me. Rankar's eyes

met mine. Mentally, I shrugged, not really wanting the little brat to go, either.

"Warm," I argued, leaning my cheek against the drakyn's back.

Rankar sighed. "Thanatos, please go tell Leara that Kinan is awake?"

I didn't see the other blue arrive or leave, but by the time Rankar snagged a chair and pulled it over, Leara and Alika stepped out of a Gate into the room. The teenager beamed at me, sliding up beside Rankar. "You're awake! Oh, Goddess, you're finally awake." She leaned forward, awkwardly hugging me over the bed railing. "Please don't leave us again."

"Never," I murmured, not one to make a promise I didn't intend to keep.

"Alika sent a message in the family chat, and I texted Treyv," she told Rankar, standing up and moving back. Her hand rested on my wrist, unwilling to let me go completely either.

I didn't mind.

"This room will fill up in a minute. But if you need anything, let me know," Alika said, standing near the end of the bed. "I only have a couple more appointments today, and I'll check back in."

"Li," I whispered. The youngest Sirach paused, Gate energy already forming. "Thank you."

"Thank you for everything," Rankar added, looking up at her.

Her smile reminded me of her mother's. "You're welcome."

As people came and went over the next hour, I fought

to keep my eyes open. The last time I fell asleep, I ended up in a weird loop of my Gifts—living the past, present, and future in an unnatural way. I would never sleep again to avoid that fate a second time.

Damienn yawned, his eyes watering from the force of it. Asher immediately followed suit, which caused me to fall in line.

"Go home. Sleep in your bed," I murmured, urging the couple to escape while they could. "I'm okay?"

Damienn nodded. "You're good, Kinan, and getting better by the minute. No more iron poisoning. No more internal bleeding. No more seizures. Rankar healed all that. You just need time to refill your tanks. Your new Gift... it took a lot out of you."

Leara volunteered to walk to the waiting room with them as they went to say goodnight to anyone hanging in there. Alone with Rankar, I forced my fingers to tighten around his. My skin craved the touch of his, as though we'd been separated a decade. "Lie with me?"

He eyed the narrow bed, and I saw his calculating mind doing the math. "I'll be little spoon," I offered, "if you help."

Shaking his head but smiling, Rankar helped maneuver me onto my side. Then he crawled in behind me and settled the cover over us. As his arm rested on my hip in the position we normally slept, I gripped his wrist and pulled his arm the rest of the way around me. He froze, and I immediately let go.

"I'm so sorry."

I had forgotten for a moment that Rankar lived his own nightmares in my need to feel him surround me. Bringing my fist to my chest, I bowed my head and concentrated on his heat warming my back. However, his arm snaked around me and his fingers intertwined with mine.

"Still green, *eirlys*. Get some rest."

I exhaled, trying not to move as the exhaustion crept over me. "Don't let me fall back into the darkness, Ran."

He pulled me closer. "I won't."

With a smile, I let my eyes close. "Soulmates."

His chest jumped as he laughed. "You're stuck with me now."

Hmming, I argued, "No, Captain, you're stuck with me."

The thought delighted me as I slid into sleep. This time, as promised, the darkness didn't await.

"Almost there," Leara cajoled, her patience with our slow after-supper walk to the nurse's station and back immeasurable.

If I hated the time I had spent on crutches, I despised using a walker more than eating my own cooking. The baby steps forced me to remember that I didn't curse in front of teenagers or the Goddess, no matter how much temptation the whispers of the nurses and doctors passing gave.

Apparently, my case had been unusual, even for a place acclimated to seeing weird stuff. Gift training started in two days, a daily session until the specialist deemed it safe enough for me to control the Cold outside the hospital environment. The Tuatha de Danaan had to be brought in from the Reykjavik Sithen, as an adult fae manifesting a latent Gift didn't happen often. No one wanted a relapse of my organs freezing, least of all me.

"Grandma Elie! Grandpa Triswon!" Leara exclaimed as we stepped into the hospital room. She ran across the room, throwing herself into Triswon's open arms and abandoning me in the doorway.

I rolled my eyes as Eliecha hurried over to make sure I didn't fall. "Oh, Snowflake. I'm sorry."

"There's nothing to be sorry for," I argued, overjoyed to see her. We'd all been worried when Mycal didn't return with them.

She wrapped her arm around my waist, reminding me that size didn't matter when it came to fae. Her tiny build easily supported my weight as she moved the walker to the side. "We can get rid of this now."

As quickly as she murmured the words, a little electricity ran from her fingers through my skin. Instantly, some of the weakness fell away. I stood more easily, leaning less on her.

"Elie," Triswon chided. "Be careful. It's only been a couple hours since…"

She waved her free hand at him. "You worry too much. This wasn't healing. She just needed a little boost." She patted my side. "Rankar took care of the healing, but I'll still come back tomorrow and help you rebuild your reserves."

Walking more easily, I moved to Triswon and wrapped my arms around him. His long sleeves allowed me to hug him without worry, and I took full advantage, pinning his arms down with my own.

"That louse of a soulsibling of mine took four hours to

find us," he grumped, fondness for Mycal coming through despite his complaint.

Leara, who'd moved to hug Eliecha, paused. "It's been three days."

"Three days!" he roared, glancing around as though something in the room would clue him in.

Eliecha sighed. "Mycal stopped at three different Sithens before he found us. We were moving around a lot, spending a lot of time in the place between places. Trying to find the perfect moment there caused us to miss an important moment here."

I moved to the recliner, and Leara grabbed one of my blankets from the bed. Since I woke up, the cold bothered me constantly.

"It'll go away, once you have more control over your Gift," Eliecha reassured me, settling into a chair across from me. "I see your Prophecy strengthened a little too. More control over one will help the other."

The hairs on the back of my neck stood on end. "I never want to go to that place again."

She patted the cover over my leg. "It's inside you, Snowflake. And *you* control *it*. Think back to the times you ordered it to do something, when you pushed your will into the darkness, and it obeyed. You didn't understand it, but the training will help with that too. Then you'll never fear that place again."

Leara pulled chairs over for her and Triswon, adding them to make a circle. "She and Rankar finally figured out they were soulmates."

Eliecha ran her fingers down the teenager's cheek. "With some help. Impeccable timing," she congratulated.

Triswon snorted. "We've hinted at it for years, but it literally takes a near-death experience for them to see it. I thought we were dense back then, but it runs in the family."

Elie's chuckle and the fondness in her eyes as she glanced at her husband made me uncomfortable, like I was witnessing something only meant for him.

"We *were* dense. Fighting fate never works out for anyone except the Goddess." Suddenly, she deflated. "Snowflake, I need to go home and rest now, but we'll come back to see you tomorrow. I just had to know you were truly okay first. We love you so much."

"I'll be here," I promised, squeezing her hand as she touched my shoulder. "Love you both."

Triswon grinned. "Love you, too, Snowflake. Give that Sirach boy hell."

Between one breath and the next, Eliecha stepped into his arms and they disappeared. The Gate happened so quickly that I hadn't even felt the energy build to create it.

"What place?" Leara asked, watching my face intently. "Do you mean the camp?"

I swallowed, rubbing my hand nervously across the blanket. "My center. When I was"—I paused, not able to say the word 'coma', even if it was true—"unconscious, I became locked inside myself. It's a dark, cold place, and my Gift of Prophecy pushed me from one vision to another. I didn't know what was past, present, or future. At one point, I wondered if I was already dead and would be trapped there for eternity, like my own private Hell."

The anxious expression on Leara's face made me realize I'd said too much. My warrior-girl already had enough to deal with, and my own personal nightmares invaded her life too much. I smiled softly, trying to bring the conversation back around. "I'm here, though. Awake and alive and with you."

She cleared her throat. "What… did you see?"

I started to brush her question off then paused. Remembering her curled up in Rankar's lap like a girl half her age, I realized her fear. We obviously needed to talk.

"It's okay, Leara. I never told him, but he knew. He looked more surprised when you admitted we had learned Welsh than when you discussed the camp. Plus, I should have taken the burden of the knowledge off you long before. I should have told him myself, once I realized it wasn't something to be ashamed of." I reached for her hand, needing a physical connection. "What is *not* okay is thinking anything that happened was your fault. You didn't cause your family's capture, and you aren't responsible for the actions of monsters."

"But I'm not sorry," Leara whispered, the tears filling her eyes breaking my heart.

"I'm not sorry, either, Leara. If I hadn't been in that cell with you, I wouldn't have you in my life. And the only thing worse than the trauma I lived through would be if you'd had to live it instead. You have nothing to apologize for." I shook her hand and squeezed. "*Nothing.* I realized what happened wasn't my fault, and if it wasn't my fault, then it absolutely was not yours. Bad people do bad things, and we were strong enough to live through it."

She launched herself at me, and I let go of her hand to wrap my arms around her back. Her shoulders shook as she sobbed against my neck. "I'm sorry," she cried.

"There's nothing for me to forgive, warrior-girl," I assured her. "You were the blessing that came from the darkness, and I thank the Goddess for you daily. I'm proud of you, Leara. You're so damned smart and skilled and compassionate."

Rocking side to side as her gasps turned to sniffles, she lifted her head and raised the cover to wipe my neck. "Promise?" she whispered. "Promise it isn't my fault?"

I rested my cheek against her damp one. "I swear, Leara, on all I hold holy, the love I consider sacred, and the blade that protects those weaker than myself that nothing that happened to me and no evil that occurred in the camp is your fault. I swear that your presence has been a blessing, a sign from the Goddess that I deserve goodness and happiness in my life. If Rankar and I never conceive, we still have the most wonderful child She could give us."

Leara's eyes filled with tears again, and she laid her head back on my shoulder. The recliner groaned as Rankar settled on the arm, one arm behind my back and the other around Leara.

He kissed the top of her head, and his hand squeezed my shoulder. "She really did."

I looked into his eyes and realized I owed him apologies. Leara had told him she'd doubted him, and I'd done the same, though he never gave me reason. I asked so much of him without giving in return. Yet here he was. Always by our side.

"I love you," I whispered to him, leaning the short distance between us to touch my lips to his. He tilted his face down, meeting me in the middle.

"I love you, too," he murmured back in Welsh.

"Gross," Leara whispered, laughing against my neck.

EPILOGUE

Anger washed over me the moment I walked back into the warded room, realizing the door had been removed. Every time I did or said something my trainer did not approve of, he found petty, inconvenient ways to punish me. This, however, pissed me off. The temperature in the room didn't drop, though, and nothing in my area froze. *Tell me that I don't have control of my Gift, you Reykjavik bastard.*

Inhaling and exhaling slowly, I moved to the chair that held the most recent distraction my family had brought me—a copy of Victor Hugo's *Les Misérables* in the original French. I stared out the window, mindlessly watching as people came and went outside. Someone knocked on the doorframe, bringing in a tray with a carafe of hot water before leaving just as quietly.

Karyn stocked me with a week's worth of dehydrated meals and tea bags at a time, so much better than anything the ACMC served. In fact, she would probably stop in tomorrow or the day after to visit and replenish my supply. Within my first week, she'd begun to bring extras after she realized that both Damienn and Alika stopped by some afternoons when they were on shift. I appreciated the company, and they enjoyed Karyn's cooking. Plus, it allowed me to talk to Alika about reinforcing to Leara that she shared no part of the blame for what happened in the camp.

Alika'd agreed immediately that she could emphasize that in their counseling sessions. After a long pause, she met my eyes. "You know it isn't your fault either, right? You didn't cause this. What happened to you in Kansas wasn't a punishment for something you did or didn't do. The only ones to blame for that hellhole are the devils who thought of it, staffed it, and filled it with demons whose only crime was to exist."

As I'd told her, knowing something wasn't your fault and always believing it wasn't were two different things. That's why Leara needed the reinforcement.

Kind of how I understood that Garfell Reykjavik didn't despise me specifically for the Sirach family seeing that Tiernia Reykjavik was a kind, compassionate, wonderful person who did not deserve to suffer for the sins of her father. He just found me a convenient target because I agreed with their assessment and hated him for his bias against a demon he'd never even met. That didn't mean I hadn't passed every test today, hadn't calmly demonstrated my carefully won control. In the past four weeks, I hadn't stepped a foot out of line or misspoke against him.

When I completed the tasks today without even a backwash of energy, I expected him to sign my release forms and send me home. I had more control over my Gifts now than I had prior to the latent one manifesting in the first place. When he ordered me to stay another month, I laughed. Except he wasn't joking.

"Let's have a real test," I offered, smiling as I leaned

forward. "If I can freeze your heart in your chest from six feet away before you can call for assistance or Gate out, I go home. If I can't, I'll stay here another month with you until I'm strong enough succeed. You game?"

While I entirely believed his death wouldn't be a loss, I couldn't kill him for being a dickbag. However, I could absolutely check myself out of the hospital. What would he do? Dislike the Sirach family more?

Not possible.

The Gift training floor had wards to prevent Gating, so I needed to leave the old-fashioned way. On four legs.

Packing my change of clothes and book into my backpack, I headed into the bathroom to strip. I rolled the clothes tight and zipped them into the bag before shifting. Then I grabbed it between my teeth and headed toward the stairs. The nurse at the station hummed to herself as she filed paperwork, and I zoomed past.

Standing on my hind legs, my paws easily depressed the handle at the stairwell as my weight pushed it open. Squeezing through, I jumped from the third floor to the second then first. Within seconds, I paced on the first-floor landing trying to figure out how to open it without being naked on cameras. My jumbo-sized paws wouldn't fit under the door, and this side opened inward.

Readjusting my hold on the bag, I stood on my hind legs and wrapped my paws around the slender handle. Backing up to lower my upper body, the handle slowly pulled downwards. I continued backwards until the door was fully open. Dropping, I ran through at full speed, thankful for the hydraulic hinges.

I followed the signs toward the emergency room,

knowing that was the main exit. Conveniently, two demons were entering, setting off the automatic door sensors. I bolted through, stopping in the parking lot.

From here, I could Gate to Asez…

Taking two steps forward, I looked up at the sun and assessed its position versus the time of day to orient myself. Then I dashed east. *Two hundred miles to Asez Holding.*

I PACED OUTSIDE Rankar's office for ten minutes before one of the guards walked by. The round door handle had eluded me, and I was *not* going to be naked in the hallway of the main compound. "You want in?" the greenie asked, his eyes a little nervous as he glanced at the door.

I head-bumped the door, and he grabbed the handle and turned. The disgusted look on his face as ocelot slobber coated his hand elicited a feline cough as he opened the door. *Yup. I even tried that.* Before he could change his mind, I slipped through the crack. He closed the door behind me.

The lower angle and enhanced sight of this form high lighted details I'd never noticed before. Indentations in the floor spoke of long hours spent in his alternate form. The smell of cougar mingled with the musky smell of Rankar proved that he walked this floor on four legs as often as he did on two. The edges of the wooden desk were smoothed by long use and likely by him rubbing against the corner to scratch bothersome itches. Through the open door to his bedroom I could see a long post bearing furrows. Either he used it to remove old claw sheaths or as a way to relieve anger.

I dropped my bag at the end of the couch to better explore the office. As I walked, I deliberately brushed against the furniture until my scent mingled with his. With a feline grin, I leapt onto his desk chair and rubbed my chin along the back. Satisfied, I carefully walked across the empty surface of the desk and leapt onto the couch. Cautious not to snag the material with my claws, I rubbed my shoulder against the back from one end to the other. Deeming my efforts satisfactory, I headed toward the bedroom.

My first stop was the scratching post. Stretched to my full height, the tips of my claws barely reached halfway up the furrows of Rankar's much larger form. Giving it up as a lost cause, I walked the three exposed sides of his bed before jumping into the middle. I sneezed, realizing that Cullyn and Caiftín had slept here recently. Moving closer to the pillows, I inhaled again. The comforting scent of Rankar filled my lungs. Curling into a ball in the corner near the pillows, I fell asleep with the scent of my lover surrounding me.

I awoke with his heat reaching for me. He leaned back against the headboard, reading a book on military history.

Masochist, I accused, crawling closer to rest my head on his stomach. He turned the page, and I rubbed my chin deliberately against his t-shirt. Still, he kept both hands on the book. I tried again, lifting my head an inch and dropping it back onto his stomach. Though it made a plop noise, he still ignored me. I huffed, affronted.

His chest jumped as he suppressed a laugh. I changed tactics, purring. Finally, he set the book on the nightstand. His fingers caressed the fur of my scruff, rubbed behind my ears, and scratched beneath my chin. "Welcome home, Kinan," he said, voice full of amusement.

He leaned his head back against the wall and closed his eyes, his fingers still stroking down my spine. I kept my eyes on him, enjoying the attention and time with him. Eventually, Hypnos and Thanatos joined us. Then Rankar's hand stopped moving.

Hypnos opened an eye and looked at me. ::Is sleep. Tired.::

While Hypnos had found me at least once a day during my five-day trip to Asez Holding, I didn't doubt that Rankar had still worried. Plus, he and the other officers had been working longer shifts in my absence. He deserved his sleep, and perhaps tomorrow I could help Rankar come up with a rotation that allowed the others an extra day off.

Trying not to wake him, I slipped from his side and padded toward the bathroom. A nudge of my body swung the door closed with a soft click. Then I pulled my energy up and changed back. My golden eyes became ice blue. Feline limbs stretched. Paws became hands and feet as the fur disappeared. Almost instantly, I was me again.

The air of the room was cooler without fur. Hurriedly, I turned on his shower and waited only long enough for it to be room temperature before stepping under the spray. A groan of relief escaped as I washed off the sand, and I felt no guilt at using a handful of Rankar's body wash.

Ah. To be clean again!

Only after climbing out of the shower and stealing one of his towels did I catch the irony. I'd rubbed my scent over Rankar's furniture when I first arrived. Then I spent the past ten minutes in the shower rubbing *his* scent all over me. Snorting, I towel-dried my hair and then wrapped the bath sheet around me before making a beeline for his dresser. Hopefully, he'd kept a few items here when he moved into the apartment with us.

Success!

I grabbed his long-sleeved shirt emblazoned with the words "An Army of One" and pulled it over my head without untying the towel. The shirt draped lower than I expected, so I didn't hold the towel when I checked a different drawer for jogging pants. I knew from experience that his jeans wouldn't fit me, even if I didn't hate the feel of denim. Bending over, I pulled on the pants and laced the drawstring at my waist.

Grabbing the towel off the floor, I turned back toward the bathroom. Hypnos stood and stretched, and when I looked, my eyes met Rankar's. He watched me intently, and a blush heated my cheeks. I moved quickly toward the bathroom and hung the damp towel over the shower curtain rod to dry.

You've gained back most of the weight you lost, and let's be honest, Rankar's seen you look pretty shitty in the past. This is nothing.

While the thought wasn't reassuring, it prompted me to step out of the bathroom. Rankar still lay on the bed, though he'd moved to the middle. It gave me room to crawl toward him. With a sigh of relief, I half-draped myself over him. Head on his shoulder, arm across his stomach, and leg over his.

Both our hearts raced, and I concentrated on slowing my breathing. Rankar's muscles relaxed under me, and his arm draped around my back to hold me to him. After a long moment, he murmured, "You okay?"

Turning my face up toward his, I smiled. "Never better. You?"

"Same, *eirlys*."

His heart beat steadily beneath my palm, and I believed him. "How did Garfell take my dismissal?"

His chest jumped with his laugh, and his knuckles rubbed the small of my back. "You lasted longer than I would have. Besides, Alika had her coworker review your chart in light of his complaints. By her coworker's assessment of the test results, you should have been cleared for release. He was just being a dick. The hospital has blacklisted him, and he won't be invited back."

I paused. "I never would have left if I thought I was a threat to anyone here, especially you or Leara."

Rankar looked down at me, his eyes startled. "No one ever believed you would. You're not that kind of person, Kinan."

Turning from my side to my stomach, I rested my chin on his chest and gripped his right hand in my left hand. "I'd never endanger you, Rankar, but I have dishonored you. Over the past two years, I had every opportunity to tell you exactly what happened in the camp, to tell you why I was no longer the person you'd grown to love when we first met. But I didn't. Leara had to. Part of it was guilt, because I thought I brought it all on myself. Some of it was shame, because I never believed I could be worthy of you after." He opened his mouth, and I covered it with my other hand. "Please let me finish. I need to explain."

His teeth raked my palm, and I put my hand back on the bed to push myself up. The inch of height gave me a renewed boost. "I went to war intending to die on the battlefield. I couldn't live without you, and I couldn't imagine you wanting to live with me. But between Locke and my own survival instinct, I made it through skirmish after skirmish. Until one of my people told me that she wouldn't still be there if I hadn't been nearby to save her, and I realized there was still good I could do. That maybe I could make up for all the terrible decisions that led me there."

I saw the tightening around his eyes, and I nodded. "I stayed away after the war because the thought of being rejected by you left my world shaky and incomplete. Except you weren't the person I doubted. It was me. My own fear, my own doubts, and my certainty that I could never forgive myself for what happened, so how could you. And it wasn't until I stopped hating myself that I stopped expecting you to hate me. *That's* when I came back to Asez. And I'm so incredibly sorry I did that to you, to us. I'm sorry that my insecurities bled onto my expectations of you when you have never in our entire relationship done anything except love me."

Rankar exhaled shakily, and I waited for him to tell me to move. However, his arm simply tightened around me. "I suspected. I tried to send Hypnos to you that first night, because the way you ended the call told me something was very wrong. I think Locke's wards on the house hid you. And when we spoke on the battlefield, you told me that you'd never *willingly* sleep with another man..."

He swallowed, pulling back whatever memories he'd conjured. "Kinan, we're immortal. I've got nothing but time to love you and care for you and worry about you.

You've been my heart since the first time we met. I don't care what happened to you while we were apart, except that I'd very much like to rip the throats out of everyone who dared to hurt you, and I hate that it still fuels your nightmares. It doesn't change my love for you. It doesn't make me love or want you less. It only makes me want to protect you with everything I have and everything I am. I'm glad you stopped hating yourself, that you stopped feeling guilty, because you are an amazing person and you don't deserve that. You did nothing to deserve that."

"I don't deserve you, but here we are," I murmured, leaning forward to kiss him.

He met my lips. His smile when I pulled back caused my heart to beat faster.

I grinned. "Whatever you're thinking, hold that thought two minutes. I want to show you what I learned."

He raised our joined hands in surrender, and I reached toward my center. Straddling his waist, I sat up and turned my face toward the ceiling as snowflakes formed over the bed and gently fluttered down. As the first one touched his cheek, his eyes glowed in delight. "That's beautiful, *eirlys!*"

Lucky for me, the humidity in the room was higher than normal after my hot shower. As he watched the flurries drift around us, I pulled moisture for my *pièce de résistance*. Keeping the small snow storm going at the same time took concentration, but every second in that hospital mastering the Gift of Cold the Goddess had dropped in my veins was worth the pride in Rankar's eyes as I lifted the newly formed ice dagger for him to see. I pressed the flat of the blade to my forehead. Now, with my heart and my head and my soul finally in agreement that we were meant to be together for eternity, I repeated the vows whispering in my head from our wedding day.

"Accept my pledge of love, Rankar. I pledge this blade, my Gifts, and my life as I pledge my soul, ever to be at your side... All that I am and all that I possess shall be yours. My love will always endure."

His eyes met mine, and he smiled. "I accept your pledge of love as I accept the pledge of your blade, soldier-girl. You know what is in my heart as I know what is in yours. My energy and my love shall ever be yours."

Setting the dagger to the side, I commanded it to stay frozen with a thought. Slowly, I touched my chilled palm to the warm skin of Rankar's neck, pulling him toward me.

"You should kiss the bride," I ordered, and he obliged.

Then we lived happily ever after.

Mostly.

Glossary of Terms with pronunciations using IPA

Alternate form /ɔltɜrnət fɔrm/ A non-native, non-humanoid form typical of some demon breeds. Tuatha de Danaan most commonly have a Terran animal form.

Arrows /ærouz/ Orion's policing force organized under Governor Domingo Martinez by Sareya Montgomery as a failsafe in case the Enlightenment turned deadly; it was disbanded during the civil war after hostilities with the US ended.

Asez Holding /əsæ houldɪŋ/ A compound near Tucumcari, New Mexico, known to the unEnlightened for breeding horses and to the Enlightened for employing paranormals. Owned by the Asez family, they also train their own security force.

Barcki Demon /bɑrkaɪ/ Demon breed native to Barcivi Plane known for having dark skin, red eyes, and horns. They also have a neutral form. Pureblooded Barcki demons tend to be peaceful, with rare exceptions. Their native language is Barcivi.

Binding /baɪndɪŋ/ A magical or energy-based restriction placed on a Gift either to lessen the strength of it or completely restrict the use of it

Bond /bɑnd/ A connection formed between a specific energy-sensitive creature and its chosen demon. Drakyn and Deylura are both capable of bonding. Demon chosen is called a bonded /bɑndəd/ or bondmate /bɑndmeɪt/.

Cariad /'karjad/ Welsh for 'love'

Center / Centering /sɛntər/ /sɛntərɪŋ/ The place where an energy-worker is closest to their energy, able to best control their Gift, and often capable of leaving behind distractions like emotion.

Chegori /ʧəgɔri/ Demon breed native to Elysii Plane known for alabaster skin, eye, and hair color. Native form appears human excepting pigmentation. They tend to be poor fighters and pride themselves on their fairness in all things, even creating Raspea as the primary language.

Council /kaʊnsəl/ The oligarchical governing body of Orion comprised of five members representing the various demon breeds present in the country

Danaan Plane /dæna pleɪn/ The original Plane inhabited by the fae millennia ago before it imploded, destroying all life who had not fled.

Deylura /deɪlʊrɑ/ An equine species native to the Kirian Plane capable of bonding with an individual demon of its choice at any age. Deylura cannot be forced to bond. They are capable of manipulating energy to create a Gate. They roam wild only on their native Plane, but they appear very similar to Arabian horses and can be bred with Terra horses.

Drakyn /dreɪkɛn/ A reptilian species native to the destroyed Danaan Plane capable of bonding with an individual demon of its choice. The dragonesque creature weighs about fifteen pounds, the size of a large housecat. They can manipulate energy to work a Gate and use Gating as their primary mode of transit, though they can fly. They can also communicate telepathically, though they usually restrict speaking to their bondmate. They avoid Terra and love playing tricks—like stealing trinkets and shiny things, hoarding baubles, or playing simple pranks.

Eirlys /eɪrlɪs/ Welsh for 'snowdrop'

Elysii Plane /iliʃaɪ pleɪn/ A thriving trade Plane centered around the culture built by the Chegori, Elysii encourages the use of Raspea in all dealings. The four native demon breeds now live in peace—Chegori, Wevran, Zksau, and Qtal—with the majority of them living outside the capital city of Mystor.

Energy /ɛnərdʒi/ A pool of power in all living beings that can only be accessed by certain demons and creatures, typically mastered with training. If too much energy is used, the pool can be depleted and ability to work the power disappears forever.

Energy-working /ɛnərdʒi-wɜrkɪŋ/ The act of manipulating one's internal energy to shield and ward, create Gates, work spells, and use Gifts.

Enlightened /ɛnˈlaɪtənd/ An adjective for a demon of any breed who knows that the extended paranormal community exists.

Enlightenment /ɛnˈlaɪtənmənt/ An event in 2005 that revealed the paranormal community to the unEnlightened on Terra.

Fae /feɪ/ Another name for the Tuatha de Danaan

Fenital /fənətɔl/ A feline predator native to the Elysii Plane approximately the size of domestic cats on Terra that hunts small rodents. Shaped like Terran cats, it has medium-length fur as soft as chinchilla and no tail.

Ferente /fɜrɛnteɪ/ Demon breed native to Kirian Plane known for their Gifts of Healing. Their native form and neutral form are the same, as they can pass for human excepting that they tend to receive colorful, cultural tattoos. Their native language is also Ferente.

Gan Treibh /gɔn tɹeɪv/ While it translates to "no clan," the Tuatha de Danaan use it to describe someone who is permanently banished from the world of the fae. The exiled fae cannot speak to, be acknowledged by, or have help from another Tuatha de Danaan lest that fae suffer the same fate.

Gate /geɪt/ A portal created from one place to another using energy. The act of using the portal is called Gating /geɪtɪŋ/.

Gift /gɪft/ An innate ability or abilities of an energy-working demon.

Ghouski /guski/ A Sithen

Human /hjumən/ Demon breed native to Terra Plane known for their inability to energy-work, with a few exceptions. Humans are the only demon breed susceptible to the Thalassemian-Therianthro Virus.

Hychydig brawd Welsh for 'little brother'

Interplanar /ɪnˈtɜrplænɜr/ Moving between Planes

Khan /kɑn/ The term for Lykos nobility; the leader of a specific pack who answers to the monarch ruling all Lykos

Kinatnya /kɪnɑtnjɑ/ Clan in the Ghouski Sithen

Kirian Plane /kɪriən pleɪn/ An isolated Plane with only one native demon breed, the Kirian Plane is best known for Ferente demons, Dcylura horses, and healing. Caravans are only encouraged to visit the capital city, Bagavo, as most of the tribes of Ferente are spread out.

Lrakavi /ʀɑkɑvɪ/ A Tulevri term of endearment that translates literally as "beloved warrior" but is often an endearment used for children

Lycanthrope /lʌɪk(ə)nˌθrəʊp/ A human infected by one of the ten L-strains of the Thalassemian-Therianthro Virus (TTV) who survives the genetic changes and begins changing into the alternate form during moon phases.

Lykos /laɪkoʊs/ A lycanthrope infected by the wolf strain of TTV-L

Mystor /mɪstɔr/ Capital city of Elysii Plane; Raspea for "center"

Native form /neɪtɪv fɔrm/ A form a demon is born with and is likely to revert to during high stress situations. Some demons' native and neutral forms are the same (e.g. humans).

Neutral form /nutrəl fɔrm/ A humanoid form that would pass for human on the Terra Plane. Not all demons have a neutral form. Those breeds tend to avoid Terra completely.

Notaio /noʊtaɪoʊ/ Italian for Notary

Nwazeh /nɑwɑzɛ/ Plant native to the Drinari Plane with spiky leaves like an aloe plant. The flower smells like candied ginger and orange blossoms and can replace comfrey. It does not grow on Terra but is available in some Sithens.

Orion /oʊraɪən/ The country of paranormals formed within the boundaries of the former US state of New Mexico after the inhabitants secede post-Enlightenment.

Orion's Vengeance /oʊraɪənz vɛndʒəns/ The name paranormals and allies use for the activities of March 29, 2006 when paranormal teams entered the five internment camps across the United States and freed all imprisoned demons without any bloodshed. See also Bloodbath

Prophecy /prɑfəsi/ A Gift that allows the energy-worker to see the past, present, and/or future depending on depth and strength of the Gift

Raspea /ræspiɑ/ Primary language of the Elysii Plane designed by the Chegori demons as a neutral trade-speak; it does not include words considered offensive, and it has been adopted by many demon breeds as a common language.

Shapeshifter /ʃeɪpˈʃɪftər/ Demon breed native to the Terra Plane who cannot energy-work naturally but does have an alternate form not controlled by the moon cycles. Shapeshifting is genetic, not viral.

Shield /ʃild/ A layer or layers of protection shaped and maintained by a demon's personal energy to reduce or prevent harm to themselves. Shields can use elements and can be built solid enough to prevent poisonous gas from penetrating. The stronger the shield, the more energy required to both build and hold it.

Sithen /sɪðɛn/ A pocket dimension similar to a Plane created by the most powerful leaders of the Tuatha de Danaan clans. A ruler or rulers lead(s) each Sithen, and the energy that created the dimension often bends to the will of the ruler. Entrances are linked to the Terra Plane as it was the most habitable but least habited Plane at the time of Danaan's destruction.

Soulmate /soʊlmeɪt/ A person whose soul is eternally linked to another's romantically. Soulmates may not both be alive at the same time and may not find each other in their lifetimes. Every person has one soulmate.

Soulsibling /soʊlsɪblɪŋ/ A person whose soul is eternally linked to another's platonically. Soulsiblings are typically not blood siblings, may not both be alive at the same time, and may not find each other in their lifetimes. Every person has one soulsibling.

Teharo Plane /tɛhɑro pleɪn/ One of the most dangerous Planes, Teharo has extreme temperatures and deadly inhabitants. Flora and fauna are illegal to export from the Plane due to their lethal nature. Only two native demon breeds remain: Tulevi and Tuveri. A third was completely eradicated. The primary language is Tulevri.

Terra Plane /tɛrə pleɪn/ Two demon breeds—humans and shapeshifters—are native to the Terra Plane, but a virus struck early in their evolution that affected only humans. If a human contracts TTV, the resulting fever either kills the infected or mutates the victim's DNA to match the strain. Many Terran demons are unEnlightened, even those who can energy-work.

Trials /traɪəlz/ A multi-day set of tasks where applicants to the Asez Holding guard compete to show their skills against fellow competitors as well as Asez Holding's officers; the applicants with the highest overall scores are accepted into the guard.

Tuatha de Danaan /tuɑ deɪ dænɑ/ Demon breed originally native to the destroyed Danaan Plane blessed with long lifespans but low conception rates. Most live in Sithens separated by their clans, and they are known as the breed with the most varied Gifts. Their native form doubles as a neutral form. Many also have an alternate (animal) form. See also fae.

Tulevi /tulɛvi/ Demon breed known for the Gift to feed from and enhance feelings of violence, chaos, and fear. Their native form provides protection against the harsh Teharan environment and includes leathery wings capable of flight. They also have a neutral form. Primary language is Tulevri.

Tulevri /tulɛvri/ Primary language of the Teharo Plane used by both remaining demon breeds

Tuveri /tuvɛri/ Demon breed known for the ability to draw energy from battle and death and a strong Gift of illusion. Their native form provides protection against the harsh Teharan environment and includes leathery wings capable of flight. They also have a neutral form. Primary language is Tulevri.

Vampire /væmpaɪr/ A human infected by the S-strain of the Thalassemian-Therianthro Virus (TTV) who survives the genetic changes. Vampires see ghosts and spirits, have an allergy to silver and sunlight, and may develop the ability to energy-work as they grow more powerful.

Void /vɔɪd/ The cold, dark place between the entrance of a Gate and the exit; if a demon becomes stuck in the place between places, the demon is considered Lost.

Ward /wɔrd/ A layer or layers of protection shaped and maintained by a demon's personal energy for an item or place. Wards can be used as a silent warning system, to keep a specific person out, or similar to a shield. If used as a shield and destroyed, the ward's excess energy snaps back to the person who created it, alerting them.

LET'S GET SOCIAL!

Follow me on Facebook.
@authorthiamackin
Follow co-creator Kat Corley also!
@katcorleywrites
Instagram: @mackinaroundtheworld
Twitter: @thiamackin

If you would like to discuss the world of Midnight Rising,
please join our Facebook group
Thia and Kat's Midnight Readers.

Visit **www.ThiaMackin.com**!

Thank you for visiting. We hope you stay!
~ Thia

Sneak Peek of *Tequila Moon*

CHAPTER 1

WHILE I DIDN'T subscribe to the saying that the best way to get to know a new town was through a bar fight, I rather enjoyed saying hello to one with a stiff drink. Normally, I chose the place myself—and Eiffel Creek, Colorado, hadn't made my list. Unfortunately, my Toyota 4Runner had other plans.

When the thermostat edged quickly toward overheating a couple hours after sunset, I pulled into a deserted gas station parking lot and popped the hood to a cloud of steam. My hand subconsciously patted the roof in reassurance before I went to the hatch to grab the toolbox and flashlight. The split in the hose didn't take long to find and not much longer to remove.

"Not funny, Sparky," I grumbled at the six-year-old vehicle.

A glance around revealed a well-lit building about a mile down the road. In under a minute, four cars pulled in. The headlights shone on a small wood-sided building, not much different than the business I stood in front of—except that one wasn't closed. At nine p.m., I doubted this blink-

and-I'd-miss-it town had a parts store open.

I closed the hood and walked to the back, tossing the busted hose inside. Flipping the flashlight to off and putting the toolbox back in the rear hatch, I pulled out a few baby wipes to clean my hands as best I could. Grease rarely cooperated. Tonight wasn't an exception; black wedged under most of my fingernails. Grumpy, I slammed the door shut so hard the license plate shuddered. "Sorry, baby," I murmured to the wagon, still frustrated but exhaling loudly to expel the pissed off.

Weighing my options left me leaning hard toward a walk. I needed a bathroom, food, and a shot of tequila or four. And I would happily cheat by Gating—using energy to create a door between the places—if the likelihood of cameras at one business or the other wasn't pretty high. Besides, maybe I'd be a mite less aggravated when I arrived if I powered myself there on my own steam.

After a quick stop to grab my purse from the passenger seat, I hit the key fob to lock the doors and set a brisk pace toward the lights down the road. The air smelled of dying leaves and snowflakes falling on the peak of the mountains in the distance. If I didn't hate the cold so much, perhaps it would be pretty. Rubbing my arms through my light jacket, I quickened my steps to a half-hearted jog.

A spotlight illuminated the words The Howling Moon on the wooden sign out front, and the name shone in blue on the side of the building. The third o was actually shaped like a crescent moon with a wolf—muzzle to the sky—in the break. My eyes rolled hard enough it hurt.

"C'mon. Clichéd much?"

Though my mutter would be impossible to hear inside

over the rock music and din of voices, I momentarily felt bad for saying it. People used what worked, and the name didn't deter anyone if the dozen cars in the parking lot was any indicator.

My hand smoothed over my auburn hair, feeling the flyaways but unable to do anything to tame them. Today had just been a travel day, so I'd gone for comfortable. My jeans were well-worn, and my faded shirt showed the double yellow lines of a highway with the Susan Sontag quotation, "I haven't been everywhere, but it's on my list." Plus, my hiking boots could have used a good scrub after my last adventure.

At least my cash spends.

I slipped inside with a thank-you when an incoming patron held the door open, taking a step to the side to orient myself. Though the music had sounded uncomfortably loud from the outside, I could still hear myself think inside. In fact, if I concentrated, I could make out the conversation at the table closest to me. I tuned them out. No need to be rude when they didn't deserve it.

Two robust dart stations were set up in one corner, neither in use. However, all four of the billiards tables enjoyed healthy Friday night crowds. The well-lit area showed quarters lined up as people claimed a spot playing the winner. It appeared that a few of the stacks of coins had a bill or two underneath as a bet. If the repair became too expensive, I could make some gas money back tomorrow night.

All but a couple tables had customers gathered around them. Luckily, only two people were at the bar—the bartender and the man he handed two beers. The patron tilted the top of one bottle toward him before hurrying back to the table where a pretty brunette waited. That left plenty of room for me to grab a bar stool and toss back a couple drinks before heading back to Sparky to sleep. If I were really lucky, the Howling Moon would offer at least a couple fried food options to get me through until morning.

"Hello, Red," the bartender greeted immediately, having watched me approach and remove my jacket. His honey-colored eyes, perfectly arched eyebrows, and carefully tousled and gelled hair spoke of a man who knew he looked damn good. Probably, he had a place nearby to take the ladies he picked up for a one-night stand. I had worked with dozens of players like him. Shit, I even liked most of them. I would never, ever fuck one, though. "What would you like?"

Gritting my teeth, I forced myself to smile sweetly then chose the seat that allowed me the best view of the room. I set my jacket on the stool beside me. "You to never call me 'Red' again, to start. Also, a double shot of tequila."

His lips twitched, apparently unperturbed by my attitude. "I'm Miguel. What would you like me to call you?"

"A cab after I'm well and truly drunk, but you have to serve me a drink first," I reminded, gesturing toward the row of golden liquor as he leaned on the counter, in no hurry to pour my drink. After a long moment of us staring at each other, I sighed. "I'm not here to flirt, Miguel. I'm thirsty."

An even voice from behind the bar interjected, "Good thing you found the bar, then. Everything else in town closed an hour ago."

Two shot glasses appeared in front of me, the hand

that placed them there disappearing so quickly I didn't catch a glimpse of the second bartender's face. However, his appearance hadn't only surprised me. Miguel jumped. Somehow, that made me feel better.

"Fucking dude. Rafferty, make some noise next time," Miguel groused, his entire attitude changing as he stood up straight. He stabbed two limes with a martini pick and set them on a plate in front of me before wiping down the already spotless countertop.

Rafferty knelt in front of a small fridge, his back to us. He restocked the contents from the box he had apparently carried in one arm while pouring and delivering two shots of tequila to me. As a mixed-bag demon with above-human strength and reflexes who'd spent my last fifteen years working in bars, I wasn't sure I could have accomplished the feat without spilling anything. Color me impressed.

I tossed back the first tequila, enjoying the familiar burn as the contents hit my stomach. Then I set my elbow on the bar and watched the closest table of billiards. The two demons—I couldn't tell if they were human or another breed—played eight-ball, the classic solids and stripes. Evenly matched, they kept pranking and distracting each other as they made their way around the table. Most people would have ended up in a brawl, but they never even looked at each other sideways.

"Did you need a menu or were you able to catch a restaurant before everything closed for the night?" the voice from earlier asked.

I turned, looking up to meet his startling blue-gray eyes. Unlike Miguel, this man hadn't spent more time in front of the mirror than I did in a week. He was tidy and handsome but not glamorous or model perfect. For example, he'd combed his hair, but he hadn't styled it. Also, his question held no flirtation. Maybe a little concern, though.

"A menu would be fantastic," I answered honestly. "Thank you."

He slid a laminated, five-by-seven paper across the bar. "Your choices are basically fried, fried, or fried."

"Excellent." I skimmed the list. "Bacon cheeseburger with mozzarella sticks, please. Also, another tequila, a little salt, with a water back."

He scribbled my food order on a piece of paper, handing it to Miguel when he stepped back behind the bar with a tray of empty beer bottles and glasses.

"Thanks, Boss," the surly flirt grumbled, pushing through the swinging door into the kitchen.

A moment later, the empty shot glass disappeared and had been replaced with a full, salt-rimmed one and a glass of ice water. When I glanced up to thank him, he had moved down the counter, efficiently popped the tops on six beers, and carried them to a table in the middle of the room. Someone flagged him at another high top, and he grinned at whatever the customer said. Dropping into the seat across from the guy, he set his elbow on the table. The other man clasped his hand, mirroring his pose. After a couple long seconds, Rafferty slammed the man's wrist against the table.

Wolf whistles and applause filled that half of the room, and if my vision wasn't failing me, a faint blush crept up the winner's neck. However, his back turned to me as he collected the empties from a couple tables before heading through the swinging door.

Heels clicked purposefully up behind me, stopping a couple feet away. Taking the second shot, I squeezed one of the limes directly into my mouth. I dropped the rind in the empty glass and turned around.

"You're new," the woman observed, not unkindly. "I'm Hazel Metcalf."

She stuck out her hand for me to shake, and I accepted it warily, knowing my Gift operated on touch. Luckily, only the tiniest zap of energy passed between us, like a spark of static electricity, before she slid onto the stool on the opposite side of me as my jacket. Whatever my Gift had set in motion for her, it would be a minor mishap or win. That meant her current karmic scales had been pretty balanced, and the consequence of our touch would fully even it out.

"I arrived in town less than an hour ago," I agreed. "Karma Delaney."

She swung her foot and grinned. "Welcome to Eiffel Creek, Karma! We're a town of 740 people, so it isn't difficult to pick out a new face."

I heard the swinging door move but didn't look to see which bartender came out. "How come you give her your name and not me?" Miguel asked, not sounding as grumpy as his words suggested. He slid a basket with a massive burger and generous order of mozzarella sticks in front of me.

"Hazel was genuine and friendly, not a practiced flirt," I explained.

He took a moment to process it. "Fair. Hey, Hazelbear. I accidentally dropped onion rings first instead of mozz.

Want a free order?"

That was quick. As expected, the effect of our touch had been small, but the little positive made me like her more as she thanked him profusely.

He asked if we needed condiments, and we agreed on ketchup before he headed back to get it. As soon as he went through the door, Hazel dropped a few dollars into the tip jar. I wanted an excuse to brush against her again so she could reap the reward for being a sweet person. Instead, I bit into the burger. Surprised by how delicious it tasted, I closed my eyes to savor it better.

Hazel laughed in delight. "Right? They use fresh ground beef. Rafferty has his own secret blend of spices to season it. I hear it's the only place worth getting a burger in town."

When Miguel stepped out, I gave him a thumbs-up, and he paused mid-step in confusion before handing Hazel the basket of onion rings and bottle of ketchup.

"She likes the sandwich," my new friend explained, squeezing a mound of red onto the checkered paper. In response, he bowed to me then slid Hazel an IPA. She removed the screw-top lid and sipped before daintily biting into an onion ring smothered in Heinz. When she slid the ketchup to me, I passed. It would be a shame to ruin the burger's flavor.

"How long are you staying?"

I shrugged a shoulder and finished chewing. "It depends. How long do you think it will take me to get a replacement hose for my Toyota?"

She frowned. "Oh no."

I shrugged again, having already mentally done the

math after she told me the town's population. "Monday, I take it?"

Her frown lines deepened. "Monday is Labor Day."

"Then Tuesday." I preferred to not sleep in Sparky for four nights without a shower. "Do you know anywhere within walking distance that I could grab a shower Sunday?"

She offered me an onion ring, and I traded her a mozzarella stick. "Everywhere is walking distance here, if you don't mind a hike. Main Street is only a mile long if you start from here, and from the center of town to the creek is just under five miles. But we don't have a lot of visitors in Eiffel Creek. Miss Grace rents out her guest suite sometimes, but she went to visit family out of state for the long weekend." Her face lit up for a second. "I can let you in at the gym, though. I planned to go in Sunday for some after-hours cleaning, and you can use the shower there!"

At cruising speed of seventy miles per hour, I truly would have missed even noticing the tiny town if Sparky hadn't run hot. Three minutes and gone. Now, I had to camp here for the weekend and shower on the goodwill of a friendly stranger to keep from stinking up my home-on-the-road.

Dammit, Sparky, couldn't you have broken down near a thriving truck stop?

"I appreciate that, Hazel. You won't get in trouble, will you?"

She waved away my concern, her eyes twinkling. "I own the gym, so definitely not. If there was a place more comfortable to sleep than a treadmill or the concrete floor, I'd offer to let you stay there."

I grinned. "I sleep in the Toyota a lot. The roads call to me if I stay any place long, and hotels are too expensive. The back seat and a well-lit truck stop are my home. What time Sunday? And is it on Main Street?"

"I'll be there eight a.m. to lunch. You just stop by whenever. Follow the main road here down a quarter mile, and it is on the left... Unless you'd rather I pick you up?" she offered, her expression earnest enough that I patted her hand. This time, the zap between us was a little stronger. I hoped something great happened to her.

"No, thank you. The walk will do me good."

She beamed at me, laying her empty beer bottle in the empty basket and piling her garbage on top. "It has been so wonderful to meet you, Karma. We have nearly double the men here in Eiffel Creek than women, and it gets crazy lonely at times."

"I am looking forward to seeing you Sunday. Is there somewhere I could buy you lunch after for the trouble?"

"We can go to The Diner. They serve breakfast all day on Sundays. Best biscuits and gravy in a hundred miles," she gushed.

From the tables, someone yelled her name. "You're up, Hazelbear!"

She grinned. "Gotta go kick his patootie. See you Sunday!"

I shook my head as she darted across the room. Stacking my empty basket under hers, I followed her example and cleaned up as much as I could. Then I dropped a ten in the tip jar and headed toward the bathroom, which was clean enough to eat off the floors. I'd been in hundreds—literally hundreds—of bars, and this one was easily the cleanest ever.

"Ready for your check and that cab, Karma?" Miguel asked when I came back to the bar, all hints of his earlier flirting gone.

I smiled at him, glad he could still learn. Of course, he'd probably poured on the charm because I was a new face in a small town. All the other girls knew his tricks. "Check, yes. Cab, no. It's a short walk, and the food soaked up most of the liquor."

While I waited for him to cash me out, I surreptitiously looked around for the more handsome bartender. *Rafferty*. Perhaps he was still in the back doing inventory? I mentally chided myself for being upset at not seeing him.

"He's already headed out," Miguel murmured, handing me my change. His eyes laughed at me, but his expression stayed customer-service friendly.

"Who?" I asked, raising a brow in question.

He grinned. "Stop back in tomorrow. I'll buy your first shot."

Slipping my jacket back on, I waved at Hazel before taking a last glance behind the bar. "Have a good night, Miguel."

When I stepped out, the temperature had dropped. Zipping my jacket, I tucked my head and started toward the truck. Though my steps were silent, a click-click-click followed me. The sound doubled my heartrate, and I turned around to walk backwards.

A big white dog followed at a safe distance. It looked like a massive white German Shepherd, maybe mixed with a Great Pyrenees. I might have thought it was a wolf if it wouldn't have been the biggest damn wolf I'd ever seen.

Also, most wolves wouldn't perk their ears at me and wag their tail when I faced them.

"Hey, big guy. You startled me," I told him—at least I assumed it was a him as big as it was—keeping my voice calm as I continued walking backwards down the road. Just in case his jaws had enough strength to puncture the energy shield that protected me, I slipped off my jacket and wrapped it around my left arm. It would protect my skin if he attacked.

His tail wagged harder, and his tongue lolled in a doggie grin. However, he didn't attempt to close the distance between us, following along as though we were just going in the same direction.

When I reached the Toyota, I clicked the unlock button on the fob. I stopped, waiting to see what the dog did before turning my back to get in. He sat down, his tail still moving. After a moment, I took a step toward him. "Are you a good boy or am I going to regret this?" I asked him, my right hand extended palm up.

He bounced in place, obviously excited at the potential attention. I grinned, no teeth, as I remembered that showing teeth could be seen as a sign of aggression in canids. "Please be a good boy," I whispered, holding my palm in front of him.

Sniffing my hand, he licked it before staring up at me expectantly. I took the hint and rubbed the damp palm on his head. "Oh shit. You're soft." My fingers caressed his warm ears then ran through the thick fur at his scruff. "You're a very good boy. And you obviously have a family somewhere, because you look too healthy and clean for a stray."

His white fur almost gleamed in the dark.

"Thanks for the love, handsome. Now go on home. It's dangerous for a lone doggie to be wandering this late. Colorado has wolves, bears, and coyotes... all kinds of things."

He barked as I moved away, and I sighed. "I'm serious. Go home, buddy."

After a moment, he stood and walked toward the abandoned gas station. Hopefully, his house was that way. I opened the back of the Toyota, found my gallon of water, and brushed my teeth quickly. Tossing my blankets and pillows into the backseat, I shut the hatch and climbed inside. Locking the doors, I curled up across the backseat. For the first few minutes, I shivered. Then my heat became trapped between the blankets. The windows fogged up as the temperature went up inside the cab, and I closed my eyes.

This was going to be a long weekend.

Made in the USA
Columbia, SC
27 June 2024